# DEADLY
## CONNECTIONS

# DEADLY
## CONNECTIONS

COLIN WADE

The Book Guild Ltd

First published in Great Britain in 2021 by
The Book Guild Ltd
9 Priory Business Park
Wistow Road, Kibworth
Leicestershire, LE8 0RX
Freephone: 0800 999 2982
www.bookguild.co.uk
Email: info@bookguild.co.uk
Twitter: @bookguild

Web: www.colinwade.co.uk
Twitter: @CPWADE1
Also by Colin Wade: *The Lost Years*
Also by Colin Wade: *Plutus*

Typeset in 11pt Sabon MT

Printed and bound in the UK by TJ Books LTD, Padstow, Cornwall

ISBN 978 1913913 373

British Library Cataloguing in Publication Data.
A catalogue record for this book is available from the British Library.

For Dad.
Rest in peace.

# 1

Gerard Le Trousain, the First Minister of Jersey, stood on the makeshift stage that had been placed at the top of the sweeping lawn, which fed down from the grand façade of the parliamentary buildings in Grouville. He looked out at the rows of seats occupied by the great and good of Jersey. The money. The entitled. Representatives of the families that had been on the island for centuries, the ones that shaped the culture and laws of this fine bailiwick.

He gestured for quiet and launched into his speech as the live TV cameras broadcast the event into every Jersey home that could be bothered to watch the rich and privileged as they indulged in one of their regular 'back-slapping' sessions.

"Ladies and gentlemen, it gives me immense pleasure and true privilege to be stood in front of you today as we celebrate the inaugural award of the *Freedom of Jersey*. My government has long considered the need for our most respected citizens to be recognised for their outstanding contribution to Jersey life and I thank the committee for their tireless work in considering all the worthy nominations. Whilst the award is mostly ceremonial, you can be sure that the winner of the award each year will benefit from unrivalled access to the highest political and social circles that this fine island has to offer."

Polite applause rippled from the crowd.

"The committee was unanimous in its selection of this year's recipient. She joined Jersey Police as a constable at the age of eighteen, working her way through all the ranks to become our chief of police three years ago. Twenty years of dedicated service and, in those last three years as our chief of police, she has led the Jersey Police service to significant year-on-year improvements in performance. Crime across all types has fallen by an average of twenty-seven per cent, fraud has fallen by sixty-three per cent, conviction rates have increased by eighteen per cent, major crime incidences have practically disappeared and satisfaction levels from the residents and tourists have improved every year. Her contribution to Jersey life is truly outstanding and I am proud to say that her achievements have made Jersey one of the safest places to live… in the world."

The applause was vigorous, coupled with a few celebratory shouts.

"Ladies and gentlemen, it is my great honour to invite Miss Sarah Braintree to the stage to receive her award."

As Sarah walked to the stage the gathered audience got to their feet. A standing ovation. The applause continued long after she was stood next to the First Minister holding the ceremonial crystal bowl that had been selected as the symbol of this new honour. Gerard gestured for quiet and invited Sarah to say a few words.

She looked over the large crowd, taking it all in.

"Wow! Firstly, let me just say what a privilege it is to receive this award and I thank Mr Le Trousain and all the other members of the committee for selecting me to receive such an honour. As a woman in my field of work it has not been an easy path. Which is why I dedicate this award to my wonderful parents who took in this poor little lost girl to their home and to their hearts when I needed them most. Their love and nurturing, particularly in my adult life, as I battled the sexism inherent in many parts of my working life, undoubtedly gave me the courage and resilience to be standing here today."

Applause broke out once again as the people near them congratulated Sarah's parents, who sat there as proud as anyone could be.

Sarah continued as the noise abated. "But of course, I also have to dedicate this award to the men and women of the Jersey Police service, whose tireless dedication and determination to keep the residents and visitors to Jersey safe have been the bedrock of our success over the last three years."

The crowd stood as one, thunderous applause once again filling the skies.

*

She was watching the live TV broadcast. She pushed the point of the knife into the palm of her hand, not enough to pierce the skin, but enough to get the pain receptors surging through her brain. As she watched the speech from the chief of police, she moved the knife several times, each time pushing the point of the knife harder and harder into her palm. As the speech came to an end, she looked curiously at the trickle of blood that was now

3

weaving its way past her wrist and along the top of her arm. She licked at it, the metallic taste making her smile. She watched the final stages of the TV broadcast.

"I hope you are ready to play my games, Sarah. I'm coming for you."

# 2

David Braithwaite loaded his golf clubs into his car. A regular Saturday routine that his wife had accepted without too much resistance. She looked after the children and he played. On Sunday they had a family day. All neat and tidy. The sort of domestic routine that many other married couples had fallen into.

But, for David, this was his smokescreen. He did a quick nine holes in the morning, which left him free in the afternoon to pursue his addiction. Unemotional sex with as many women as he could snare.

He had been using an online dating site for some time that specialised in people seeking discreet affairs. His hit rate of successful one-off sexual encounters had been amazing, and as he got in his car, he checked the message from the woman he had arranged to see that day. Lily Smedley. She was in her mid-thirties, allegedly, and described herself as having shoulder-length blonde hair, a pretty, slightly worn-in face and a decent figure. The nature of the site meant pictures weren't a thing.

They had arranged to meet in a car park up on the north coast. She wanted to walk along the rugged coast path and stop for a picnic. His mind wandered at the possibilities.

*Alfresco sex. I like it. A little bit of danger. Being caught in the act.*

He smiled as he drove to the golf course, ready for another day of illicit escapades.

It was nearly 2pm when he drove into the car park, a little way north of St John's Church. He parked up and got out, looking around for his date. There were a couple of cars in the car park but there was no obvious presence in any of the vehicles.

"Hello, you must be my date."

David jumped. Where the hell had she come from?

"Oh, hi. Lily?"

"Yes." She thrust her hand out in greeting. "I'm Lily, and you must be David."

"Yes, it's lovely to meet you," he replied. David was pleased with what had turned up. She had described herself really well; her full breasts and curvy figure were particularly commanding his attention. He could feel the lust rising in him instantly. Some of the women on the website were, let's say, creative with their descriptions, and there had been a few times when his need for sex had overridden his disappointment at how 'visually challenging' some of these women had been. Today was different, though, and he stood there with a stupid, goofy smile spread across his face.

Lily looked at him with an amused expression on her face, seemingly reading every perverted thought in his mind. "Come on, then, let's find a place to eat this lovely picnic I have prepared, and then maybe we can see if we can turn some of those naughty thoughts that are flying through your head at the moment into reality. You dirty boy."

With that she wandered off towards the coast path. David admired the rear view as the summer dress she was wearing clung to her shapely rear. He must have lingered too long in the moment of growing lust, because she was suddenly looking around wondering why he hadn't followed her.

"Are you coming?"

"Oh, yes. Sorry."

They walked for a while, taking in the spectacular views of the sea and rocky vista that dominated this part of the north Jersey coast. The temperature was in the mid-twenties and the slight sea breeze made for a pleasant experience. A few minutes later, Lily stopped.

"This will do."

She laid the mat out on a rocky outcrop about thirty yards from the main footpath, looking out to sea. They sat next to each other as she started to unpack and prepare the picnic. David didn't take too much notice of what she was doing, but a few minutes later he was presented with a lovely plate of bread, salad, cheese, beetroot and quiche. He started to devour it. Hungry for the sustenance that he hoped he would need for the naughty, alfresco sex that might follow. A gust of wind blew up Lily's dress, revealing pink lingerie. His eyes almost popped out of his head and the familiar stirrings down below put his mind in a dilemma. Should he finish his picnic or make his move?

He placed his hand mid-way up her exposed thigh.

She stopped looking out to sea and looked down at his hand, meeting his gaze with a smirk. "Eat your picnic, you randy sod. There is plenty of time for that."

She smoothed down her dress. David removed his hand and started to eat frantically, desperate to consummate their little adventure.

He had finished everything but the salad, always a complete waste of food energy in his eyes, but Lily looked at him expectantly as though she was saying *finish your plate and you'll get some.*

He took a massive mouthful. The reaction was instant.

David's lips started to tingle; his throat started to constrict. He grabbed the EpiPen out of his jacket and fumbled with the cap, trying to prime it. His throat continued to constrict and his face started to swell. He was having trouble seeing what he was doing. Through blurred vision he looked at Lily, pleading for her help. She sat there, watching him, doing nothing.

\*

Sarah Braintree sat in her garden, nursing a cool drink, revelling in her first proper day off for several weeks. The workload and her big awards event the previous day had all but consumed her, giving her no time to take a breath. She lived in the lodge on her parents' sprawling estate, a gift from them for her twenty-fifth birthday. As she lay on her sunbed, taking in the warmth of the sun, she once again thanked god, or whoever it was that shaped people's destinies, for bringing these wonderful people into her life.

She wasn't sure how long she had been laid there, the sun having gradually lulled her into a semi-sleep state, but she was suddenly brought to by the ringing of her phone.

She glanced at the screen and her heart sank. It was

Jo Millar, her deputy, who was supposed to be in Gold command all weekend to give her a break. The fact he was ringing her was not a good sign.

"Jo, what's up?"

"Ma'am, I'm sorry to bother you and I wouldn't do it unless it was absolutely necessary."

"I know, Jo. What is it?"

"We have a suspected murder."

"What!"

"I'm afraid so, ma'am – a body has been found on the north coast."

"Jesus, why do they think it's murder?"

"From the ME's initial assessment, he seems to have died from an anaphylactic shock."

"Well, that's hardly cause for a murder suspicion."

"I know, ma'am, but there was a note left on the body. It seems there is no doubt someone deliberately caused this man to have the allergic reaction that killed him."

"What does the note say?"

"I think you need to come in and see it, ma'am. I am setting up an incident room at St Helier Police Station and putting a team together to investigate. We are having a briefing at 7pm."

Sarah cursed under her breath. "OK, Jo, I'll be in at around 6.30pm. I want to be briefed on this thing before we speak to the investigative team."

Sarah hung up and punched the cushion on the sunbed. She could not believe what was happening. The day after she had been lauded as this heroine that had reduced major crimes like these to practically nothing, somebody decides to start murdering people.

"Unbelievable!" she shouted at no one in particular.

She got off the sunbed and went in the house to get ready. So much for a relaxing weekend. Someone was really fucking with her karma.

# 3

She sat watching the evening news, desperately hoping for some negative press coverage of the police and that *bitch* Sarah Braintree. Her mind wandered back to the events of the afternoon.

*God he was a loser. Thinking he was going to get his end away in broad daylight. Just like all the other bastards that have blighted my life.*

She watched some more. Nothing. No coverage whatsoever. The knife was in front of her. She wanted to cut herself again. She stared at it, her attention split between the TV coverage and the release she would get if she dug it deep into her palm or scraped it across her arm. As her hand went for the knife, the news reader started reading a story that clicked her back to reality.

*We are just getting some breaking news. We have unconfirmed reports that a body was found on the north coast above St John's Church. The police are making no comment on this story at the moment, but we will bring updates as we get them.*

She smiled. They had found him, which meant they should have her note. *No comment on this story at the moment.* An interesting statement, she thought, the classic public denial tactic. She hoped Sarah was now having a really bad time.

She took off the blonde wig. Lily Smedley had done her job. Now it was time for someone else. Maybe a redhead this time.

*

Sarah arrived at St Helier Police Station and went straight to her office. Jo was waiting for her.

"Come in, Jo."

"Ma'am."

"So, what have we got?"

"Well, as I said on the phone, ma'am, the victim appears to have died of an anaphylactic shock, we assume brought on by something he ate. The coroner is doing the PM now and we should get the results later tonight or first thing in the morning. Now, ordinarily we would have put this down as a tragic accident, except for this."

He passed her the note. Sarah sat grim-faced as the true horror of what she was reading started to sink in.

*This man was a loser and deserved to die. Cheating on his wife and thinking he could get away with it. But it served my purpose. To get your attention so we can play my little game.*

*You will get a series of clues. Solve each one and you will find the location of my first act finale, the first of three acts that will prove how lame the police are and how clever I am. The lives of many*

*Jersey residents are in your hands. I expect you to fail, but here is the first clue:*

*'What have a baby koala and a baby kangaroo got in common?'*

*Can you work out the deadly connections?*

"What in god's name is this? What do they mean *'first of three acts'* and *'the lives of many Jersey residents are in your hands'*? Are they planning mass murder?"

"We can discuss more with the team in a minute, but the preliminary assessment of this note seems to suggest we have a psychopath on our hands seemingly determined to make us look stupid and kill lots of people."

"But... but where has this come from? Why now? What is it that has triggered this person to start this so-called deadly game today? If we truly have a psychopath on our hands, they must have been harbouring this resentment for some time. Something has set them off."

"It's early days, ma'am. We need to get boots on the ground. Talk to the wife of the deceased. See if she can give us any insight as to why her husband was up on the north coast. We need to work through the implications of this note and prepare a robust response. The press has already got hold of this and we are going to have to contain any sensationalist headlines that could cause panic on the island. We don't want people thinking we have lost our grip."

Sarah rubbed her face. It was nearly 7pm. "OK, let's meet the team and get this thing moving. No one is going to make a mug out of me."

They went down two flights of stairs to the incident room that had been hastily kitted out. The main room had a large incident board at one end of the room, with numerous computer kits set up around the perimeter. Chairs and a table were set up in the middle of the room. Two side rooms were set up. One for the commander and one for interviews. As Sarah entered, the team were already there, all bolting up at her presence.

"Please sit down," she said, trying to calm the mood, belying the knots in her own stomach. "Right, can we do introductions?"

Jo took over. "Ma'am, we have DCI Steph Brown, DS Mark Adams and DC Lisa Johnson."

Sarah nodded at each one, a sombre 'ma'am' coming back in response.

Jo continued. "We should also be joined by the CSI who examined the scene."

Sarah nodded an acknowledgment. "OK, I'm sure I don't need to tell you how important it is that we get a grip on this thing urgently. I know it is breaking command protocol, but I am going to take personal command of this investigation. I would like the side room set up so I can operate out of here on almost a permanent basis. Jo here is going to take over the majority of my other chief officer commitments to allow me time to focus on this."

There was a general murmuring of compliance coupled with an unmistakable look of surprise on the two senior officers' faces. Sarah knew she was breaking one of the golden rules of effective police investigation teams – *don't let the senior commanders interfere* – but she was determined not to let this get away from her. She had worked too hard for some lunatic to suddenly railroad her success.

She pushed on, commanding the room. "Right, here is what I want over the next twenty-four hours. DCI Brown, I want you and DC Johnson to go and see the widow of the victim. Find out all you can about his movements and why he was up on the north coast. DS Adams, speak to the comms team and get out a public appeal for witnesses. It seems like this was done in broad daylight and there must have been other people around. Then, I want you all to analyse this note. Do some initial profiling on what this maniac is saying and intending to do next. For my part, I will speak to the CSI about any forensics and the medical examiner about the post-mortem. We'll meet back here at 3pm tomorrow."

Sarah dismissed the team and walked into the room she was going to use as her command centre. She looked around. It was clean and functional. There was a lovely view out to St Helier harbour. She fired up her laptop and tried to forget the relaxing plans she originally had for the weekend. She hoped to god they could wrap this up quickly and she could return to her normal job.

\*

Her phone beeped. A text message.

*You have her. She is completely engaged.*

She smiled and swigged the last of the whisky that was swirling around in the glass. Tomorrow she would start planning her second killing.

# 4

Sarah woke with a start. Her sleep had been restless and fitful. Through bleary eyes she checked her phone. Two emails caught her attention. The CSI had their preliminary findings and the post-mortem results were in from the medical examiner. She forced her body to get moving, and within forty minutes she had showered, eaten a functional breakfast and was on her way to St Helier Police Station.

She called ahead, and the CSI was ready and waiting for her in the new command office. The rest of the team were out, doing the tasking she had set the previous evening.

"Hello, my name is Sarah."

"Pleased to meet you, ma'am, I'm Jennifer Colney, Senior Crime Scene Investigator."

"Nice to meet you, Jennifer. What have you got for me?"

"I'm afraid not much. The note you were given last night didn't give us anything. A few smudged prints, but nothing we could get a fix on. The paper and ink used were both in common use so no real clues from that. The crime scene was also inconclusive. There was food debris around the victim and the only hair we found that was not his was artificial—"

"Artificial?"

"Yes, from a blonde wig."

"Can we pin down who produced the wig?"

"Initial investigations suggest not. We would need more to make this a realistic line of enquiry."

"Well, I suppose we know one thing. The perpetrator was wearing a disguise, if we consider a wig as a disguise. Do we therefore assume it was a woman?"

"Nothing conclusive to support that, ma'am."

"What about defensive wounds?"

"Nothing at all. I think the PM will confirm that he died from an anaphylactic shock, which killed him quickly. The victim had an EpiPen in his hand but didn't manage to use it in time. It seems the murderer didn't need to do any more than watch him die."

"Jesus. That is cold. Thank you, Jennifer. Can I keep you assigned to the investigation team in case we need any more from you?"

"Of course, ma'am."

Sarah got up and made herself a coffee. Her stress levels were already rising. The forensics were non-existent. She desperately hoped the team would come up with something.

An hour later she walked over to the ME's building to find out the results of the post-mortem. She met a Dr Jason Dingle.

"Dr Dingle, I'm Sarah Braintree, chief officer of the Jersey Police."

"Nice to meet you, Sarah. We don't usually get someone of your stature over here."

"I know, I have decided to take personal command of this situation. I can't let this get out of hand, the day after

I have been lauded as a freaking heroine for eradicating major crime on the island."

"Yes, I saw you on the telly. All a bit inconvenient."

"That's the understatement of the week. What have you got for me?"

"Well, pretty straight forward. His stomach contents confirm he ate a picnic-style meal – bread, cheese, beetroot, that type of thing – but what killed him was the peanut dressing on the salad. Seems he had a severe allergy to nuts. I can only conjecture that the perp knew this, as there is no evidence of adrenalin being administered from his EpiPen. If their intentions had been good, I'm sure they would have helped him administer his shot, which would have at least given him time to get to hospital."

"Any other forensic signs?"

"No, I can't find any evidence of transference of body fluids or other non-victim entities."

"OK, Doctor, thank you."

Sarah left and headed for the little patisserie. The couple of slices of toast she had for breakfast had long since been burned off, and she needed coffee and as much sugar as she could stuff down her throat before she went back to the command centre. She couldn't help feeling that this was the start of something horrendous. They had no breaks so far and the implication of the note suggested this killer wasn't finished. She grabbed some money out of her bag and eyed the sweet treats on view. *Sod the diet. Today is a bad fucking day already.*

\*

DCI Steph Brown and DC Lisa Johnson knocked on the door of the large detached house just outside Gorey. A well-tended garden set it off and the views out to the coast were breath-taking.

Steph raised her eyebrows. "Clearly one of the Jersey rich," she mumbled under her breath.

A middle-aged woman answered the door, looking stressed and tired, the bags under her eyes dark and prominent.

"Mrs Braithwaite. I'm DCI Brown and this is DC Johnson. Can we come in?"

She let them in without comment and gestured them into the large sitting room. The inside of the house matched the outside. Large, expensive sofas dominated the room; a plasma TV on the wall and beautiful flowers in several expensive vases brightened the room, seemingly at odds with the sombre mood they had expected to encounter.

Mrs Braithwaite offered them refreshments, but they declined, keen to get on with finding out what she knew.

Steph started. "Mrs Braithwaite, please let me first offer my condolences. The team and I are determined to find out what happened to your husband. Can you firstly tell us why he was up on the north coast?"

Mrs Braithwaite had not looked at Steph the whole time she had been speaking and for a few seconds she didn't seem to be cognisant. There was no movement and no acknowledgement that she had heard Steph's question.

"Mrs Braithwaite?"

Mrs Braithwaite snapped out of her daze and looked up. Steph had expected to see tears or some sort of signs of grieving, but her face was rigid and angry. The words tumbled out in a tirade of bitterness.

"I'm sure he was with one of his many sluts. You see, DCI Brown, I knew all about his stupid little deceit. Going off to golf every Saturday, pretending he was there all day. He was so stupid and indiscreet, never tried to hide his shenanigans. Friends of mine told me what he was doing within hours of his first little adventure. It didn't take much for me to hack into his laptop and find that disgusting website he is… was using to meet these bimbos. He never cared about me or the children, so you will forgive me if I don't play the part of the grieving widow."

Steph tried not to show her surprise at what she had just heard and Lisa just kept her head down, frantically writing down all that Mrs Braithwaite was saying.

"How long had this been going on, Mrs Braithwaite?"

"Oh, I dunno, about six months."

"Why did you put up with it?"

"Look around. He is the one with the money. If I walked out with the children, we would have nothing. I guess I hoped that one day something like this might happen, to free us from the scumbag."

"Where were you on Saturday afternoon, Mrs Braithwaite?"

Mrs Braithwaite glared at Steph and let out a sarcastic laugh. "My god. Really? Do you really think I would sit here and spout off about how much I hated the man if I had killed him myself? I had hoped you would have more common sense than that."

"Just routine, Mrs Braithwaite. We have to rule you out, so I ask again, where were you on Saturday afternoon?"

"I was shopping with the kids. I am sure there are a hundred people that can verify that."

"I just need one, Mrs Braithwaite."

# 5

It was mid-afternoon when the investigation team all gathered for the daily briefing. Sarah took command and started the meeting.

"We've had the forensics report from CSI Colney and it is non-existent. The only piece of hard evidence is that the perp was wearing a blonde wig, which is practically impossible to trace. The PM confirmed he died from an anaphylactic shock as a result of a peanut dressing on the salad he ate. The ME confirmed that he did not have time to administer his adrenalin and he conjectures that the perp watched him die, making no attempt to help with the drugs that would have saved his life. This seems to support the theory that this was murder, as per the note that was left on the body. There was no evidence of bodily fluid transfer from the perp or any other forensics. It seems the perp did not touch the victim directly, merely murdering him through the food they prepared. This suggests some prior knowledge of his condition."

Steph stepped in. "I can help with that, ma'am. We interviewed the widow, who seemingly knew about him meeting other women for sex. She found the website he was using. We persuaded the owners of the website to give us access to his details, and he does mention on his profile that he has a severe nut allergy."

"OK, so what about the perp?"

"Well, the website administrators confirmed that he had a date booked with a woman called Lily Smedley. Her profile was completely fake. In fact, she stole the identity and address of an eighty-five-year-old wheelchair-bound lady from St Brelade, who was somewhat surprised when we contacted her to ask why she had been on the north coast on Saturday. There are no pictures on the website, just a vague description stating she was blonde."

"No pictures, there's a surprise. That would be too easy. Anyhow, what about the wife? Is she in the frame? Sounds like she had motive."

"I don't think so, ma'am. She was clearly angry with him but had been putting up with this for six months. Seems he had all the money and she refused to walk out with the kids if it would make them homeless and destitute."

"Are we sure she didn't just snap? She would know about his food allergies better than anyone."

"Lisa is checking her alibi for that afternoon, but I'm pretty sure she is not in the frame."

Sarah turned her attention to Mark. "DS Adams, what about the witness appeal?"

"Yes, it went out on the lunchtime news and will continue through the news and print media for the next couple of days."

"Any hits?"

"No, not yet."

Sarah rubbed her face in frustration. "Jesus, people,

this is not good. We have barely anything. Can we even confirm the perp was a woman?"

There was a general murmuring of negativity as most of them tried to avoid direct eye contact with Sarah.

She pushed on. "What about the note? Has anyone done any profiling on it?"

Mark responded. "I have had an initial look, ma'am, but none of the team are profiling experts. We would normally buy this in."

The stress of the situation was already testing Sarah's patience, and for some reason she had taken an instant dislike to Mark, but she held her frustrations in check. The team needed a calm, focused leader, not a loose cannon.

She gritted her teeth and carried on. "OK, DS Adams, that is a fair point. I will have a look at whether we can get some expert profiling support. Tell me what you think."

"Well, the pure interpretation of the note suggests the perp is planning further killings and is wanting to play some sort of riddle game with us. The tone of the first sentence does suggest this is a woman who dislikes men, such as our victim. The reference to three acts suggests some sort of interest in theatre, and the general language seems to confirm her hatred for the police. The answer to the riddle is Joey."

Sarah perked up. "Joey?"

"Yes, a baby kangaroo and a baby koala are both called a Joey."

"What does that mean? Is she, and I agree the perp is most likely a woman… giving us the name of her next victim?"

"I don't know, ma'am, but everything points to her starting a killing spree."

"Great, so we have a potential serial killer on our hands."

The room remained quiet. Sarah couldn't work out whether they were intimidated by her presence, by her rank or were just a bit ineffectual. She wondered whether she had made a mistake by taking this on... after all, she was the chief of police, not a plodding detective.

She batted away the doubts in her head and continued. "DCI Brown, DC Johnson, what are your next steps?"

"Ma'am, Lisa and I are going to check out the wife's alibi tomorrow and will speak to the online dating firm again to see if we can get anything else. We are wondering, with their help, whether any of our tech boys can trace back where the fake Lily Smedley profile was created."

"OK, sounds reasonable. What about you, DS Adams?"

"I will follow up with comms about the witness appeal, and I thought I would scout the local villages around the murder scene, do some door-to-door, see if anyone has seen anything."

"Good, get some uniform to help you and let's reconvene the same time tomorrow. I don't like being so much on the back foot with this one, and if the note is a real threat this lunatic could be planning her next murder at any time. Get to it, everyone."

The team dispersed, and Sarah went back into her office, poured herself a coffee and sat in her chair staring out of the window that looked out onto St Helier harbour.

"Why? Why now?" she said quietly to herself as the hit of caffeine calmed her nerves.

*

She stood at the window of her second-floor flat, looking over the sweeping vista of St Aubin's Bay. The sun was out and the seagulls were making their usual haunting calls as the tourists milled about along the seafront. It was a view that would brighten most people's day but, for her, it just brought back bad memories. A view that so often framed the traumatic periods of her life, a seemingly constant reminder of being stuck on an island. Even now in her adult life she did not have the means to escape. She could never hold down a job for very long, her demons constantly eating away at her, making her restless. She was always efficient and functional in her many jobs. People liked her, but there was always something that made her jump ship. Someone getting too close; someone asking difficult questions.

She looked at the pokey flat, barely furnished with no soul. It kept her safe and dry, but the deadline of the monthly rent payment was a constant stressor.

She saw the knife, resting on the kitchen counter, glistening in the sunlight that was streaming through the window. Like some shiny present waiting to be played with. She picked it up and placed it at the top of her forearm, pushing the blade lightly against the skin. The skin bowed at the pressure. Immediately she took it away, watching as the indentation slowly disappeared as the skin plumped back to its normal shape. The demons in her head were urging her on.

*Go on. Do it harder this time. Make yourself bleed.*

The knife hovered over her arm as her confused mind battled with itself, the rational side of her brain trying to win out, trying to stop her cutting herself again. As her torment grew her phone beeped. She stopped. She dropped the knife and unlocked her phone.

*All going to plan so far. Time to ramp it up.*

She smiled, the text easing her torment. The deadly game she was playing was the only thing that would heal her wounds. Sarah had to pay for what she had done.

# 6

It was gone 9pm when Sarah turned into the long driveway that led to her parents' mansion. As she made the manoeuvre to start up the drive she had to slam on her brakes. A man was standing there, blocking her way. She glared at him as he came around to the side of her car. She buzzed her window down.

"What the hell are you doing? I could have run you over."

"Miss Braintree, I'm Jeff Godley from the *Jersey Herald*. I wanted a comment on the murder on the north coast."

"What the hell do you think you are doing, coming to my house and hassling me like this? You have had the witness appeal and that is all we are saying at this time. Now get off my property or I will arrest you for trespassing."

"So, I can quote you as refusing to answer my questions?"

Sarah started to buzz the window shut, but as it reached full closure, he shouted something at her that made her stop in her tracks.

"What about the note on the body, Miss Braintree? What does that mean?"

She froze. How on earth did he know about the note? That information had not been made public. She buzzed the window down again, trying to remain calm. "What note?"

"Oh, come now, Miss Braintree, we both know that the murderer left a note, so why don't you make it easy on yourself and answer my questions… otherwise I might just have to speculate that the police are hiding something."

Sarah buzzed her window back shut and drove away.

As she turned into the parking space next to the lodge, she turned the car off and smashed her fists on the steering wheel.

"What the fuck is going on?"

\*

Sarah had stewed all night on the run-in with the reporter. As she sat at her breakfast bar, drinking her second cup of coffee, after another night of broken sleep, she phoned her deputy.

"Jo, it's Sarah."

"Morning, ma'am, what can I do for you?"

"We have a problem, Jo. I was doorstepped by a reporter last night who knew about the note on the victim. The only people that know about the note are the investigation team."

"What? You think we have a mole?"

"Well, I can't think of another explanation. What do you know about the team you put together? I have to say my first impressions of them all is not good. They all seem a bit wet."

"DCI Brown and DC Johnson work together regularly on the main proactive CID team and have an excellent arrest record. DS Adams has a reputation for being a bit of a terrier – good on detail, never lets anything drop. He was recommended to me by the DCI that covers the west. Jennifer, the CSI, is one of the best we have."

"Actually, yes, Jennifer really impressed me. Although she didn't find much on the victim her approach when she was de-briefing me was thorough and professional."

"So, what do you want me to do?"

"I dunno. I have no idea where he could have got that information. I need to keep a tight leash on this team and hope they start getting a bit more gumption."

"They might just be a bit scared of you, ma'am. It's not every day your chief takes personal command of an op."

"I know, I know. I'm breaking every rule in the command handbook, but if one of them is selling our secrets to a bloody reporter, it's a good job I'm in their faces. I will not tolerate anything like this. If I catch one of them, they will be out of their job within seconds, with my boot firmly up their arse."

"Understood, ma'am. Let me know if there is anything I can do."

*

It was still early, a few hours before they both had to be at work. He rolled over on his back, his breathing heavy, the smell of sex filling the room.

"Phew, you are good."

"Ah, you say the nicest things. You weren't too bad yourself."

He leant over towards her and looked her straight in the face, still flushed with the intense mutual orgasms they had so skilfully engineered.

"Thank you for what you did yesterday."

"Yesterday?"

"Yeh, you know, giving me that tip about the note. It really shit her up when I confronted her about it."

"Be careful, Jeff. You'll get me in loads of trouble if she works out the information came from me."

"I know, babe. Don't worry, I'll play it cool. Protecting my sources and all that."

They cuddled as the inevitable post-sex sleep threatened to consume them. Jeff was off in seconds, not noticing the troubled look that had come over her face.

# 7

Sarah arrived at St Helier Police Station just after 9am and went straight into see the resource manager, who seemed completely unfazed by her sudden unannounced presence.

"Morning, boss lady, what can I do for you?"

"Good to see you are your normally bubbly self, Lydia."

"Keep happy, boss. That's what I say. Don't let the bastards get you down."

"Yeh, indeed. Lydia, what is the resource and tasking profile of our senior detective team at the moment?"

Lydia knew everything about everything when it came to who was deployed where and raised a mischievous eyebrow. "Fallen out with your new team already?"

Sarah tried not to smile at the banter. She always liked the fact that Lydia paid little adherence to her rank and status. Too many people she encountered were 'yes men and women', too willing to tell her what they thought she wanted to hear.

"No, but I do have some concerns. We might have a potential leak and I want to explore my options if we need to swap some of them out."

"The problem is all your most experienced detectives

are on the fraud and money laundering case and are having massive success in shutting it down. You know how much Mr Le Trousain and the moneyed on this island value that."

"Yeh, but they might change their mind if this lunatic does what she is threatening and starts killing more people."

"You have a good team there, Sarah. All about your age, with some decent service and good performance records. I'm sure they'll come good, and if there is a bad apple in there, I'm sure we can wheedle them out pretty quickly."

"Thanks, Lydia. We'll leave it for now, but I might need you to work your magic if the shit hits the fan."

"No problem, boss lady. Always at your command."

As Sarah walked out, she stopped in classic *Columbo* style. "Actually, Lydia, one more thing. What about profilers? Where do we normally get the really good ones from?"

"The National Crime Agency on the mainland. They are the best if you want expert profilers."

"Thanks, Lydia."

\*

The daily de-brief was uneventful. Sarah had decided to keep the run-in with the reporter to herself. She wanted to watch the dynamics of the team for a bit, suss out whether anyone was giving off the wrong signals. After an hour of chat, she was none the wiser. Whilst no one was exactly 'pulling up trees', they all seemed to be on task.

The next twenty-four hours were equally frustrating, with progress painfully slow. Steph and Lisa had verified the wife's alibi, but the tech team had not much success in tracking down the origin of the fake profile. Mark had some positive response from both the witness appeal and the door-to-door, with a number of sightings of a blonde woman seemingly hanging about in the car park near where the victim had been found. The problem was beyond the blonde hair and a summer dress, the descriptions were patchy.

Sarah kept pushing them to get on with proper grunt detective work. Work the evidence, work the public, get out and about. Something had to start going their way. She couldn't help but fear that this killer was ready to strike again, and she couldn't shake the feeling that there was something badly off with the team.

# 8

Shane D'Varne slowly stirred the rich tomato sauce he had made to go with the pasta that would form the main course of the meal he was preparing for his date. He thought a night in might be better than being out in public. He was a single man, but due to his hugely influential role as the state Treasury Minister he didn't need people gossiping about his love life.

He had found her on a dating website, not one he particularly approved of, due to its apparent focus on extramarital affairs, but the options for finding women in Jersey were limited and he needed the discretion. She was called Daisy, in her mid-thirties and she described herself as having striking red hair and an appealing, attractive face. Due to the type of site it was, there were no photos, so he was never sure whether the person he was supposedly dating was actually genuine. Somebody had warned him about 'catfishing' or some word like that. Part of the youth of today's lingo that described this modern phenomenon of people duping silly old fools like him with fake online profiles.

As he put his avocado starter in the fridge and gave the sauce another stir his doorbell rang. He looked at his watch. She was very prompt.

As he opened the door, he gave the visitor a curious look. She did actually look like the description on the website. Maybe he wasn't such an old fool after all.

"Hi, I'm Daisy, it's super to meet you."

Shane was a bit taken aback. Her accent was full on Jersey posh and as he gestured her into his home, he wondered to himself why he was so surprised.

She walked into the sitting room with poise and balance, clearly a proper lady, although the plunging neckline of her top, which revealed a decent firm cleavage, seemed to be at odds with his first impression.

Shane realised how ill prepared he was for the dating scene. He had barely said a word to her as she sat down on his sofa, crossing a pair of very shapely legs.

"So, do you want the sex now or after we have eaten?"

He stood there with his mouth open, trying to take in what she had just said. "Err... what... um... I'm..."

She roared with laughter. "Oh, darling, you are so precious. You should see your face. I'm sorry, just my little joke."

"Oh, right. Ha, ha, very funny. Err, can I get you a glass of champagne?"

"Now you are talking, darling. I would love one."

Shane walked back into the kitchen to find the champagne, completely wrong-footed by this sassy, confident woman that was sat in his home. Did she really expect them to have sex on the first date?

After a rather awkward few minutes Shane invited her into the dining room and served the avocado starter. She ate it slowly and appreciatively, savouring every mouthful.

"Mmm, you can clearly cook, Mr D'Varne."

"Oh, thank you, glad you enjoyed it, but please, call me Shane."

"OK, Shane, tell me a bit about yourself."

"Err, a bit boring, really. Single. Work for the Jersey government as the Treasury Minister—"

"Ooh," she interrupted, "you sound quite important. Do you use this dating site a lot?"

"Well, on occasions. Not sure I really approve of its 'raison d'etre', but I struggle to meet women."

"Do you use these women for sex?"

"Um, well, I'm not sure that is really any of your business—"

"Oh, come now, Shaney waney, don't be bashful. Its 'raison d'etre', as you so quaintly put it, is to help people fuck each other's brains out."

Shane flinched at the crudeness of her comment. "I guess, and of course sex is nice on occasion."

Daisy smiled at him. "You're actually really nice. What a shame."

Shane got up to get the main course, curious about the exchange. What did she mean, 'what a shame'?

He busied himself in the kitchen, finishing off the sauce and draining the pasta. He cut up some basil to go on the top. As he walked back into the dining room, she was sat there, drinking a glass of red wine.

"I poured us both a glass. I hope you don't mind?"

"No, of course not." He placed the meal in front of her. "Enjoy."

She smiled and started to eat. The silence was a bit uncomfortable and Shane noticed that she kept looking at his wine glass. "The wine's lovely," she said, seemingly willing him to drink it.

Shane finished his mouthful and picked up the glass. A nice red merlot he had picked up from one of the local vineyards for just such an occasion. He took a deep slug.

As the wine flowed down his throat, he noticed Daisy had stopped eating, staring at him expectantly. A few seconds later, as the horrendous pain consumed his body, he realised why.

"What a shame," she mouthed as her image faded from his conscious vision and he slumped over the table, his face landing unceremoniously in his pasta.

# 9

Sarah bolted awake at the annoying tinkling of her mobile phone. She tried to clear her blurry vision to see it was 5.25am.

"What the…"

She swiped the screen.

"Sarah, it's Gerard Le Trousain, I need you in my office now."

"What? Why?"

"Now, Sarah. I can't discuss this over the phone."

The call was abruptly ended and Sarah sat in her bed dumbfounded. Mr Le Trousain was not normally rude. What on earth had got his goat?

Sarah hurriedly got ready and drove to the government buildings in Grouville. Mercifully it was still early and the roads were clear. Just after 6am she was sat in his office, nursing a soothing cup of tea.

Gerard walked in, ashen-faced.

Sarah sat up. "What is it? What has happened?"

"Shane D'Varne has been murdered, Sarah. His body was found slumped in his dinner by his housekeeper when she turned up for work this morning."

"Jesus, what time does she start work?"

"Early, she looks after Mr D'Varne's every need including making sure he is in here by 7am each morning."

"Why do they think it's murder? Couldn't he have just had a heart attack or something?"

"Because there was a note, Sarah. Just like the other one."

Suddenly, for Sarah, the world felt like it had stopped on its axis. Gerard was still talking to her, but she wasn't hearing the words. Everything was a blur, unreal, unbelievable. Another murder. It just couldn't be true.

"Sarah, are you listening to me?"

She was bolted out of her malaise by Gerard's obvious irritation. "God, yes, sorry. I just can't believe it. I need to get to the scene and find out what the team are doing. I'm so sorry, Gerard. I will get this sorted."

"You had better, Sarah. Shane was a dear friend of mine and I don't need to remind you what an embarrassment this is for me, a couple of days after lauding you as a bloody heroine on this island."

"God, yes, I'm sorry—"

Gerard interrupted her uncharacteristic stumbling over her words. "And of course, this doesn't help. What the hell is going on here?"

Sarah stared at the front page of the *Jersey Herald* that Gerard had slammed down on the desk in front of her. The headline made her heart sink. That reporter had done what he threatened.

*JERSEY'S TOP COP REFUSES TO ANSWER QUESTIONS ABOUT ISLAND MURDER. POLICE DENYING SADISTIC NOTE LEFT*

*ON THE BODY. PUBLIC HAVE A RIGHT TO
KNOW WHAT IS GOING ON.*

Sarah put her head in her hands as she read the poisonous words. "Gerard, I'm so sorry. This reporter doorstepped me at my home talking about the note. No one but the investigation team know about it. I am working with my deputy to find out how this information could have got to him. I did refuse to comment as it will jeopardise the investigation, but he is clearly chasing sensationalist headlines."

"Christ, Sarah, this is an absolute disaster. How have you let this thing get out of control so quickly?"

Sarah tried to regain some of the ground. "The best thing I can do, Gerard, is get to this second crime scene and start working my arse off to sort this out. I will get onto our comms team to smooth this over."

"OK, but I want results, Sarah, and I want them soon."

Sarah left quickly, his words stinging her ears. She phoned Steph straight away and got the victim's address. The whole team were already there.

*

Twenty minutes later, Sarah walked into the plush second-floor apartment overlooking the sea in La Rocque, part of a gated community for more of the rich and famous of Jersey. The whole team were there, with CSI Colney in full flow. As Sarah walked in there was a general murmuring of greeting.

"What have we got, Jennifer?"

"Well, my initial assessment is some type of poisoning. You see these areas of red patchy skin, coupled with skin lesions? They are classic signs of a high exposure to poison, probably something like arsenic. The ME is on his way and I'm sure the post-mortem will confirm exactly what killed him. I have taken samples of the food and wine, but it is almost certainly something he drank for it to get into his system in the sort of quantities that killed him so quickly."

"What about the perp?"

"As you can see, clear evidence of a second person having been present. I have taken a few prints and swabbed the glass and plates to see if I can get any DNA. I'll know more when I can get these back to the lab."

Sarah turned to Steph. "What have you got, DCI Brown?"

"Ma'am. We've got a grainy CCTV image from the building's security camera showing a woman entering the building around 7pm. The picture does not really pick up her face, but she is a redhead, fairly slim build, probably in her thirties or forties."

"Is it the same perp?"

"We think so. If she wore a wig at the first scene, it's perfectly feasible that she wore a different colour wig this time, but the images aren't clear enough to be conclusive. We have spoken to the website admin team again, for the dating site used by the first victim, and they confirmed that Mr D'Varne had arranged a date through their site with a Daisy Smith. Lisa will check it out, but if the MO is the same, the profile will be another fake one. Of course, ma'am, the thing that really tells us this is the same perp is this note."

Sarah took the bagged note and steeled herself for what she was about to read.

*The game is moving fast. As I predicted, you floundered around with victim number one. Did you get my description... blonde women in a summer dress... well, I waited around in that car park long enough to get seen, but of course people don't really see you... do they?*

*Victim two here was actually a rather nice man, not like that loser I killed first. What a shame he had to die so we could continue our game.*

*Here is clue number two: 'if you search the internet, will you find the answer?'*

*There will be a third clue before my final act of round one, which will be a very public display of your incompetence.*

*Can you work out the deadly connections?*

As she finished reading, she shook her head. "This bitch is goading us. What have we concluded from the note?"

Mark took the lead. "The language is similar, ma'am. Clearly she feels she has the upper hand on us and is demonstrating a hatred for our profession. She seems to want to humiliate us for reasons that are not yet clear. I have to say that the clue is much less clear than the last one. I really don't know what she means about searching on the internet. Is she maybe referring to the name of a search engine, like Yahoo or Google, or is she referencing the act of searching, so the answer is surfing? To be honest, I need more time to profile this, as none of the possible answers

I have come up with have any obvious connection to the name Joey."

Sarah sighed. For the first time as chief officer of Jersey Police, she felt completely out of control. How had this one individual managed to turn her life upside down in a few days? Jennifer was just finishing her work, so Sarah pulled the team together to task them out.

"Right, once again I don't need to tell you what a fucking disaster this is. I was summoned to see Mr Le Trousain at stupid o'clock this morning because, if you don't already know, this is the Treasury Minister and a personal friend of his. We also have a reporter stirring up shit about the first murder referencing a note on the victim. We are all over the *Jersey Herald* this morning. I have no idea how he found out about the note, but I don't need to tell you that I will kick two bells of shit out of anyone I find leaking confidential investigation details to the press."

Sarah paused for dramatic impact, but none of the team seemed to flinch at the mention of leaked information.

"I want a briefing tomorrow morning at 8am. For the rest of the day, I expect you all to be putting in the hard yards. DCI Brown and DC Johnson, talk to that website again and find out all you can about these fake profiles. She must have left a trail somewhere. Then, I want all of you to do door-to-door in the local area. Find some evidence, find some more CCTV. She can't avoid all surveillance, surely. DS Adams, can you guard the scene until the ME gets here and supervise his work? Jennifer, I want your preliminary report at the meeting tomorrow. For my part I'm going to smooth over this PR disaster—"

Sarah's flow was interrupted by the beep of Mark's phone, who tried to avoid her obvious displeased look as he checked the message.

"Sorry, ma'am, but the uniform guarding the gate has said that the TV and press are outside asking for a statement about what is happening."

"What!" Sarah walked to the window to look back towards the gated entrance. The local TV cameras were there and a familiar face she really didn't want to see. "How the hell are they on this so quickly?"

Mark responded. "I guess the forensic van and our vehicles are fairly conspicuous. I'm guessing one of the local residents has tipped them off."

"Jesus wept. OK, get on with my tasking, and DS Adams, make sure the ME can get in without being hassled. I will call our comms team to agree a strategy. For now, say 'no comment', but I'm almost certainly going to have to front this out."

They all dispersed, the mood in the room sullen and dark.

# 10

It was mid-morning as she sat aimlessly watching the TV, hoping for something on the local news that would tell her they had found the second victim. She hated the waiting. The rush she had from the act and the unbridled joy she experienced as she wrote each note, filled her body with adrenalin. The problem was the high didn't last long, and she got home drained and exhausted. The come-down, the waiting, just served her demons. Once again she had the knife pressed to her wrists, the nervous excitement coming back in waves and raging through her body. A red mark appeared as she pushed harder, her eyes bulging with the anticipation. She let out a scream and dropped the knife.

\*

Sarah walked to the gate that protected the community from the outside world. She saw the reporter that had doorstepped her and allowed herself an inner smile. She had agreed a statement with her head of comms, and it was time to get her own back.

She walked through the gate to be met by a small

crowd of reporters and a camera team from the local TV station. As usual, they all started shouting questions at once. She gestured for silence as the camera started to roll.

"It is with some regret that I must inform you that Shane D'Varne, the Treasury Minister of the Jersey government, has been murdered in his home last night. This follows the murder of esteemed local businessman David Braithwaite on Saturday. We believe that both these killings have been committed by the same woman, who seems determined to strike fear into our island community. I can assure you that the Jersey Police are treating this as their top priority and will not rest until the perpetrator of these heinous acts is safely behind bars. As always, we welcome any information from the public who may have seen anything around either murder scene. The woman is in her thirties or forties and is disguising herself by wearing a blonde wig at the first scene and a red wig at the second. She is using a dating website to meet her victims and we urge all men using these sites to be careful about who they are meeting. My success as your chief of police, which was recently celebrated by the honour of receiving the inaugural Freedom of Jersey accolade, has been built on an excellent rapport with the public of Jersey. This is why I am disappointed that the *Jersey Herald* and its reporter Jeff Godley, who is standing in front of me now, chose to chase sensationalist headlines in their paper this morning. I can assure you that we will always share as much information as we can with the public but will understandably hold back on key evidence if it would be detrimental to the investigation by releasing this information too early. Thank you for listening to my statement and we have no further comment at this time."

Despite the clamour for more information, Sarah turned around and ignored the multiple shouts for further comment. As she did, she stared down Jeff Godley, who gave her an arrogant, unnerving smirk. She walked through the gate, wondering what he might do next.

*

It was nearly 11pm and Sarah stared at her reflection in the mirror. The day had been long and arduous. She had left the team to get on with their investigations, desperately hoping for some good news in the morning.

As she studied her reflection, she was shocked at what was looking back at her. Her eyes were sunken, her skin was blotchy, and her hair was lank and lifeless. And, *my god, is that a grey hair?* At thirty-eight years old, she had no illusions that her face would start to rapidly show signs of the stresses and strains she was constantly under in her role. She knew she had never been much to look at: a sharp, angular face with piggy eyes had led people to describe her as unconventionally pretty. She often felt this was just a kind way of saying she was just a bit ugly. It was the same as a kid. She had always been the plain, odd-looking one. Having never met her real parents, she never knew where she got this odd combination of looks from.

Her drive and determination to get to where she wanted to in her police career had masked this unconscious worry. The worry about whether anyone would really want to love someone that looked like her. The constant fight against sexism and the need to be rough and tough as she climbed the career ladder had undoubtedly put men off, and real relationships had been few and far between. She slapped some skin cream over her face and got into bed, desperately hoping that tomorrow would bring a breakthrough.

\*

The sex was once again passionate and satisfying. As they lay in bed, Jeff Godley stared at his partner, who had a mischievous look on her face.

"What's that look for?"

"She marked your card this morning."

"Huh, if you're talking about your boss, that bitch thinks she's too clever. She is making a mistake if she underestimates me."

"What exactly have you got against her? She seems quite nice."

"I have my reasons."

His partner sat up and fixed him with a concerned look. "What is going on here, Jeff? I don't mind feeding you bits of information, but I'm not going to lose my job over it, so if you have something I should know about, spit it out."

"Don't worry, you'll find out soon enough."

With that he rolled over and closed his eyes, leaving her confused and a little unnerved.

# 11

The team assembled on time in the incident room. The incident board had been updated with all the pictures and information from the Shane D'Varne murder, alongside the details of the first one.

Sarah started the briefing. "I have the preliminary report from the medical examiner and he has confirmed that Mr D'Varne died from a massive dose of arsenic, ingested through the wine he was drinking. Again, there is no evidence of any non-victim fluids or other substances. It seems she somehow slipped it in his drink and waited for him to die. Jennifer, does this match your findings?"

"Yes, ma'am, as I said at the scene, it appeared to be poisoning from the condition of the skin, and the wine sample does contain high levels of arsenic. The guy had no chance with that dosage. I did manage to get one decent thumbprint from the wine bottle and a DNA sample from the fork, where she left some saliva. There are no matches on either sample on any of our databases, suggesting she has not been known to the police before. The good news is that we can do a match against these samples if we get any suspects."

"OK, thanks, Jennifer. DS Adams, what have you got?"

"The door-to-door gave us some confirmation that a redhead was seen walking into the building, but no one saw her getting out of a car or taxi—"

"Actually, that is a good point. How is she getting to these places? Can we check the local taxi firms to see if they dropped a redhead off around that time?"

"Yes, ma'am, we'll get on to that. In terms of the profiling, I have written every word I could think of that might be the answer to the clue on the board, but I'm struggling to see the links to Joey."

The team all looked around at the board and stared at it, the little cogs whirring but seemingly no flashes of inspiration.

Sarah changed her focus to Steph and Lisa. "What about the website? Any progress?"

"Actually, yes, ma'am. We discussed how the punters use the site to see whether we could track activity such as someone setting up new profiles or booking dates. There are around 450 male profiles on the site and just over 270 female profiles. They confirmed that there have not been any new female profiles added over the last three days, meaning the perp probably set up several fake profiles in one go. They checked, though, and there is no evidence of a user setting up multiple profiles, meaning she is using different aliases each time."

"OK. Anything else?"

"Yes, the good news is that the site administrator can tell us which people have booked dates, because it is a condition of the site that all liaisons are booked through the website. Now, whilst there can be between fifteen to twenty dates each day, I'm proposing we contact the men booked on dates over the next few nights to see if we can track her down. It seems the best break we have had so far."

They waited for Sarah to respond, all tensed up as they wondered whether the 'ice queen' would give them any credit.

Eventually she spoke. "OK, DCI Brown, that seems like a good step, but I do hope we are not wasting time on a wild goose chase. This woman is clearly very clever and may stop using the site, but I guess it's a credible line of enquiry. Anything else from anyone?"

There was a collective non-committal, slightly embarrassed grunt from the team as the meeting drifted to its conclusion and the team dispersed.

Sarah got up and walked into her office. She stared out of the window, her gut churning as the lack of progress on the case escalated her body's stress responses. She looked back out to the main incident room as the team slowly trudged out. She shook her head. What was wrong with them? Apart from the money laundering case, this was the biggest thing that had hit the Jersey Police since she had been chief, but the team were acting like they were trying to track down a couple of shoplifters. She sipped her coffee. Was she the problem? Had she made a mistake in taking command? Was her rank intimidating them and affecting their performance? She shook the doubts away. They had to respect her decision and get over whatever issues they had. She sat down and continued to watch the seagulls flock over the harbour, hoping that something would start going her way.

\*

Sarah continued to stew on the outcome of the briefing. She picked up the phone to call her deputy. He answered straight away.

"Jo, this team is doing my head in. Is this really the best we have?"

"The problem is, ma'am, you have seventy-five detectives deployed on the fraud and money laundering case. They are so close to taking this whole enterprise down, we can't afford to re-deploy them at this crucial stage."

"OK, but I can't believe this is the best of what is left. DS Adams doesn't seem to have any energy for the case. DCI Brown seems vaguely competent but is grabbing at straws, and I don't think I have even heard DC Johnson speak. Thank god for Jennifer. She at least seems to be good at her job."

"The strange thing is that DCI Brown and DS Adams practically kicked my door down when they heard about the first murder. They were desperate to be on the team. I think it's just a bit of 'stage fright'. I'm sure they will come good but let me know if there is anything I can do."

"Can you review the resource profile of the money laundering case with Lydia to see if there is any chance of releasing any more resources? I will speak to her about getting a professional profiler from the mainland. I need someone to properly profile the perp."

"OK, ma'am, will do."

Sarah stared out of the window again. The boats were bobbing about gently in the harbour, backlit by a beautiful sunny day. The locals and tourists were buzzing around enjoying the weather and making the ice-cream sellers happy with the long queues seeking refreshment from the burning sun. She shook her head at the normality of it all. Was the killer mingling amongst them, selecting her next victim?

# 12

She saw him sat at the bar. He looked like just the right mark. Sufficiently desperate and sufficiently drunk. She wasn't going to use the website again, not since that *bitch* Sarah had blabbed about it in her press conference. Tonight she was being an opportunist and she loved it.

She sidled up to him, deliberately brushing his arm to attract his attention, whilst thrusting her cleavage directly into his eyeline. It had the desired effect as he looked at it before he slowly raised his inebriated face to look at her.

"Hi, sexy, now you look like a man up for a good time."

He instinctively pulled back from her gaze, vaguely taken aback by what she had said, almost falling off the bar stool in the process. She put a firm hand behind his back to steady him. After a minute he managed to string a vaguely coherent sentence together.

"Ya na, I bloody well am, my fair maiden. Where dush you want to do it?"

"I think you need to go and buy some protection. I ain't a slut, you know. Safe sex is still important."

"Oh, yeh, of corsh." With that he stumbled off the stall and made for the toilets, fumbling around in his pocket for some change.

She sat on the stool and ordered him another whisky, discreetly adding her magic killing potion as she set it down at the bar.

A few minutes later, he emerged from the toilets, waving the packet of condoms with not an ounce of discretion. She tried not to show her utter contempt for him as he stumbled back to his stool.

"I'm ready, baby."

"Pipe down, big boy. I just need to freshen up. Drink up and I will be back in a minute."

He turned to his glass, utterly compliant. She slipped the note in his pocket and walked out of the bar.

\*

Sarah had barely let her head touch the pillow when her life was once again interrupted by the tinkling of her phone. The sense of dread as she picked up the phone was palpable. It was Steph.

"Ma'am, I'm sorry to bother you but there has been another one. At Randolph's bar in St Ouen. The team are assembling and I assume you want to be there."

"My god. This woman is killing every few days. I'll be there in half an hour."

Sarah sat up, stress gripping her, the familiar knotted feeling in her stomach increasing by the minute. In these moments she wished for someone lying in bed next to her. Someone that could keep her calm, keep her on track, tell her that everything was going to work out. As she looked at the empty space in her bed, she realised a tear was rolling down her cheek.

She quickly wiped it away. What was happening to her? She never cried. Not even at sad movies. She splashed some water on her face, got dressed and set off to the crime scene.

*

It was around 11.30pm when Sarah arrived at the bar in St Ouen. The now all-too-familiar scene of her team going through the motions of securing and examining the scene greeted her as she walked in.

Jennifer was examining a man that was sprawled on the floor by the bar. A broken glass was next to the body. His face had the same marks as the previous victim.

"Is this another one, Jennifer? The same perp? The same MO?"

"I'm afraid so, ma'am. Almost certainly arsenic poisoning again, administered via the whisky in the glass that has shattered on the floor."

She changed her focus to the rest of the team who all seemed to be hanging around aimlessly, like this was just another 'day in the office'. "DCI Brown, was this date booked on the website?"

"I'm afraid not, ma'am. We made contact with the male side of the dates that had been arranged tonight. We had a range of responses from downright outrage at being contacted by the police, from a website that was supposed to have discretion as one of its key principles, to men who were genuinely concerned about this 'black widow'. But, in the end, none of them seemed to be dating a woman that matched our description. This was backed up by us checking the ID in his wallet. He did not use the website that the other two victims used."

"Well, I did warn you not to go on a wild goose chase with this. This woman is clever. She almost certainly watched my press conference where I mentioned the website. Maybe that was a mistake on my part. Anyway, let's focus on what we can control. What about witnesses?"

"Actually, ma'am, lots of witnesses confirmed that an attractive woman, brunette, probably in her late thirties, was seen talking to the victim at the bar. A number of people thought she was a prostitute because she was dressed very sexily and seemed to proposition him to have sex. It seems their interaction was brief. He was very drunk but apparently went to the gents to get condoms. When he came back, someone heard her say she was going to freshen up and she would be back shortly. A few minutes later he falls off his stool, dead. The barman confirmed that she bought him a whisky, but no one can remember seeing her putting anything in the drink. There is no CCTV in here."

"Well, at least we have something this time. She doesn't seem worried about being seen. Do we have any forensics, Jennifer?"

"Yes, I have another really good fingerprint. I agree with you, though, ma'am, she doesn't seem to be worrying about the forensics or who sees her. She must know we don't have anything on her to be this brash."

"Right, detectives, let's get all these witness statements processed and see if there is any CCTV in the local area that can give us a sighting. DS Adams, did you get anywhere with the taxi firms?"

"No, ma'am, I have spoken to all the firms in the area and they didn't pick up anyone that matched her description around the time of the previous two crime scenes."

"Damn it! She must be using her own car. Surely we can look at some of the traffic cameras around the scenes to see if the same car appears?"

"We can try, ma'am, but as you know the traffic cameras on the island are fairly sporadic."

Sarah's rage was building. There was something about Mark that got her heckles up every time. She had to remain professional, but he was testing her limits. With all the furore she forgot the killer's signature. The note. As she calmed down from her simmering rage, she looked over to Jennifer, who seemed to read her mind.

"It's over there, ma'am. Bagged on the counter."

Sarah walked carefully around the crime scene. The last thing she needed was to compromise evidence. She picked up the bag and read the now all-too-familiar rantings of this mad bitch. The first line took her breath away.

*Are you enjoying this yet, Sarah?*

# 13

She opened the door to her flat, the blood still rushing through her veins. A new high, better than the last two. The game was exciting, driving her on, helping her battle her demons. The thought of Sarah stood at another crime scene, baffled and stressed, gave her such joy.

She put her bag down and looked in the mirror. Her boobs looked great, stood up like a couple of perky melons. She turned around to look at her arse. The dress shaped it well. She nodded admiringly at what she was seeing.

"Not bad. Not bad at all."

She slipped the dress off, still admiring what she saw. That loser was never going to see the nice lingerie she was wearing, but it made her feel good. Confident and sassy. Empowering her to play the role she had so expertly executed tonight.

She walked back into the main living area. The knife was on the side. She picked it up. She stared at it for a few minutes.

"Not tonight."

\*

Sarah must have given out an audible gasp, because the whole team turned to look at her. She turned away from their gaze and read the whole note, utterly dumbfounded by this new development. Someone was making this personal.

*Are you enjoying this yet, Sarah? You and your pathetic team really are slow. I told you the game would be fast, but you seem happy to plod along... Oh god how funny am I... that is why they call you the plod. LOL!*

*Here we have victim number three, killed by a brunette in a sexy dress... well, at least I'm guessing that's how your so-called witnesses described me. Another drunk loser who accepted the promise of sex without a flicker of regret for his wife. The prick didn't even try to take off his wedding ring.*

*So, this is my penultimate step in act one. On Saturday, I will demonstrate your total incompetence. There will be mass causalities in a very public way unless you can solve the clues and find the location of my act one crescendo... and, of course, catch me.*

*Here's your final clue.*

*'Six is the magic number. You have two so far, and this is the one where Lewinsky and Hunter join them in their coffee shop. What was the name of that coffee shop? Work it out and you may have the location of Saturday's fun and games.'*

*Can you work out the deadly connections?*

Sarah tried to compose herself and called the team over to the other side of the room, away from everything that was going on.

"What do you three make of this?"

Mark started, seemingly taking the mantle of the lead profiler. "Well, the obvious first point is she is now making this personal. Whether she saw you on the TV and decided to focus on you is unclear, but I guess it is an unsettling development for you personally."

Sarah sat steely-faced. She had never let a man think she was vulnerable and she wasn't about to give this prick the satisfaction. "Carry on, DS Adams."

"We seem to have someone who is oozing self-confidence, both in her written words and her apparent certainty that witnesses and forensics will not expose her. The reference to a brunette suggests she was wearing another wig, or maybe that is her real hair colour. Another male victim and her obvious disdain for these people suggests she is someone that hates men. She continues to goad us, clearly feeling superior to us in every way. I must admit her clues are baffling me."

Sarah looked to Steph and Lisa for any sort of inspiration, but all she got was blank, tired faces. Her inner monologue kept addling her mind. Was this team just incompetent? Had she been overworking them? Or was there something else at play here? Something she wasn't seeing?

She shook the doubts from her mind and decided not to pursue anything else tonight due to the lateness of the hour.

"OK, get the scene processed and handed back to the

owners. Make sure all the witness statements are signed and properly indexed. Find out if the victim has any next of kin and make sure someone informs them tonight. Otherwise, I will see you at the station in the morning for a 9.30am briefing. I need you all fresh and alert, so get some sleep. We need to solve this lunatic's riddles and work out what the hell she is planning on Saturday."

\*

Jeff Godley stirred. His partner was just getting into bed. He bolted up.

"Where have you been?"

She didn't answer.

"Shit, there's been another one. Hasn't there? Why the hell wasn't I told?"

"I'm not your bloody PA. Why haven't your dozy newspaper people told you about it, if you are supposed to be so well connected?"

"It wouldn't have hurt you to tip me off. I would have loved to have seen her face. She must be frantic."

"Go to sleep, Jeff. I have a lot to do in the morning."

She rolled over, away from his gaze.

Jeff got his phone out and started texting his work colleagues. This story was going to make him famous if it was the last thing he did. A triple murder was big news in anyone's book and he needed to get ahead of it before the mainland newspapers started sniffing this out. He set his alarm for 5am.

# 14

Jeff Godley arrived at St Helier Police Station at 7am, hoping to doorstep Sarah once again, to watch her squirm at his presence and his insightful comments, but the sight that greeted him made his heart sink. They had been too late, too slow off the mark. The media circus was in town. TV and newspaper reporters were stacked in rows around the entrance, being poorly marshalled by some hard done by uniformed coppers. They were all there, the UK mainland media, Sky, NBC and some French media he hadn't seen before. Suddenly this had become world news, and he cursed at the sloppiness of his tinpot newspaper firm.

He mingled with the throng, trying to listen into their narrative, but there wasn't anything new. All the noise seemed to be about the third murder the previous night and the expectation that Sarah Braintree was due out at 9am to make a statement. He stewed at the situation. This was not what he wanted, not how he wanted to make her pay for what she had done to him. He couldn't be just another face in a crowd. She had to know he was always going to be there. In her face and in her nightmares. He decided the best option for now was to wrestle his way to the front of the media scrum, front and centre, so he was one of the first faces she saw.

*

It was just after 9am when Sarah Braintree emerged at the front of St Helier Police Station to the world's media. She was shocked at how one more murder could suddenly turn this from the local Jersey media in her face to the world scrutinising her every move. She steeled herself and started her pre-prepared statement.

"Ladies and gentlemen. It is with some regret that I must confirm that there has been a third murder on this island, at Randolph's bar in St Ouen, last night. The victim was poisoned with arsenic, administered in a glass of whisky. We believe this is the same woman that has committed the previous two murders. She is brash and confident, seemingly unconcerned with being identified. However, despite numerous witness statements from people in the bar last night, we are no nearer identifying who she is. She appears to be targeting men in the forty-five to fifty-five age range, duping them into intimate situations through the promise of sex, leaving the victims vulnerable to her deadly intentions. We therefore warn any men that are approached by an attractive woman offering sex to be very careful and report any such situations to the police. It is imperative that we catch this woman and put a stop to her murderous trail through this island, so I once again appeal to the public for their help in this matter. We are particularly keen to identify any vehicles that may have been seen around any of the crime scenes which appeared suspicious or out of place. I can re-assure the public of Jersey that I will not rest until she is caught and arrested. I will also be procuring some additional specialist support from the National Crime Agency on the mainland to assist with this investigation. Thank you for your time today and we will issue further statements as necessary."

As she finished her statement, the inevitable flurry of flash bulbs started and multiple questions were bombarded at her. She had agreed with the PR team and Mr Le Trousain that she would do no more than read out the statement. She stepped away from the lectern, consumed by the wall of noise. This wasn't the day she had expected to become a global face and, as she looked back to the throng of cameras and reporters, she saw Jeff Godley smirking at her, clearly revelling in her discomfort.

*

She watched the TV coverage. Finally, she was world news, and Sarah was front and centre, squirming as she made appeal after appeal for help. *Incompetent fools*, she thought to herself. She was satisfied they had nothing on her, as she was sure Sarah would have issued a photofit with a better description. She couldn't believe how easy it was not to be noticed, despite her brashness and bravado. The wigs helped, but the great public of Jersey were as pathetic as those plodding detectives, too wrapped up in their own sad little lives to give Sarah the help she so desperately needed. She let out a booming laugh, picked up the knife and ran her finger along the blade, a small trickle of blood appearing as she cut.

She eventually sucked the wound and stopped the bleeding, calmed by the action. She went into the kitchen and got everything ready on the kitchen table for her *act one finale*.

She lined up the empty water bottles and filled them with her special cocktail. She attached the specially prepared labels.

*STRAWBERRY-FLAVOURED WATER. WITH THE COMPLIMENTS OF JERSEY POLICE.*

# 15

Sarah sat in the command suite, frantically doodling on the pad in front of her. It was midday on Saturday, the day the multiple killer had promised to escalate her killing spree. She was trying to get some inspiration, trying to solve the stupid clues that this *bitch* had been goading her with.

The team had worked hard over the last twenty-four hours, but nobody was nearer to solving the clues from the notes or advancing the investigation based on good old-fashioned police work. She had a decision to make. She had to do the best she could for the public of Jersey and was relieved that, so far, no major incidents had been reported.

The team were all there as she walked into the main part of the incident room, all looking apprehensive at her presence and worsening mood. Sarah was never one for hiding her feelings. Her face was one of those that belied everything she was thinking and the team were all tensed up.

"Right, team, I am assuming that we have not made any progress overnight on solving these riddles?"

There was a general embarrassed murmuring, confirming what Sarah suspected.

She turned her attentions to Steph. "DCI Brown, yesterday you gave us all a list of events that are happening today. Have you been able to advance our intel or update the threat, risk and harm assessments on each of the events?"

"Yes, ma'am, the team have been working round the clock, contacting the organisers, assessing potential attendance numbers and profiling the layouts of the events."

"Good, and what conclusions have you come to?"

"Well, ma'am, there are twenty-four events happening across the island that have been advertised quite widely, but there are three that we would recommend as deserving of our attention due to the threat, risk and harm profile."

"OK, go on."

"There is a large event at Jersey Zoo, celebrating their sixty-year anniversary, which is expected to attract larger than normal crowds. There is also a medieval day at Gorey Castle, jousting and stuff, which is also expecting bigger crowds than normal. The final event is at Coronation Park. This is much smaller than the other two, but there are lots of stalls, children's rides and a pop-up waterpark that the organisers say is attracting a lot of attention, particularly from the local community. They had already approached us to get some advice on stewarding and crowd control because the event is free, and with the weather so nice, they might get more than they bargained for."

"What is the current deployment profile at these events?"

"The local inspectors covering the zoo and castle already have two serials deployed from the moment the events started this morning. They have not reported any instances so far. The event at Coronation Park starts in just under an hour at 1pm. I understand they are deploying now to make sure the event doesn't run into any crowd problems as it starts."

"What else do we have?"

"We have three police support units ready across the island to be deployed at the first sign of any trouble."

Sarah sat pensively, scanning the faces in the room, all of them seemingly poised to respond to whatever direction she would give. She stood up and filled her coffee cup. The room remained silent.

"OK, if we are no nearer working out the answers to her stupid riddles, I'm inclined to deploy one PSU to each event. They should remain discreet but ready for action. I can't afford for this woman to create havoc on our island and I agree with the threat assessments you have made. She seemed to imply that she was going to target a large event and these three seem like the most lik—"

"Oh my god, ma'am. I've worked it out."

Everyone turned around to see who had interrupted the chief. It was DC Lisa Johnson.

Sarah was genuinely surprised. She really didn't think she had ever heard Lisa speak more than a couple of words, always seemingly deferring to Steph.

"Sorry, DC Johnson. What did you say?"

"I've worked it out, ma'am. The riddles."

*

She was already in place, enjoying the sunshine, the bottles in her bag ready to be left at strategic points for the maximum impact. Her phone beeped. She opened the text message.

*Get ready. It's go time. No doubt she will deploy every available officer to the scene. Good luck.*

She smiled to herself. The wounds on her hand were sore, but she put that all out of her mind. Sarah Braintree was about to get the full extent of her wrath. She played it out in her mind.

*Thirty years, Sarah. Thirty years I've waited to pay you back for what you did to me.*

# 16

Sarah was beside herself. Had this vaguely incompetent team finally caught her a break?

"What is it, DC Johnson? What is the answer?"

"It's *Friends*, ma'am."

"What? The TV show?"

"Yes, ma'am. The answer to the first clue was Joey. The last note talks about Lewinsky and Hunter. She is referencing famous people with the same names as the characters on *Friends*. Monica Lewinsky and Rachel Hunter. The second clue is quite clever. She is referring to a search engine. It's Bing, Chandler's second name on the programme. You see, Joey, Chandler, Monica and Rachel. All characters from *Friends*. She says that six is the magic number because there are six of them, when you add Phoebe and Ross. Sorry, I can't believe I didn't see it before. It's one of my favourite shows."

"No need to apologise, DC Johnson. I'm glad someone is on it. How does this solve the final clue then?"

"Well, the name of the coffee shop in the show is Central Perk – it's a pun around Central Park in New York, where the show is based."

"Central Park? There isn't anywhere on Jersey called Central Park. What the hell type of clue is that?"

Mark interjected. "Actually, ma'am, there is. It's what the locals call Coronation Park. I'm not sure how they came to give it this alternative name, but I think it something to do with it being in the central part of the south coastline. She's targeting the event at Coronation Park."

The next few minutes was a blur of noise. Instructions being barked out by Sarah, radio contact made with all the available sergeants and inspectors to deploy to Coronation Park, kit being picked up and put on as everyone in the room headed for their date with destiny.

Sarah's final rally cry left them in no doubt about her mood. "Come on, team. Time to nail this bitch."

*

She sat eating an ice cream, watching the gorillas. She loved the way they sat, staring at people, almost goading them. Gentle giants but with the potential to kill you with one swipe. Kind of like her, but she didn't hit; she didn't touch. She was far more subtle than that.

She smiled as she heard the faint wailing of sirens, seemingly moving away from the zoo towards the park. She watched as people picked up the bottles and started drinking the contents. She couldn't wait to see Sarah's face.

*

Sarah and the team arrived at the park just before 1pm. As she alighted from her vehicle, she realised the decision to deploy all available resources had made the surrounding area sound like some major emergency was going down, sirens coming from every direction. She could see several members of the public looking concerned and she realised they were being too gung-ho.

She got straight on the radio. "All units, this is Chief Braintree. Turn off your sirens. I repeat, turn off your sirens. Maintain your deployments but ease down on the approach to the park. Public are looking concerned and I don't want the perp to be spooked. Set up the perimeters at each exit of the park and await my instructions."

She grabbed the investigation team together. "Right, you heard my instructions. I want the perimeters swamped with our guys, but I do not want the public or our perp spooked. DCI Brown, please take DS Adams and DC Johnson into the park and liaise with the local sergeants. I want a calm but focused recce of the crowds. We need to find her and what she is up to. Hopefully the PSUs are in place to cut off any escape routes if our perp decides to run. I'm going to mingle and try to give the impression that this is just some nice neighbourhood event. I want immediate radio updates if you spot anything suspicious."

The team deployed and Sarah scanned the growing crowd. "Where are you? Where are you?" she muttered to herself.

She started to walk into the main part of the park. The air was filled with the excited giggles and squeals of the children, enjoying the rides and splashing about in the waterpark. A number of people greeted her warmly and she chatted to them without fully engaging in what they were saying. Her mind was racing, her eyes constantly darting from place to place, desperately hoping for a break.

She stepped away from the crowds and got on the radio, seeking updates from each unit. Her heart sank as the same response came back. "Nothing to report, ma'am."

She started to patrol the perimeter, checking in with each of the police support units, who were locked and loaded, itching to jump into action. The nervous tension was palpable and Sarah tried to keep them calm but focused.

She returned to the main park. DC Johnson gave her an update on the interior recce, but nothing untoward had been spotted and nothing had happened.

She paced around, looking at every face, twitching at anyone that seemed like they were wearing a wig, but nobody was matching the description.

The afternoon dragged on, Sarah tensing up as every minute passed. She desperately didn't want another murder or the multiple casualties that the perp had promised, but perversely she felt like something needed to happen, to release the nervous energy coursing through her whole team.

It was nearly 5pm and the event was winding down.

She called her team together. "What's going on?"

DCI Brown took the lead. "I don't know, ma'am. Nothing has happened. We have been all over the event and there have been no incidents. The PSUs haven't reported anything suspicious either."

"Do you think we have stopped her doing what she planned? Did we work out her silly riddles in time and our presence has made her change her plans?"

The team all looked at her, seemingly unable to give her the re-assurances she needed.

"What about the other events you profiled, DCI Brown?"

"Nothing, ma'am. I have been in contact with the event commanders and they haven't reported anything either."

"This just doesn't make sense. Did we make a mistake? Why hasn't she carried out her threats?"

# 17

It was nearly 11pm and Sarah sat watching the end of the news, glad that she wasn't featuring as today's headline. She checked her phone and emails. Nothing had been reported to her since all the events had finished. She allowed herself a brief smile and happier thoughts to invade her psyche. *So, you are not as clever as you thought... bitch.*

She lay down, hoping for some uninterrupted sleep. Tomorrow was going to be an interesting day, trying to work out what their next move was going to be.

*

Jeff Godley sat on the sofa, with his partner. "Come on. What happened today?"

"I'm not telling you, Jeff. Just back off."

"You were expecting her to strike again. Weren't you?"

"Look, Jeff, stop being so morbid. The fact that the murderess bitch hasn't carried out her threats is a good thing. I know your only motivation in life is to sell your bloody newspaper but the rest of us quite like our normal, uneventful lives."

"OK, sorry. Shall we—"

"No, Jeff, not tonight. I'm really not in the mood."

*

She sank her third whisky; the nervous excitement not being dulled by the alcohol. Her plan had worked perfectly. As usual, the waiting was killing her. Her final act of round one was a slow burner, designed to lull Sarah into thinking she had won, but the longer she waited for the high of seeing her actions bear fruit, the worse her demons became. She looked at the knife. Picked it up. Put it down. Picked it up. Let out a guttural scream and threw it across the room.

*

Sarah stirred. Her phone was ringing. She looked at the time. 4.53am.

"What the hell is this?" Her mouth was dry, but she managed to utter a response to the call.

A familiar voice was on the end of the line. "Ma'am, it's Jo."

"What's up, Jo? I'm guessing this is not good news."

"I'm afraid not, ma'am. We have thirteen people that have been admitted to the general hospital in St Helier with suspected poisoning. Three are already dead and the rest are in a critical condition."

Sarah was suddenly wide awake and frantic. "What? How? Nothing happened today. How is that possible?"

"The preliminary assessment is that they have

been poisoned by anti-freeze. It seems the effects of the poisoning can take up to twelve hours to appear, but once they set in, they can be fatal."

"Oh my god, Jo. This can't be happening. This is what she promised. Get the team together. I will be there in twenty minutes."

It was just before 5.30am that the whole team gathered in the command suite. Jo, her deputy who had been on Gold command overnight, had been the one to deal with the initial incident reports and was ready to de-brief.

"OK, DCO Millar is here to give us an update on what has been going on over the last couple of hours. I know we are all tired, but please focus on what he has to say. We have a major incident here."

"Thank you, ma'am. At 12.37am this morning, the first casualty, a twenty-three-year-old woman, was admitted to the general hospital in St Helier. They were admitted with severe vomiting. At first the hospital thought she had drunk too much and left her too sleep it off, once they controlled her sickness. Within thirty minutes of her initial diagnosis her heartbeat started to spike, she had multiple convulsions and went into major organ failure. She died soon after. Within an hour of this first person being admitted, the hospital was swamped with another twelve people exhibiting similar symptoms. They declared a major incident and called us. Two more people have died and the other ten are fighting for their lives."

The room was silent.

DCO Millar carried on. "We did catch a break, though. One of the victims, who seems to be less seriously affected than some of the others, brought something into the hospital which we think is key to explaining what happened."

Sarah nodded for Jo to carry on.

"He brought in a bottle that he said was given out for free at the event he was at this afternoon. It was labelled as strawberry-flavoured water, but he said he started to feel weird about an hour after he drank it. He still had the bottle with him and brought it into the hospital when his symptoms got worse. We quickly seized it as evidence, and the preliminary analysis by CSI suggests the bottle contained the main chemical components of anti-freeze. Ingestion of the amounts that we think people consumed is almost always fatal."

Sarah shook her head. "Jesus Christ. Do we think this is her? Is this the outcome of her threats?"

"It seems probable, ma'am, but of course we don't have her signature move. No note."

Sarah pondered the point. "It's a good point, but she promised multiple casualties. I guess her approach has changed. She doesn't seem to have any bodies to place the note on, at least not at the scene…" Sarah stopped herself. "My god, Jo. I've just realised. Where were these bottles given out? Was it at Coronation Park?"

"I'm afraid not, ma'am. It seems they were all given out at the zoo."

"What? But we solved her clues. The location was Coronation Park. I don't understand."

"I can only conclude, ma'am, that this was all part of her sick game. She has deliberately deceived us about the location of her killing spree."

Sarah rubbed her face in frustration. "Can this get any worse?"

"I'm afraid it can, ma'am. The poisoned bottles had labels on them saying they were with the compliments of the Jersey Police."

# 18

It was just after 9am as Sarah Braintree stood outside the office of Gerard Le Trousain, steeling herself for the inevitable onslaught. She couldn't believe how much her stock had fallen in just one week. A few minutes later the door opened and Gerard's facial expression told her all she needed to know about how this meeting was going to go. He wasted no time in launching into his tirade.

"This is an absolute disaster, Sarah. I'm told we have six dead and six more in a critical condition, with only one coherent survivor of this outrage. What the hell is going on? How have you lost grip of this island so quickly based on one woman's determination to strike fear into the public? She is making you look a fool, Sarah, and the press are having a field day."

"I'm sorry, Gerard, we are doing everyth—"

"But you're not, are you, Sarah? You are not doing everything you can, otherwise this murderess bitch would be in one of our cells."

"Look, Gerard, the team are working around the clock on this one and I have a profiler from the mainland turning up later today, but we don't have enough bodies on the ground to cover all the lines of enquiry."

"Not enough bodies! I have just given you the highest budget settlement ever awarded to the police and you have the audacity to tell me you don't have enough resources."

"Myself and my deputy have been keeping the resourcing profile under constant review, but we are struggling to release resources from the money laundering investigation. At last count we had seventy-five of our best detectives on that investigation and I'm told they are about a week away from busting this whole thing wide open. Don't forget we are having to co-ordinate with Interpol, the French Secret Service, MI6 and the CIA on this one. We can't drop the ball now."

The shouting stopped as they both stared at each other, trying to calm their stress levels, trying to get to some rational place where clear thinking was the only way forward. Gerard turned away from the confrontation and looked out of the window. Sarah stood, not moving, waiting for his next move.

After a few minutes Gerard turned around and gestured for Sarah to sit. He barked into his intercom. "Celia. Coffee. Now."

An uncomfortable vibe hung over the room, as they waited for the coffee to be brought in.

Eventually, Gerard spoke. "OK, Sarah, I'm sorry. I know you are working hard on this, but you have to understand what a nightmare this is for the government after such a long period of stability under your stewardship. I hate the fact that we are world news. We need to find her and stop her."

Sarah filled her coffee cup and took a sip, the caffeine hit immediately calming her mood. "I know, Gerard. I understand that more than anyone. The profiler is key. We need someone that can focus our investigations by giving us a more detailed analysis of the perp. If we can reduce the suspects list by focusing on a clear profile, we will have a better chance of closing in on the perp. We have some good fingerprints and a DNA sample from the second crime scene. If we can focus our energies on the right type of person, we will get her. She can't hide for ever."

"Well, I hope you are right, Sarah. We need a break on this one, but I have to agree, I can't afford for you to drop the ball on the money laundering case. The policing committee has some very powerful people on it that have been directly affected by these organised crime groups that think they can use Jersey as some sort of haven to deal in their dirty cash. We need results on both these cases, and soon."

Sarah finished her coffee and made her excuses to leave.

*

She stood naked in front of the mirror, smiling to herself at what she was seeing. The knife had remained on the side. Untouched. The buzz of the previous day still calming her nerves.

"You are as fit as fuck, Miss Crohan. Not like Sarah. Ugly, spotty, piggy-eyed Sarah. How she must wonder what I look like now. Well, the time is coming, Sarah. The time is coming."

*

Sarah walked back into the incident room. The place was empty. The team was out dealing with the victims, trying to piece together what happened. The CSI team all over the zoo, trying to find something. A small forensic breakthrough that would get them on the front foot.

She examined the incident board, the three previous victims staring down at her, goading her. The team hadn't had time to add the latest victims. How many more faces would there be? Haunting her. Gerard had said there was six victims, but Sarah knew there was likely to be more by the end of the day. People fighting for their lives because of one woman.

She put the coffee machine on and walked into her office. She froze. In the middle of the desk was an envelope. What was written on it made her heart sink.

# 19

Sarah crashed through the door of the post room, like some elephant in musk. The post-room team had the double shock of the sudden uninvited guest and the simultaneous realisation that the person making the noise was the big boss. They all stood open-mouthed, not knowing what to do or what to say. Sarah stood rigid, trying to quell her rage, but nothing was going to stop her offloading.

"There is an envelope on my desk, in the incident room. Who put it there?"

Maureen Baxter, the post-room manager, had to step up. "I don't know what you mean, ma'am. We haven't delivered any post to your team yet today."

"It's on my desk. A handwritten envelope. No postage. Someone handed this into the station and someone put it on my desk. Now tell me who dealt with it."

Maureen looked around at her team. They all shook their heads. "We don't know anything about it, ma'am. You can see from the blank expressions on my team's face that they don't know what you are talking about."

Sarah's rage was not quelling. "The envelope is almost certainly from the woman that has been murdering people at will across this island. There could be key forensic evidence on it and someone in here has just handled it like some normal piece of post. Do you know how important it is that we catch this perp? You may have compromised key evidence."

"With the greatest of respect, ma'am, that is totally unfair. I'm telling you that no one in this team has seen or handled the envelope you are talking about. We would always be alert to non-post-marked letters. We know they can often be suspicious and would always call an officer in if we had any concerns. But I can assure you, we have not seen your envelope."

Sarah let out a frustrated scream and stormed out, leaving a somewhat bemused post-room team behind her.

*

Sarah sat at her desk. The envelope lay there untouched. The words taunted her.

*Sarah Braintree, Chief of Police. The blood of Jersey residents on her hands.*

The incident room was still empty. The team was not due back for a couple of hours. She stood up and paced the room. What should she do? If the post room had not handled this envelope, how the hell had it got put on her desk? Were the forensics already compromised?

After an uncharacteristically long period of indecision, Sarah took action. She grabbed some crime scene gloves and picked up the envelope, being careful to touch as little of it as she could. A single piece of paper slipped out and she steeled herself for what she was about to read.

*Hello, Sarah. I'm guessing you're not enjoying our little game. So, you solved my riddles and swarmed Coronation Park. I was impressed someone knew the Central Park thing, something that only true Jersey people would know. I'm guessing it wasn't you that cracked that one.*

*But of course, you failed, as I predicted you would, because you naively believed I would actually be at the place I so cryptically hid within my riddles. Did you really think I would be that stupid? Give you a chance to catch me when we have so much more of the game to play? I laughed as the coppers, who were still at the zoo, didn't pay me an ounce of attention or seem interested in the bottles I had left around. I mean, what sort of coppers are you training these days?*

*I have to be happy, though. Your incompetence allowed me to complete act one without a glitch. You see, this first act was all about your total humiliation, to show the public of Jersey who you really are. Not that false heroine that was being celebrated at that frankly puke-inducing ceremony. From all the media coverage, I think I can safely put a tick in that box.*

*So, we move onto acts two and three. Act two will give you a clue as to why, and act three will tell you who is behind this. And, yes, more people will have to die so we can complete our game of deadly connections.*

*Get ready, Sarah. The fun is really about to begin.*

Sarah read it over and over, trying to contain her rage. Who on earth was this person? Someone that hated her so much. Someone that was prepared to kill innocent person after innocent person, just to get at Sarah. It didn't make sense. There was no one she could think of that fitted that profile.

She grabbed an evidence bag, depositing the letter and the envelope, sealing it shut. She documented the timing of the evidence being bagged, desperately hoping they were not too late to get some form of forensics from it.

She sat back in her chair and closed her eyes, playing through in her mind what she would do about tasking the team when they came back later that afternoon. She wasn't sure whether the stress and tiredness had caught up with her, making her doze off, but she was suddenly aware of a distant voice, calling to her from her subconscious.

"Are you Sarah Braintree?"

Sarah bolted too. As she re-orientated herself, she saw a slim, attractive woman with short-cropped mousy-brown hair stood in the doorway of her office. She sat up, trying not to look like someone who had just taken a power nap at her desk. She quickly stood up, trying to maintain a degree of professionalism whilst struggling to clear her fuggy head. The woman seemed to sense her disarray and continued to speak, trying to give her an 'out' from an embarrassing situation.

"I'm Jessica Fletcher, the profiler you requested. I work for the National Crime Agency on the mainland and, before you say anything, I have heard all the jokes about *Murder She Wrote*."

Sarah looked perplexed. "*Murder She Wrote?*"

"Yeah, the TV programme. *Murder She Wrote*. Jessica Fletcher is the main character."

"Oh, I see. Sorry, I don't watch much TV and not a programme I have ever heard of."

"Ah, figures."

An awkward silence fell on the conversation, Sarah staring at this visitor in her midst, strangely unnerved by her presence. She couldn't work out why she had such a strange first impression of this person. Sarah eventually shook herself out of the malaise and got back in control.

"Right, Jessica, it's great to meet you. Sorry for being a bit out of it when you arrived. As you can imagine, I have rather a lot on my mind at the moment."

"That's not a problem, Sarah."

Sarah stopped at the use of her forename. Jessica looked at her quizzically.

Sarah smiled. "Do you know, Jessica, please do call me Sarah. I know the rank protocol is important, but I do get fed up with all the ma'am this and ma'am that. A bit of informality is nice."

"Oh, god, sorry, I should have thought—"

"No, it's fine. As I said, it's nice to introduce a bit of informality to proceedings. It feels like everyone is wound up like a tight spring at the moment."

As they both relaxed a bit, having navigated the awkward introductions, Jessica saw the bagged note on the desk and picked it up. "What's this?"

"The latest note from our perp. Somewhat of a signature move on her part, leaving notes after each murder."

Jessica scanned it. "Jesus, this is some piece of work."

"Well, Jessica, this is what you are here for. The team will be back in about an hour. We will do introductions and then get the team to take you through the evidence. I'm guessing you are aware that the latest atrocity was multiple victims. The team haven't had time to write up the board yet."

"Yes, I had the basics, but a full de-brief will be important for me to complete a comprehensive profile."

"How long do you think that will take? This perp doesn't seem to want to slow down her murderous spree."

"I'll work round the clock, Sarah. Two days, max."

"That's great, Jessica. I can't help feeling that she is out there somewhere plotting her next move."

# 20

It was a little after 4pm when the whole team convened in the incident room. Sarah made the introductions to Jessica, with only DC Johnson stifling a laugh at the mention of her name.

Jessica smiled. "Glad to see at least one person gets the joke."

Lisa looked embarrassed. "Sorry, ma'am, but that must be a pain to deal with, especially in our environment."

Mark looked confused. "Eh, what? I don't get it."

Jessica carried on unflustered. "*Murder She Wrote*, DS Adams. Jessica Fletcher is the main character."

"Oh, god, yeah, how funny."

Sarah became impatient with the team's apparent desire to have a laugh in the middle of Jersey's worst crime crisis in a decade.

She cut across the conversation. "OK, can we focus, please? Jessica has an important job to do if we are going to stop this woman's killing spree. We need your updates from today and then you all need to brief her on the evidence we have. Don't expect to get home early tonight. This all needs to be done before you go."

Once again, Sarah had firmly brought the mood down

and the room returned to the quiet, uptight vibe that usually hung over every briefing.

Sarah ignored the obvious dissatisfaction in the room and cracked on. "OK, the first thing is that we have a note from the perp. It was hand-delivered to the station and left on my desk. Does anyone know anything about this?"

Sarah scanned the faces, all of which seemed genuinely shocked at the turn of events.

"I checked with the post room and they claim they did not handle it. So, I ask again. Does anyone know anything about this?"

Steph stepped up. "Are you accusing us of something, ma'am?"

There was a stand-off as the room fell silent, wondering how Sarah would react to Steph's challenge.

Eventually Sarah responded in a calm, authoritative tone that belied the rage she was feeling. "No, DCI Brown, I'm not accusing anyone of anything, but I would like some idea as to how this envelope got on my desk when nobody in the station apparently handled it."

There was nothing else forthcoming. Steph wisely deciding that she had got away with one moment of insubordination and was not about to risk another one.

"Well, as part of your briefing with Jessica, I want you all to read this note and draw your own conclusions. It will no doubt be another key tool in helping Jessica develop our profile. Once you are done with it, please pass it to Jennifer for forensic analysis. In the meantime, I will be investigating how this envelope got here."

Sarah scanned the faces again. She didn't know why she was suspicious of this development, but she believed the post-room team knew nothing of this envelope and she couldn't think how else it would have got on her desk. Was someone in her team playing mind games? She stared at DS Adams. *Hmm?*

Sarah's private pondering must have lasted longer than she realised, as she suddenly noticed everyone was staring at her, waiting for her next move. She shook herself out of the daydream and got back in command mode.

"Right, DCI Brown. What is your team's update?"

"At the time of leaving the hospital, there were nine fatalities. However, the doctors are quite confident that the other four will survive. For some reason they seem more resistant and are responding to the anti-poison medication."

"Are they awake? Coherent?"

"Not really. The man that gave us the bottle and the relations that were with some of the victims at the zoo all give the same story. They picked up the bottles from small baskets that were left around the zoo. They didn't see anyone leaving the bottles and didn't question why they were free due to the message on them."

"Next steps?"

"Well, we will keep in touch with the hospital and go back and interview the other three if they recover sufficiently to answer our questions. DS Adams has put out the witness appeal for people who were at the zoo on the day. They had thousands of visitors. Someone must have seen something. Otherwise the team will work with Jessica to take her through the evidence."

"OK. Jennifer. What's the update from your work?"

"Practically non-existent, forensic-wise. The sites where the bottles were left were used by hundreds of people, so no chance of getting any sort of forensics. We obviously did a comprehensive analysis of the bottle the gentlemen brought in and verified that the contents were anti-freeze. Again, because the bottle had been touched by multiple people, we could not get a fix on any specific fingerprints or DNA."

Sarah shook her head. "You see, Jessica, this perp is either forensically aware or just damn lucky. We have a couple of fingerprints and one potential DNA sample from the crime scenes, but that's it. It's really frustrating."

Jessica nodded sympathetically.

"Actually, that reminds me, Jessica. We need to get your fingerprints and DNA so we can rule out any forensics that you inadvertently leave at future crime scenes. DCI Brown, can you organise that and liaise with Jennifer to get our records updated?"

"Of course, ma'am."

Sarah closed down the briefing and went back into her office. The team started de-briefing Jessica.

\*

It was nearly 11pm as Jennifer Colney opened the front door. The air was still close from the heat of the day and the slightly cooler interior of the flat was a welcome relief. She desperately needed to sleep and the lack of sound in the flat made her think her partner must already be 'away with the fairies'.

As she stepped through the entrance hall, she peered into the living room. He was slumped in the chair, an empty bottle of beer hanging precariously from his hand.

"Oh fuck," she muttered under her breath.

She tried to unpack her stuff, desperately hoping not to stir him, but it didn't work.

"Jefiner, my gorjus woman. How the fook ish it goin'?"

"Go back to sleep, Jeff. You're drunk and I don't want anything to do with you when you are like this."

"Yus ish such a party pooper. Come heres and gis us a hug."

"No, Jeff. What the fuck has brought this on?"

Jeff tried to focus. His mood seemed to change from inept drunk to something more sinister. "Wha hash 'brought this on'?" He tried to do the double-finger gesture when he repeated back Jennifer's words but just made himself look at bit stupid and uncoordinated. It didn't stop him chuntering on. "Yur *bitch* of a boss. Thas is wha' hash fooked me off. We've loshed the plot. The stupid newsh... er... paper peeps hash been too slow. Ish world news now, 'parently no longer our exclusif."

"So what? I don't know what you've got against my boss, anyway. She seems a really nice person."

"I hates her. Hates her."

Jeff's tirade seemed to drift off as he struggled with his focus and conscious state. Jennifer moved towards where he was sat to remove the bottle he was holding.

As she leant towards him the sudden movement shocked her. Jeff swung a punch, landing it square on Jennifer's cheek. It knocked her back, stumbling over the coffee table, landing in an unceremonious heap by the other chair.

The next few moments seemed to happen in slow motion. Jennifer instinctively touched her cheek. Blood on her fingers. As she tried to process what had happened, the coffee table moved as Jeff tried to stand up. She looked at his face, contorted with rage. He was not finished. She scrambled up from her prone position. As she turned, she screamed as one of his hands grabbed at her skirt. She slapped his hand away, but he seemed to have an inner strength and his grip remained firm, despite his intoxicated state. She tried to pull away again, but he was using the leverage of holding Jennifer to propel himself forward. She tried to spin round to disorientate him and his grip weakened. He grabbed at her with his other hand but just made himself stumble against the coffee table. Suddenly free of his grip, she stood a few yards away, staring at his now-stooped frame. The shock of the violence consumed her and she kicked him straight in the face. He landed in a heap.

Jennifer grabbed her bag and bolted out of the front door. Ever since she had started working on this case, her relationship with Jeff Godley had become more and more difficult. Now she knew what she had to do.

*

Sarah Braintree applied her face cream, the dark rings under her eyes not getting any better as the stress of the situation consumed her every waking hour. Having Jessica on board was a relief. As she prepared for bed, she kept looking at her phone, expecting it to ring, to disturb her attempts at sleep once more. This perp did not seem to be slowing down and Sarah was expecting news of another murder any time soon. She got into bed and hoped for a night of unbroken sleep.

*

She lay in bed, pleased with her day's work. She hadn't cut herself for two days now. Ramping up the game against Sarah seemed to be keeping the demons at bay. She closed her eyes and let her unconscious work through her next move. It was time for act two.

# 21

Sarah Braintree arrived at the incident room a little after 9am. The team were finishing their morning briefings, ready to set off on their investigative tasking. Jessica was deep into the evidence, focusing on developing the profile that the team so desperately needed. Sarah didn't seek to disturb the re-assuring industry that the team seemed to be showing. She exchanged basic pleasantries with each of the team and wandered into her office. More than anything she was relieved they didn't have another murder to deal with. As she went to sit down, she realised someone was missing.

"Err, team. Where is Jennifer?"

Mark responded. "We don't know, ma'am. She hasn't come in yet. Probably just running a bit late."

Sarah returned to her office and started to plough through her emails, wondering why the normally reliable Jennifer was not where she was supposed to be.

Half an hour later, after most of the team had dispersed, she got her answer.

*

DS Mark Adams sat in the CCTV room at Jersey Zoo. He had picked up all the responses to the witness appeal from the comms team, which gave a mixed description of the woman that many had seen leaving the bottles around the zoo. What was consistent was her hair colour. Blonde.

The only CCTV the zoo had was at the entrance turnstiles. He started looking through the footage from the first minute the gates were open. He had a pretty good idea what he was looking for. Half an hour in, he found it.

*

Sarah was still beavering away at her emails when she realised someone was stood in the doorway. She looked up.

"Oh my god, Jennifer, are you OK? What happened?"

Jennifer Colney instinctively put her hand up to the large contusion that was clearly visible on her cheek. She started to cry.

Sarah leapt up from her desk and ushered her to sit down. "Now come on, Jennifer. Tell me what happened. Can I get you a coffee?"

"Yes, thank you, ma'am. That would be nice."

Sarah hurriedly grabbed a coffee and shot Jessica a concerned glance, who was the only one of the team left in the incident room. She mouthed a *can I help?*, but Sarah shook her head. Sarah shut the door and encouraged Jennifer to tell her everything.

There was a brief pause as Jennifer took a slurp of coffee and tried to contain her emotions.

Eventually she spoke. "Ma'am. I'm sorry. I've got something to tell you. Something I should have told you as soon as I was assigned to the team."

Sarah tried to remain calm and professional. "OK, go on."

"I've been really stupid and really disloyal to you. I've been seeing... god, this is hard... err... I've been having a relationship with Jeff Godley, the reporter from the *Herald*."

"What!" Sarah immediately regretted the tone of her reaction and ushered Jennifer to carry on.

Jennifer didn't seem fazed. "I know, ma'am. I don't why I did it. He isn't a very nice man, but the sex was... err... sorry, TMI. He was drunk last night and lashed out at me. It's not the first time it's happened and last night I knew it had to end, so I walked out. I crashed at a friend's, but haven't had much sleep."

"I'm sorry that happened to you, Jennifer. We should arrest him for assault."

"No, just hear me out. There's more. Our relationship was good at the start but as soon as this story broke, he changed. He hates you. He keeps going on about something you did to him, but when I pushed him for details, he just clammed up."

"But I don't even know him, beyond the minimal contact I had with him on the press side. What on earth could be making him hate me? I've never done anything to him that could spark such a reaction."

As Sarah ranted on, she could tell by Jennifer's facial expression that there was more to say. "Is that all, Jennifer?"

"No, ma'am. I haven't told you the worst bit yet, and before I tell you, I realise that you will expect my resignation."

Sarah raised her eyebrows. "OK, let me be the judge of that."

"When this investigation started, he kept asking me for information about what was going on. He kept trying to get what he called 'the inside track'. I'm afraid I was the one that told him about the notes on the victims. I'm so sorry. I knew it was wrong as soon as I did it and I haven't told him anything else, which I think is why he turned violent."

Sarah was trying to contain her emotions. At least she now knew where the leak had come from, but she was struggling to quell her rage at what Jennifer had told her.

There was a brief, uncomfortable pause as both sides seemed to be paralysed by the revelations that hung in the air.

Sarah managed to calm herself and spoke first. "Look, Jennifer, I can't say I'm not furious with you for what you did. It was highly unprofessional, but I can tell that you are genuinely sorry and got duped by the emotions that can sometimes consume you in a highly charged relationship. Whatever you did, you don't deserve the violence this bastard has meted out. You are a good CSI, Jennifer, and I don't expect your resignation. The best thing you can do is put it behind you and put all your energies into solving these murders."

Jennifer visibly relaxed, relieved at the clemency shown by Sarah. "Of course, ma'am. You will have my complete focus and no more cock-ups."

Sarah gave a strained smile. "Going back to your Mr Godley, I'm genuinely confused by his hatred for me, but it does raise an interesting question."

Jennifer gave an encouraging nod.

"Do you think he is working with the woman that is murdering all these people?"

# 22

Sarah sent Jennifer home for a rest until later that afternoon when she asked all the team back for the daily briefing. As the team gathered in the incident room, they 'caffeined up' and devoured the chocolate hobnobs that Sarah had supplied.

Sarah brought them to order. "Right, team. We have a lot to get through this evening. I need updates from your investigations today and I am pleased to tell you that Jessica has completed the profiling of our perp."

There were lots of enthusiastic nods in Jessica's direction. Everyone was clearly impressed with the speed of her work.

"But, before we do that, I need to update you on a serious development in this case. As you can see, Jennifer has an injury to her face. Now, whilst Jennifer would prefer to keep her private life out of the picture, we have agreed that you need to know what happened as we believe it has a material impact on our investigations."

Jennifer looked a bit embarrassed and the others had various looks of concern on their faces, whilst trying to hide their intrigue around the revelations that were about to be revealed. Lisa touched Jennifer's hand in a small act of sympathy.

"Until last night, Jennifer was in a relationship with Jeff Godley, the reporter from the *Herald*. The one that has been hounding our investigation. It seems that Mr Godley had been trying to exploit his relationship with Jennifer by trying to persuade her to divulge information about the case. He did manage to glean information about the notes on the victim, but when Jennifer refused to give him any more, he became violent."

Jennifer fixed her gaze on Sarah, not wanting to catch anyone's eye as her private life was laid bare.

Sarah pushed on. "During these exchanges he professed a level of hatred for me. To date, I'm totally confused about this, having hardly met the man, but his vitriol has the hallmarks of our perp. Now, I'm sure Jessica's profiling will confirm we are looking for a woman, which raises the uncomfortable question as to whether he is working with her. My belief is that he is now a significant person of interest and I want him brought in for questioning. DCI Brown, I want you and DC Johnson to arrest him tomorrow on assault charges and conspiracy to murder. We need time to question him about his assault on Jennifer and the possible involvement in these murders. As much as I would like to watch the weasel squirm, his apparent obsession with me means I will have to stay at arm's length. Can I rely on you two to focus on that tomorrow?"

"Yes, ma'am," they chorused.

"OK, thank you both. Can you give the team your update from today's investigation work?"

DCI Brown took the lead. "Yes, ma'am, we have continued to interview relations of the victims and one of the survivors was able to talk to us for a while. The stories are much the same as before. It seems the bottles didn't appear until lunchtime and the odd witness statement from this group, coupled with the public appeal, appear to paint quite a clear description of the woman that left the bottles. She is described as slim, pretty, with long blonde hair. It seems that all witnesses believe this was her real hair and not a wig. I liaised with DS Adams during the day and this helped him focus his search on CCTV."

Sarah turned to Mark. "Do you have an update, DS Adams?"

"Err, well, a bit. Jersey Zoo only has CCTV on the entrance gates. I spent a couple of hours yesterday going through the footage, using the description we were given. Apart from you, ma'am, I didn't find much."

"Sorry! What do you mean, 'apart from you, ma'am'?"

"Well, you were on the CCTV. First thing in the morning."

"I'm not sure what relevance my being on the CCTV has to your work, DS Adams. I went to the zoo and Gorey Castle to check in with the event commanders as part of my morning briefings."

"Sorry, ma'am, I just meant I was looking for blonde woman and you are…"

"Yes, DS Adams, I'm blonde, but the description also said slim and pretty."

Sarah's comment floored the room. Total silence. Shock. Embarrassment. No one quite knew what to make of it. Sarah didn't crack jokes. Ever. Was she being self-deprecating or was this some plot to nail Mark to the wall? She held a firm, unflinching expression, fixed on Mark.

He looked down, trying to avert his gaze, hoping for the earth to open up and swallow him. The uncomfortable silence was broken by Lisa trying, but failing, to stifle a laugh. As Mark still had his head down, Sarah looked at Lisa and cracked a smirk. The others picked up on the subtle exchange and visibly relaxed.

Sarah pushed on. "Apart from your obsession with me, DS Adams, what else did you find?"

Mark kept his gaze down, attempting to dig himself out of the hole. "Err, well, nothing conclusive. The quality of the images is not great. I'm not convinced by any of the possible hits we had. I have downloaded all their footage from the day, which I have back at our CCTV suite. I'll continue to go through it tomorrow. If the witnesses say the bottles were placed around lunchtime, it's possible she arrived later in the day. I haven't looked past 11am yet."

Sarah's disdain for Mark was clear to see. She didn't say anything, but the steely look she fixed on Mark told him exactly what she thought about his update. She couldn't work out what his issues were and why he had only done half a job again. As the uncomfortable vibe returned to the room, Sarah's phone beeped. "Ah, the pizzas are here. Let's take a short break and then Jessica can tell us all about her profiling."

# 23

After a good feed, the mood in the room had lightened as another round of coffees washed down the last remnants of the pizzas. Sarah coaxed them back to the matter in hand.

"Right, everyone. I hope you are sufficiently refreshed and ready for Jessica's briefing. I can't tell you how important this work is on sharpening our investigation. I'm a little surprised she hasn't struck again, but I'm grateful for small mercies. So, Jessica, please give us your detailed profiling of this psychopath."

Jessica stood up, calm and confident, all eyes on her, hungry for the wisdom she was about to impart.

"Thank you, Sarah. Firstly, I must just pick you up on the use of the word psychopath. Whilst there is no doubt that the perp has clear psychopathic traits, we should actually describe her as a sociopath. A person with psychopathic traits tends to be quite obviously troubled with clear anti-social, often overtly violent behaviour. They stick out as someone you would want to avoid. Our perp isn't like that. She is a classic sociopath. Whilst sociopaths do share many of the anti-social and violent aspects of a person with psychopathic traits, they are much harder to spot because they hide them well. Sociopaths are charming, intelligent, manipulative, intense and spontaneous. They blend in, often being the life and soul of a party. People like them, are drawn to them. They can function within any normal social or work environment."

"So how do we spot them?" Sarah probed.

"Well, that rather depends on how skilled their sociopathic tendencies are, but the key point is that they lie. Constantly. They become so caught up in their version of the truth that they are continually deceiving people, and it is often this deceit that can catch them out. They will show no remorse and are incapable of love or empathy. They are also intensely competitive. If we have any chance of catching this killer, we need to probe these characteristics when any suspects are identified."

"Thank you, Jessica. Any questions so far, team?"

Mark raised his hand. Sarah was still steaming at him but let it go.

"Yes, DS Adams, what is your question?"

"Thank you, ma'am. Jessica, are you saying that this perp is just like a normal person on the street, someone in front of us in the queue at the coffee shop, our next-door neighbour or someone standing in this room right now?"

Jessica smiled. "Well, I think being in this room is stretching it a bit, DS Adams, but I understand your point. She will be able to interact with others without particularly raising suspicion and so, yes, she could be the person standing next to you in a shop or indeed one of your neighbours."

There was a general murmuring of acknowledgement from the team. Sarah nodded for Jessica to continue.

"OK, let's validate these sociopathic characteristics against what we know about our perp. Firstly, let's consider the competitiveness. She is clearly demonstrating a desire to win by the game she is forcing us to play. She is goading us, challenging us to be as clever as she is. She wants to play a game and she will be determined to win. Secondly, let's consider the lack of remorse. In the first two murders she watched the victims die, appearing to be completely detached from the events that she had instigated. Thirdly, let's consider the charm and manipulation traits. In the first three murders she shows a high level of confidence and bravado. She has charmed these men to be comfortable in her company, making them relax and drop their guard, giving her the opportunity to strike without fear of them fighting back against her deadly intentions. There is also an element of spontaneity. She clearly reacted to Sarah mentioning in her TV appeal that she used the website to find men. The third murder was different. She visited the bar and picked the mark on the fly. A spontaneous, adaptable approach to what she set out to achieve. Finally, let's consider the intensity point. She is moving fast. She is murdering people every few days. She is consumed by the game, consumed by her apparent hatred of Sarah. She is not going to stop and is not going to slow down until she feels she has won this game. The so-called 'grand finale of act one' shows an escalation in this intensity. She wanted to demonstrate her control over this situation, with once again little remorse for how many people she killed."

The room was silent but focused, hanging on to every word Jessica was saying.

"Now, let's look at other aspects of her profile. Despite everything I have said about her ability to blend in, she is clearly very troubled. Her focus on Sarah is interesting. There is something in her past that has deep-seated trauma attached to it, and for some reason she associates this with Sarah. I am guessing that she is between thirty and forty years old, which means this trauma could have occurred any time in that period. It may even be as far back as childhood. Another theory is that it may be more recent, possibly linked to someone you put away, Sarah. I think you need to consider any key incidents in your life, Sarah, particularly where others were involved, that might explain this, as well as looking at all your key cases and arrests. I am sure the answer to this perp's obsession with you lies in one of those areas. What I can be sure about is that she has harboured this resentment for some time and the trigger for her murderous spree was seeing you given that award. Her last note pretty much confirms that."

Sarah puffed out her cheeks. "OK, Jessica, it gives me something to think about."

"A few other things. She undoubtedly lives alone. She will not have a meaningful relationship because she is incapable of sustaining one. She uses sex as a weapon, evidenced by the way she manipulated the first three victims, but, and this is crucial, I don't believe she has had many, if any, sexual relationships."

Jessica could see the surprised looks on the team's faces at that revelation.

"Let me explain. From what we can gather, she is an overtly sexual person, dressing and acting provocatively. But, the word acting is key here. She is playing a role, which ultimately does not end with any physical contact. She is not touching the victims when she kills them. She isn't strangling them or stabbing them. She is administering poison or exploiting health issues, none of which require her to have any physical contact with the victims. This is why forensics are so limited. I really believe that the trauma she has experienced is somehow connected to intimacy issues. She doesn't want to touch the victims and she certainly would not have sex with them."

The room was transfixed by the volume of information that Jessica was pouring out.

Lisa piped up. "God, this is just like an episode of *Criminal Minds*. It's fantastic."

Jessica smiled and cracked on. "My final point is that you could do with a technical focus. I'm sure there is a way of using public records to filter down a list of suspects that match my profile, as I believe this is a resident of Jersey and not a tourist. They should also look at how she obtained the arsenic. This is not something that is readily available. She may have ordered it online and, if so, there will be a trail somewhere."

Sarah reacted first. "Wow, Jessica, that's an amazing piece of work. What do you think she will do next?"

"She is going to kill again, and soon. She has intimated that we are about to go into act two, which means, in all likelihood, a return to her signature move of notes on the victims and a fresh set of clues. She seems to have a real interest in TV and the theatre. I am certain the way to crack her riddles should again focus on those areas."

"I agree, Jessica, she does seem to want to carry on with these stupid riddles. DC Johnson. Should this happen, I am going to put you in charge of deciphering them, as you did such a good job with the first set of clues."

Lisa looked a bit embarrassed but nodded in acknowledgement. Mark just stewed.

As the briefing seemed to be drifting to its natural conclusion Sarah took command. "OK, take five, grab a coffee and when we come back, we need to discuss an action plan for the next few days."

When everyone gathered back in the incident room, Sarah sensed that Jessica's presentation had energised the room. She was determined to exploit it.

"Right, team, let's focus. Firstly, Jessica, thank you for an excellent piece of work. I'm sure everyone can see the benefit of bringing you in. Your profile has given us a renewed focus on finding our perp. For my part, I will focus on what Jessica suggested, examining key moments in my life that could give us some lines of enquiry, as well as looking back at my old cases. DCI Brown, I want to start being proactive. I am convinced she is going to strike again, so tomorrow evening I want an operation focused on flooding the key areas of the night-time economy with visible uniformed presence. I think she will be prowling for another victim. I want our resources out there, disrupting her efforts. Please liaise with Lydia about getting that sorted."

"Of course, ma'am."

"Also, Mr Le Trousain's government has given us unprecedented temporary powers to stop and search any member of the public that fits Jessica's profiling. Please make sure everyone assigned to the operation is made aware of this. If she is out there tomorrow night, I do not want her slipping through our fingers."

There were appreciative nods from the team.

"DS Adams. I want you to work with comms and get her description out there. We seem to have a pretty good idea what she looks like, so exploit that. Also, get the CCTV review work finished tomorrow. She has to be on there somewhere."

"Understood, ma'am."

"Also DCI Brown, I want Jeff Godley arrested and questioned."

"No problem, ma'am. I will get the operation sorted tonight to give Lisa and me time to deal with him in the day."

"Good. Good. Finally, I agree with Jessica that we need some focus on the technical side. If we can get a list of possible suspects, we may be able to target our investigation better."

DS Adams could sense more work was coming his way. "Err, that's sounds good, ma'am, but who is going to do that? There are only three of us on the team and I'm sure the tasking you have given us tomorrow will more than occupy our time."

Sarah bit her tongue, because despite her growing annoyance with DS Adams' attitude and general performance, she knew he had a point.

"You are right, DS Adams. I will speak to Deputy Millar again about detective resources. We can't carry on dealing with a major investigation on such scarce resources."

The team dispersed, with Mark somewhat aghast that he had actually got a positive response from Sarah, who went back into her office, beckoning Jessica to follow her.

"Do we have a chance now, Jessica? A chance to catch this perp?"

"Oh, I think so, Sarah. The team seem re-energised. It's only a matter of time before we get her."

"Thank you, Jessica. You really are a breath of fresh air."

As the office emptied, Sarah realised Jennifer was still sat in the room, not moving. "Are you OK, Jennifer?"

"Yes, ma'am. I guess I don't know what to do now."

"Look, take a day off. Sort yourself out in terms of where you are going to live and then come back in when you are ready. I'm sure we are going to need your skills again soon."

# 24

It was late, just past 1am, as sleep alluded her. Outside her bedroom window, the sea was lapping the coastline, high tide making the noise of the water splashing on the mix of sand and shingle seem louder than usual. It was like the sea was goading her, reminding her of the isolation she had always felt being stuck on this island, the demons never far away.

She picked up the knife and pressed it against the top part of her forearm, teeth gritted, watching as the skin bowed and the familiar red line appeared as blood rose rapidly to the surface. She held it there, closing her eyes to savour the feeling, the relief. The knife dropped and she looked at the bloody mark. Her mind eased. She was ready. Ready to start again.

*

Sarah woke with a start. She picked up her phone. Nothing was on it. What had made her stir from a troubled sleep? She looked at the time on her phone. It was 1.13am. She sighed, a mix of relief that she wasn't being woken by another murder but a constant sense of angst as Jessica's words stuck in her head. What was it about her that this murderer hated so much? Who could she be? When in her life had this person become so fixated with Sarah? And what about Jeff Godley. How was he connected to this? She rolled over and tried to settle her mind.

*

The next morning, Sarah went straight in to see her deputy, Jo Millar. The stifling weather had finally broken and she was oddly refreshed by the rain that had deluged her as she ran from her car to the station. Jo, her rock in these difficult times, was where he always was. At his desk, beavering away.

"Morning, Jo, any developments overnight?"

"Morning, ma'am, thankfully not. Very quiet all round."

"Hmm, I don't like this. Feels like we are just waiting for something bad to happen."

"Yes, I know. I have been briefed on the profiler's work. Seems very comprehensive."

"Yes, she has done a great job and I have asked her to stick around. She believes another murder is imminent and I will need her to update her profile as this thing develops. Has DCI Brown briefed you on this evening's operation?"

"Yes, we have a significant uniformed presence ready to be deployed, backed up by a couple of PSUs. I have signed off her operational plan. It just needs your review and sign-off."

"Good, I'm certain she will strike again tonight. She hasn't waited long between kills, and if we had nothing overnight, I'm even more certain that she won't be able to wait any longer."

"That's fine, ma'am. I'm about to head home for a sleep and I will be back on to support the operation at 6pm."

"Thanks, Jo. I really appreciate your support."

Sarah made her way to the incident room. The team were all there. She exchanged the usual pleasantries, got a coffee and went into her office. A few moments later DCI Brown put her head round the door.

"Ma'am, DC Johnson and I are just off to arrest Mr Godley. Have you had a chance to look at the ops plan for tonight?"

Sarah smiled. "Don't let that sleazy bastard worm his way out of this one, DCI Brown. I want him nailed to the floor. As for the op, I have just seen DCO Millar. He has signed off your plan, so I will just do a quick glance over it. Assume all is in order and thank you for what you are doing."

DCI Brown seemed surprised at the warmth of Sarah's words and left the room before she had a chance to return to her usual ice queen persona.

Sarah reviewed and signed off the ops plan before going back into the main room to re-fill her coffee. DS Adams had left without comment. *Stupid wanker*, Sarah thought to herself. She had a private bet with herself that he would once again not come up with any tangible leads. Jessica was the only one left, seemingly consumed with the case notes.

"Are you OK, Jessica? What are you focusing on?"

"Hi, Sarah. I'm just re-reviewing all the evidence. Making sure I haven't missed anything."

"Don't be so hard on yourself, Jessica. That profiling was amazing."

"Thanks, Sarah, but we mustn't be complacent. This perp will evolve and adapt. I need to try and predict her mindset. Get ahead of her."

Sarah walked back into her office, strangely calmed by Jessica's presence. She desperately wanted to stop this woman from killing again, but she knew Jessica's work had at least given them a renewed focus. Thinking about the profiling reminded her about the need for tech support. She picked up the phone to call Lydia, the resource manager.

"Lydia. Sarah Braintree."

"Morning, boss lady. What can I do for you?"

"Lydia, our profiler feels we need some tech support to produce a possible list of suspects from Jersey residents, based on her profile. We should be able to use public records to do this."

"OK. DCO Millar and I have been reviewing the resource profile of the money laundering case on a daily basis. Now, as you know, they are close to cracking the whole thing, so taking resources away at this critical time is tricky... but I think I might have an answer for you."

"Don't leave me hanging, Lydia."

"Well, we have a new DC, Cassandra Kennon, who came to us with a degree in cyber technology. That girl is an absolute computer whiz and has been helping the money laundering team no end. But, her work is pretty much done and we both believe we can afford to transfer her over to your team for most of her time over the coming days."

"Lydia, that's amazing. When can she start?"

"I'll get her to report to you at 9am tomorrow."

"Thanks, Lydia. You're a star."

Sarah stood up and looked out of the window down towards St Helier harbour. The rain was still lashing down and the tourists that were yesterday queuing up for ice creams were now bombing around under umbrellas, trying to find a dry shop, restaurant or bar to shelter in. She wondered to herself whether the bad weather would stop the perp striking tonight.

"Not a chance," she muttered to herself.

# 25

DS Adams sat in the CCTV suite, carefully going through the footage. He navigated to where he was the day before. The frames that showed the perp. Clear and unmistakable. He opened up the editing tool on the CCTV software, clicked on the frames and pressed 'DELETE'.

He sat back in his chair, smug and satisfied. She didn't like him and he didn't like her. Revenge had been a long time coming and he was going to enjoy watching Sarah's world fall apart.

As he revelled in the satisfaction, an email popped into his inbox from the comms team. As he read it, he smiled to himself. A significant breakthrough from a witness statement. He would play this one carefully. This might just be the thing that would win him some brownie points with the ice queen. As much as he loved playing the incompetent detective, he had to play a fine line. He couldn't afford to get kicked off the case. Not now. This might just be enough to keep her sweet. The ops briefing wasn't due for another seven hours, but he decided to hit her with this now. He got up and went down to the incident room.

*

Sarah spent most of the morning trawling through the recent major case history of Jersey Police, trying to find something that might give her a clue as to who this perp was and the reason for her hatred. After three hours, nothing had stuck. As chief, her direct involvement in these cases was, at best, tenuous, not enough for someone to hold a grudge against her personally. None of the criminals her team had put away matched the profile. She wondered whether the perp was the wife of someone that they had convicted, but Jessica's profile went against this idea. As she sat back to contemplate her next step, she heard the incident room door open. DS Adams stood in the doorway looking like an excitable puppy.

She stood up and walked into the main room, staring expectantly at DS Adams.

"We've got a breakthrough, ma'am."

"What? On the CCTV?"

"Oh, no."

Sarah's facial expression, as ever, told DS Adams that he needed to crack on and deliver her something.

"From the witness appeal, ma'am. Despite all the other witness statements stating that she was a blonde, and that it wasn't a wig, we have a witness that has come through to refute that."

Jessica was the only other person in the room. She stopped what she was doing and turned to listen. Sarah prompted him to continue.

"We have a witness that states he spoke to a woman matching our description who was stood right next to one of the baskets where the bottles were left. After their brief conversation, she smiled, wished him a good day and walked off. But crucially, he said he is absolutely convinced she was wearing a wig because he spotted several strands of brown hair peeking out from under the line of the hairpiece. He has also agreed to work with our photofit guys to develop a composite of what she looks like."

Sarah had to smile as she reflected that maybe she had lost that little bet with herself.

"OK, so this witness is telling us that we are not looking for a natural blonde. He thinks she actually has brown hair?"

"Well, yes, it seems so."

"Has this helped with your CCTV work?"

"To be honest, no. I have been trawling through looking for women with long blonde hair but have not found any convincing matches. Now I don't know whether she put the wig on after she entered the zoo."

Sarah couldn't read this one. Was Mark making more excuses, only doing the most basic detective work that seemed to be his MO? Or was he genuinely energised by this breakthrough? He certainly seemed more motivated than usual.

"OK, DS Adams, good work. Can you supervise the witness statement and composite work? Bring an update to the briefing later."

"OK, ma'am." With that DS Adams walked out of the incident room.

Sarah looked at Jessica. "Well, well. What do you make of that?"

"I'll be honest, I'm not surprised. I did find the witness statements from the zoo incompatible with what we know of this woman. I can't see that she would be as slack as walking around without some form of disguise. This witness testimony seems to fit better with my profile."

"That's good and even better if we can get a proper description of her, but this cast doubts on her hair colour. We are going to have to update our advice about who the team stop and search on tonight's op."

# 26

Steph and Lisa parked up outside the offices of the *Jersey Herald*. They walked into reception and asked for Jeff Godley. They waited a few minutes before a door opened just beyond the lifts. He walked towards them with a mix of curiosity and a slight edge of concern.

"Well, well. Two of Jersey's finest. What can I do for you?"

In a swift motion, Lisa grabbed his arms and cuffed him while Steph read him his rights. "Jeff Godley, we are arresting you on charges of common assault and conspiracy to murder. Anything you say can and will be used—"

"You what. Are you completely insane? I haven't done anything."

Steph finished reading him his rights, ignoring his protestations. They manhandled him out of reception and into the waiting police car, leaving a bemused receptionist behind him.

Half an hour later, Jeff Godley was ensconced in one of the interview rooms at St Helier Police Station, sipping a cup of lukewarm muddy liquid that purported to be tea.

Steph and Lisa entered, turned on the recording equipment and started the interview.

"Mr Godley, I'm DCI Brown and this is DC Johnson. This is a formal interview under caution, related to the allegations of common assault and conspiracy to murder. You are reminded that you have the right to formal counsel during these interviews."

"I don't need a lawyer. I'm not guilty of any crime."

"OK, so to be clear for the recording, Mr Godley, you are waiving your right to legal representation."

"Yes."

"Right, Mr Godley, let's start with the allegations of common assault against Jennifer Colney."

"She's a lying bitch."

"What has she lied about, Mr Godley?"

"I dunno. You tell me."

"She alleges that on the evening of Sunday 13th June, you attacked her in a drunken rage, punching her in the face, resulting in abrasions to her cheek. She also sustained minor bruising to her back and legs as the force of the punch made her fall back over the coffee table."

Jeff Godley leant forward. "Yeh, I was drunk, but I don't even remember talking to her. When I woke up, she was gone. Simple as that."

"You deny hitting Miss Colney?"

"Like I said, I was drunk. Don't remember a thing and, if I'm not mistaken, this comes down to my word against hers. Does she have anyone that can corroborate these allegations?"

Jeff could see DCI Brown twitch at his challenge. He knew he was on the front foot, but the questions kept coming.

"How many times have you hit Miss Colney?"

"I don't know what you mean."

"On how many separate occasions during your relationship with Miss Colney have you hit her?"

"I refuse to answer that question and I re-state that any allegations are her word against mine. You have no case."

"How do you explain the injury to Miss Colney's face?"

"As I already said, I haven't seen her, so how can I explain something I haven't seen?"

Steph tried not to show her exasperation with his answers. She changed tack. "OK, Mr Godley, do you deny exploiting your relationship with Miss Colney to get inside information on the current multiple murder case that we are investigating?"

He smiled at the question, arrogance coming off him in spades. "Sex is great, DCI Brown. Don't you agree?"

"It has its moments, Mr Godley. Is that your way of telling me that you obtained information from Miss Colney during your 'pillow talk'?"

He smiled.

"Does that smile mean 'yes', Mr Godley? It would be helpful if you could confirm for the recording."

"Yes."

"So, once Miss Colney stopped giving you information you started hitting her?"

Jeff Godley's expression changed, his smile dropped and he sat back in his chair, arms crossed and defiant.

"Mr Godley?"

No answer. "OK, for the purposes of the recording, Mr Godley is refusing to answer the question."

There was a brief pause as Steph attempted to ramp up the tension with silence.

"Can you explain your connection to the multiple murder case currently terrorising this island?"

Jeff uncrossed his arms, the question interesting him, re-engaging him. He leant forward. "Connection? What on earth makes you think I have any connection to these murders? You are on a serious fishing exercise, DCI Brown, if you think you can fit me up on this one."

"So you deny any connection to the case?"

"Of course. I can't even begin to imagine what 'evidence' you think you have that might connect me."

"Well, apart from your interest in obtaining information about the case, your apparent hatred for our chief of police bears all the hallmarks of our killer."

His smile was back. "My interest in getting information in this case is because I'm a fucking journalist. That's what we do. As for your chief, I don't think I'm the only one that hates her. Don't you agree, DCI Brown?"

Without warning, Steph turned the recording off and ended the interview, directing Lisa to take Mr Godley back to the custody cells.

They re-convened in the custody suite kitchen. "What the hell was that all about, Steph? Why did you let him rattle you?"

"We have no case against him, Lisa. What the hell is the chief playing at? We can't prove he assaulted Jennifer and we have nothing other than her testimony that suggests any personal issues with the chief. We are going to have to let him go."

After Steph had left the room, Lisa sipped her tea, her

mind racing. *What the hell just happened? Something isn't right about this situation. Steph would not have normally acted like that, giving up so easily. What on earth is going on?*

# 27

It was half an hour before the evening's operational briefing. Sarah was finishing off her preparations when Steph walked into her office.

"DCI Brown. What can I do for you? I hope you are dealing with our Mr Godley."

"Actually, ma'am, that's what I want to talk to you about."

"OK. I'm guessing from your demeanour that it's not going well."

"We have no case, ma'am. Whilst I completely believe everything that Jennifer has told us, we have no way of corroborating her testimony. He kept stating that it was his word against hers… and he's right. A good lawyer will get him off in a second."

Sarah rubbed her face. "What about the links to the murders?"

"He just laughed them off. Said… err…"

"It's OK, DCI Brown, don't worry about my sensibilities. I'm sure he wasn't complimentary about me."

"…err, sorry, ma'am, when I asked him why he appeared to be spouting bile about you he retorted by saying that lots of people hate you."

Sarah put on an amused expression. "Did he now?"

"We can't keep him in custody, ma'am. We have nothing to go on."

Sarah drummed her fingers on the table, staring out of the window. After a few minutes she turned back to Steph.

"I'm not happy with this. I want to get some justice for Jennifer, but maybe I have been a bit premature by asking you to bring him in. If he is working with the perp, maybe we need him out and about. He's so arrogant, he's bound to trip up somewhere. Let him go and maybe get some surveillance on him."

"OK, I'll get him released." With that Steph left the room, slightly surprised at how calmly Sarah had handled the situation.

As Steph walked out, Sarah noticed that Jennifer was in the incident room. She called her in, welcomed her back and explained the situation. A day of rest and new living arrangements seemed to have re-energised Jennifer. She took the news on board with limited emotion, a weak smile at Sarah's closing comment.

"We will get him, Jennifer. I promise."

*

Sarah pulled the team together just after 7pm for the evening's operational briefing. The room was full of nervous energy.

"Right, team, we have an important night ahead of us. As you know, based on Jessica's profiling work, we are predicting that our perp will strike again tonight. We don't believe she is using dating websites any longer, which means she is likely to be finding her next victim on the fly. This is why tonight's operation will flood the night-time economy and the main road network with police resources. The Jersey government has granted us extraordinary temporary powers to stop and search anyone that fits the profile. Therefore, the focus of tonight's operation is to stop any woman on her own, either on foot or in a vehicle, that matches the profile. There will be roadblocks on all the major routes to facilitate the vehicle searches. We will ask for voluntary DNA samples. Anybody refusing this can be brought in for extra questioning."

Sarah paused to check that everyone was paying attention. The focus was there.

"Be aware that there is one small issue with the description of the perp. We had a significant update from a witness at the zoo whom we believe spoke to the perp. He has worked with our team to develop a composite of what she looks like. The major problem is that he is convinced she was wearing a blonde wig, going against the multiple witness statements we had from other members of the public who were at the zoo on Saturday. He states he saw strands of brown hair. DS Adams has therefore worked with the team to develop two composites, one with long blonde hair and one with shorter brown hair. These pictures have been sent to all officers on duty tonight."

Sarah paused as the team looked at the hard copy prints that Mark handed round. As she scanned the room, one person seemed to flinch at the pictures. *An interesting reaction*, she thought to herself. She made a mental note to follow that up in private. She cracked on.

"OK, so in terms of deployment, we have uniformed teams manning the roadblocks on the major routes across Jersey. We also have a police team in each of the main locations across Jersey where there is a high proportion of pubs and restaurants. The focus of our core team will be St Helier, with three teams of uniformed officers assisting us. DCI Brown, DS Adams and DC Johnson will be out on the ground in St Helier co-ordinating this work. I will be in the control room with DCO Millar, co-ordinating the island-wide operation. Jessica and Jennifer can join me in the control room."

There was a general murmuring of consent as the briefing was brought to an end. The game was on.

# 28

The Duty Inspector Stuart Hill wasn't fazed by the exalted company that was gathered around him in the force control room, as he settled in for the night's operation. He was the central point for all officers to report any developments in their search for the murderer. The room was dominated by a map of Jersey on the large plasma screen, with officers' locations plotted through the GPS technology on their phones and radios.

Sarah, as ever, was eager to crack on. "Right, DI Hill, tell me what we are seeing on the screen."

"Well, ma'am, these black dots are each of the officers we have deployed across Jersey. If you hover over any of these dots you can see their call sign and the identification of the officer in question. As you can see the deployment plan is in place. They should report any significant developments to me via the radio and I will deploy additional officers to support them."

"OK, sounds good."

Sarah gave a strained smile to Jo, Jennifer and Jessica as she settled in, hoping for some action, a break in the case that just might get her back on track.

All officers had the same script. They were tasked to

stop any females on their own that matched the profile and composites. They were told to ask about their movements on Saturday, recording details of any stated alibis to enable these to be followed up and checked. They were to ask each woman for a voluntary DNA sample and their contact details should further follow up be required.

As the evening dragged on, nothing dramatic happened. DI Hill checked in regularly with each sergeant that was leading their respective teams on the ground. They reported a steady flow of 'stop and searches' on women that fitted the profile, but nothing suspicious had arisen. All the women had complied with the request to provide DNA, had answered the officers' questions without any drama and provided their follow-up details. As DI Hill reported the progress, Sarah was becoming more agitated.

"What do you make of this, Jessica?"

"Give it time, Sarah. We still have a couple of hours to go. If she is out tonight, someone will catch her."

Sarah shot Jo a look that said she didn't share Jessica's optimism. She changed focus.

"Jennifer. Have you got your lab set up to start processing the DNA samples in the morning?"

"Yes, ma'am. The DNA sample from the second crime scene is logged into the system. I just need to process each swab collected tonight and run it against our sample. If we get a hit, we will arrest the suspect and run a second confirmatory sample alongside fingerprint analysis."

Sarah nodded, re-assured by Jennifer's professionalism despite everything she had been coping with over the last few weeks. The thought of Jennifer's circumstances pricked her conscience. She gestured for Jo to join her in the kitchen, not wanting to give Jennifer any more stress. "Jo, have we released Jeff Godley?"

"Not yet, ma'am. We will release him well within the PACE timescales but didn't really want him running around St Helier as a loose cannon while we run this op."

"Good idea. Have you been able to find anyone from the surveillance team that can keep an eye on him?"

"Yes, I have asked the DI to release someone from the money laundering case. We are close to putting that to bed and I think we can take a calculated risk with releasing resources."

"That's good, Jo, and Lydia says we are getting another DC tomorrow. A computer whiz."

"Yes, DC Kennon. She is a diamond at that stuff. Helped us no end on the laundering case."

Sarah took the coffees she made on the pretence of speaking to Jo back into the main control room. Nothing new had happened in the short time she was out of the room.

Another hour passed with nothing significant to report. Sarah stood up and grabbed her fluorescent jacket. "I can't stand sitting here anymore. Jennifer, I suggest you go home, get some rest and be ready to start your work in the morning. Jo, Jessica, let's get out on the ground and meet the team in St Helier."

Everyone jumped at Sarah's instructions. She thanked DI Hill for his work and flew out of the room. They walked up from the police HQ building towards the main town centre. They met Steph, Mark and Lisa in Broad Street. It was nearly 1am and the streets were relatively quiet. They bought coffees on their way up and these were handed round, the three detectives grateful for the pick-me-up. The rain that had deluged the capital earlier in the day had eased off, but the scorching temperatures of the previous days had long gone and there was a decided chill in the air. Sarah's stress levels were easy to detect as she spoke through gulps of coffee.

"What's your assessment, DCI Brown?"

"We have stopped nineteen women that matched the profile and description. All of them spoke to us willingly, seemingly keen to help us and provided us with a DNA sample. We have their alibis recorded and their contact details. I can't say we found anything odd about any of them."

Steph looked to Mark and Lisa for re-assurance, and they nodded their support for her pitch.

Jessica interjected. "The thing is, Steph, remember that this perp is a sociopath. She will have been comfortable in this environment, not at all fazed by being stopped and questioned. She will have been energised by the thrill of the game, playing the role she set up for herself tonight. There is every chance that one of the women you spoke to was the perp."

Steph screwed her face up. "So how are we supposed to catch her?"

"As I said in my profiling, catch her in a lie. Look for exaggerated answers, embellishments on a normal conversation, over-confidence."

"I honestly can't say we met anyone like that tonight. Do you two agree?"

Mark and Lisa nodded their agreement.

"OK, maybe she hasn't been in the capital tonight, but I guess you have their DNA samples and alibis to check, in case we catch a break."

The mood in the team seemed flat. Sarah tried to pick them up.

"Look, DI Hill says we have stopped another twenty-three women across the island, all of whom have given their DNA and other details. It gives us something to go on. Jennifer will be processing the DNA samples tomorrow against the DNA hit we had at the second crime scene. You guys need to start working through the alibis to see if you can find any anomalies. We also have a new DC starting with us tomorrow who is going to focus on the technical angles that Jessica suggested. Now go home, get some rest and we will meet for a briefing at 10.30am."

The team logged off with the control room and dispersed.

As Sarah started to walk back to the station with Jo, she couldn't help but blurt out what was on her mind. "What have I done, Jo? How could I have got this so wrong? I have wasted all these resources on a wild goose chase."

"You don't know that, ma'am. We might have got something tonight."

"I don't think so, Jo. She has outwitted us... me, again."

# 29

Mark stood for a moment with Jessica and Lisa, letting the bosses walk out of sight. "Well, that was a bust. Do you think our chief is losing it, wasting our time like that?"

Jessica responded first. "You need some faith, Mark. Remember she is being directed by my advice. I am confident we have the right focus now."

Mark shrugged. "OK, but she doesn't seem to have a clue what she is doing."

His comments trailed off into the night as the other two drank the last of their coffee, trying to find a way out of the uncomfortable vibe that Mark had created.

Lisa tried to change the focus of the chat. "So where are you staying, Jessica?"

"Oh, in a little B&B up the road. About five minutes' walk away."

"Really? My mum runs a B&B around here. What's it called?"

"Oh, god, something lame like Sunny View. It's in that funny-named street, Journ... something."

"Journeaux Street?"

"Yeah, that's it. Is that your mum's place?"

"No, hers is a bit further up in Roussel Street."

As the conversation trailed off, Mark made to leave and stumbled over his footing. Lisa went to grab him.

"Are you OK, Mark?"

He righted himself. "Yeah, fine, just a bit tired. Need to get to bed. My flat is only a few minutes away, I'll be fine."

As the other two went their separate ways, Mark started walking up the road, along York Street and into the Parade, past a number of fast-food shops that were still buzzing with late-night customers trying to soak up the alcohol they had consumed. The smells were drawing him in, but he resisted, the tiredness consuming him. Every step felt like a huge effort and his mind was fuzzy. He cracked on, willing his tired body on. A few minutes later he finally turned into Westmount Road, his flat on the corner overlooking the People's Park.

As he fumbled for his keys, he heard a noise: a twig cracking under someone's foot. He stopped and looked around. He put his hand against his front door to steady himself. What was wrong with him? Why did he feel so woozy? He went to put the key in the lock when another sound stopped him.

"Is someone there?"

There was no answer. He stepped away from the door and moved around to the side of the building. There was no one there. He stopped and listened, all the time fighting the chronic tiredness. After a few moments, satisfied that he was just spooking himself unnecessarily, he went back round to his front door. As he turned the corner, he had to stifle a scream as a face loomed up at him. After a few seconds, trying to get over the shock, he relaxed.

"Oh, it's you. What are you doing here? You frightened me half to death."

# 30

The birds sitting in the tree outside her window were well into their morning chorus as she ran her finger along the rough edge of the scar that was now forming on the top part of her left forearm. It settled her. The previous night had gone well. She had outfoxed Sarah once again and the thrill of another kill had kept the demons at bay for another night, the knife laying untouched on the side.

The memory of the kill jolted her back into action. She washed her hands again. She had to touch the victim this time. It was necessary, but it ramped up her anxieties. Every touch made her heave. No one could touch her anymore, not since... her mind drifted off. She looked at the knife again. A tear escaped. She brushed it away quickly, looking at her reflection in the mirror.

"Don't worry, little Lucy, we are about to end thirty years of pain. He is next."

*

Sarah had survived on five hours' sleep and was back in the incident room at 8am. None of the team were in. She turned on the coffee machine and fired up her laptop. She checked the overnight briefing from DI Hill. Nothing else had happened. No murders. No more suspects. She sat back in her chair and looked out at the view of the sea. The wind had now picked up sweeping ominous-looking black clouds across the bay, a metaphor for her mood.

She ploughed through the emails and got her thoughts in order for the morning briefing. A few minutes before 9am, there was a knock on her door. Sarah looked up. A young woman with spiky red hair and a smart blouse/skirt combo was stood in the doorway.

"Ah, you must be DC Kennon?"

The DC took a step forward and offered a handshake. "Yes, ma'am. It's an honour to work with you."

Sarah was slightly taken aback by the compliment. They came so infrequently these days, especially from the rank and file. She was just about to launch into her welcome when her phone rang. She grimaced at the interruption but picked her phone up to see who was calling. It was Gerard Le Trousain.

"I'm sorry, DC Kennon. I need to take this. Grab yourself a coffee. I won't be a minute." Sarah swiped the green button. "Gerard. How can I help you?"

He clearly wasn't in the mood for pleasantries. "What happened last night, Sarah? I need an update. I don't have time now, but I want to see you at 12.30pm today in my office. Can you ring my PA and confirm?"

Sarah hardly had time to confirm when the phone was disconnected. *OK, so that's how it's going to be*, she thought to herself.

She called Cassandra back in, trying to concentrate on giving her a positive welcome, while agonising over the extra pressure that Gerard was placing on her every minute of every day.

"So, what do you know about the case, DC Kennon?"

"Well, it's hard to ignore, ma'am. I have been keeping up with the force briefings and I spoke to Lisa – sorry, DC Johnson about it yesterday. I'm raring to go."

"Good. Good. I understand you are a computer whiz, so I need you to start on two things. Firstly, get a briefing from Jessica, our profiler from the mainland. I want you to use public records to see if we can narrow down a suspect list based on the profiling she did."

"Actually, ma'am, I've already started on that. Lisa mentioned it yesterday. Based on the public records there are 1,453 single women on Jersey in that age bracket, assuming we are focusing only on islanders and not tourists."

Sarah raised her eyebrows. "Wow. That shows some commitment, DC Kennon. Well done, but do speak to Jessica to refine the search. We can't do anything with that many names."

"Of course, ma'am."

"Secondly, I want you to research how someone might have obtained arsenic, which was used in the second and third murders. This is not a readily available commodity and I am not aware of anywhere on Jersey that sells it, legally or otherwise. I need you to look at routes via the internet and how this could have got past customs and import checks."

"No problem, ma'am. I suspect this is dark web stuff."

"Dark web?"

"Yes, the part of the internet the average punter can't see, where criminals do all their business."

"Oh, right, sounds good. OK, get to it. We have a briefing in an hour where you can meet the team."

*

It was a little before 10.30am and Sarah could hear the buzz in the room as the team gathered. As she walked in to start the briefing she stopped and scanned the room.

"Where is DS Adams?"

Steph responded. "We don't know, ma'am. He hasn't turned up yet."

"Have you tried to phone him?"

"Yeah, a couple of times, but the calls just go to voicemail."

"For god's sake. What's he playing at?"

Lisa pitched in. "Actually, ma'am, at the end of our shift last night he did seem a bit wobbly on his feet. He said he was just tired, but it's possible he was coming down with something and is just in bed trying to sleep it off."

Sarah pondered what Lisa had said. "OK, I know we are working round the clock on this one and that no one has had any time off for nearly ten days. I realise that you are all probably on your knees, but we have to keep going. If DS Adams is ill, I would have still expected him to call in. DC Johnson, can you keep trying to contact him, and if he hasn't emerged by lunchtime, go to his flat and see if you can stir him. In the meantime, I will see if I can get you some days off, but it will have to be one of you at a time."

There were positive murmurings in the room.

Sarah pressed on. "OK. Hopefully you have all introduced yourself to DC Kennon, who will initially be providing the technical support that Jessica suggested we needed. She will be working with Jessica today to try to develop a suspect list from the public records of Jersey residents. I have also asked her to look at how the perp may have obtained arsenic."

There were lots of welcoming smiles in Cassandra's direction.

"Jennifer will be processing the DNA samples collected last night against the sample we obtained at the second crime scene."

"Yes, ma'am, the team are already working on it. I should have the results by the end of the day."

"Good, well done, Jennifer. DCI Brown and DC Johnson will focus on reviewing the alibis from last night and hopefully waking up our errant DS. For my part, I have been summoned to see Mr Trousain at lunchtime. I will try to protect you from the heat that he is applying, but do focus on the tasks in hand. We are only going to get some space to do our jobs if I can keep reporting progress to him."

The briefing came to an end and the team dispersed. Sarah walked back into her office and stared out of the window. The ominous clouds had formed into something darker and threatening. The metaphor kept strengthening.

*

Sarah arrived early for her meeting with Gerard Le Trousain. He was running late. She sat down, enjoying the hit of caffeine and the sugar rush provided by the mini Danish pastries that were an ever-present fixture in the waiting area outside his office.

Fifteen minutes late, she was called in. He made a poor attempt at a welcome, but Sarah knew he was still in a bad mood and was not expecting an easy ride.

"What's the latest, Sarah? I do hope you made some progress last night."

"Well, it's a bit early to say, but we stopped forty-three women last night that matched the profile and the witness descriptions from the zoo. They all gave DNA samples willingly and the CSI team are processing them as we speak."

"That doesn't sound very optimistic."

"Why?"

"Well, surely the perp would not want to give their DNA willingly if they suspect we have a sample to compare it with."

"Let's wait and see, Gerard. Our profiler seems to think that this perp is uber-confident and will not have been fazed by being stopped. We'll know if we've had a hit by the end of the day."

"You're not filling me with great confidence, Sarah. What else?"

"We took alibis from each of these women and the detective team are following those up today. The profiling work is really helping us to sharpen our focus and we have a new DC in the team today who is providing technical support to produce a suspect list based on public records."

"So, you think she is a Jersey resident and not some tourist who decided to visit our island for a murder spree?"

"Yes, our profiler is quite certain about that."

Gerard gave a look of surprise that told Sarah he didn't share her faith. His next line confirmed as much. "The problem is, Sarah, your operation didn't actually catch the perp. We have no one in custody."

Sarah held her ground. "That's true, but there were also no murders last night. We may well have disrupted her plans."

Gerard shook his head. "You're clutching at straws, Sarah. I think last night's operation was a complete waste of time."

As the awkward vibe hung in the room, the tension was interrupted by the tinkle of Sarah's phone. She ignored Gerard's look of disapproval to see who was calling.

"Sorry, Gerard, can I take this? It's my DC."

He waved her away, without comment.

She answered. "DC Johnson, what is it?"

Lisa's voice cracked with emotion. "Ma'am, we are at Mark's flat. We had to bust the door down. He's not asleep, ma'am. He's dead."

# 31

Sarah rushed out of the room, making no attempt to explain what she was doing to Gerard. The last thing she needed was more of his disapproval. She tore through reception and jumped in her car, which was parked out the front of the building. As she drove to Mark's flat her mind was racing.

*Is this our murderer? How did we miss her, and why was Mark her next victim?*

As she arrived, most of the team were already there. Steph and Lisa were guarding the scene. Jessica was just inside the door, watching Jennifer process the scene. Sarah tried to give a sympathetic shoulder rub to a clearly upset Lisa. Steph's face was resolute and she didn't seem to need the same attention. Sarah quickly donned the forensic coveralls and walked in under the police tape. She nodded an acknowledgement to Jessica.

"What have we got, Jennifer? Is this our killer?"

"I'm not sure it is, ma'am. Look in that evidence bag."

Sarah walked over to the table where Jennifer had placed the evidence bag. Inside was a fully plunged syringe.

"What is this?"

"From the blue tint on his nails and lips, together with some discolouration on his tongue, I'm guessing this is a heroin overdose."

"What! DS Adams was a heroin addict?"

"Well, I'm not sure we can call him an addict. He may just have taken this one hit and got it badly wrong. It can happen. He surely would have been picked up on our random drug testing programme if he was using regularly."

"I don't understand. Why?"

"I hate to say this, ma'am, but it may have been a reaction to how hard we are all working. It's not uncommon for people to use drugs on an occasional basis as a pick-me-up."

"Oh my god." Sarah sat down on one of the chairs, away from the crime scene. She put her head in her hands. *Have I driven him to this?*

Jennifer could sense Sarah's distress and tried to change focus, as she suddenly spotted something. "Ma'am. I've just realised there is something wrong with this crime scene."

Sarah looked up, trying to regain some composure. "Wrong?"

"Yes. Mark was right-handed, wasn't he?"

"Err... yeh, I think so. What's the relevance?"

"It's the position of the needle mark. The syringe was in Mark's left hand when I found the body, and the location of the injection site, under his right armpit, would suggest an injection with his left hand. It's not impossible for him to have done that, but it is very unusual for people not to favour their dominant hand when doing something like this."

"Are you saying that someone helped him inject the drugs?"

"It's possible, and it's also odd that the syringe was still in his hand. If he injected this himself, he would have dropped or put the syringe down. The overdose would not have killed him instantly, giving him time to savour the hit. He would not have done that still holding the needle."

"You are saying this could be a murder scene rather than accidental suicide?"

"I wouldn't rule it out at this stage."

Sarah looked at Jessica. "What do you make of this?"

"I'm not sure, Sarah. There doesn't seem to be any of her signatures here."

There was a short delay as Sarah processed what Jessica had said. "Oh, no note?"

Jennifer looked up, overhearing their conversation. "Jessica's right. There is no note."

Sarah looked at the scene again, trying to see something that would explain what this was. She looked back at Jessica. "Is there anything you can do here at the moment?"

"I don't think so, Sarah. Without something that gives us a sense that this our perp striking again, I should probably get back to help Cassie."

Sarah was once again surprised by Jessica's informality. They had only known her for a few hours and yet Jessica was already calling her Cassie. As Jessica left, she reverted back to surveying the scene as Jennifer beavered away. She was trying to envisage the different scenarios. Was this suicide or was this murder? As her brain filled up with possible options Jennifer found something.

"Ma'am. I have a single blonde hair, underneath the body. Can you pass me an evidence bag?"

"Real or fake?"

Jennifer held it up to the light. "It's real."

"Not a wig then."

"No, so no connection to the wig hair we found at the first crime scene."

"Did he have a girlfriend?"

"I don't know, ma'am."

Jennifer continued to process the scene as they both considered the possibilities. As much as Sarah disliked Mark and his sloppy attitude to work, she just couldn't see him as the type to do this. What was killing Sarah was the fear that this was a murder unconnected to the main case.

After a few more minutes Sarah decided she could do no more. She went outside to speak to Steph and Lisa. "DC Johnson, are you OK to carry on with your shift today or do you want to go home?"

"I want to carry on, ma'am. We have to stop this woman."

"Actually, DC Johnson, Jennifer is not yet sure what this is. It could be an accidental suicide, an overdose of heroin."

Lisa response was unusually forceful. "That's crap, ma'am. Mark was not a druggie. Someone did this to him. He was feeling unwell at the end of the shift, unsteady on his feet. They need to find out what was in his system before the drugs were injected. I'm sure this is murder."

"But there's no note, DC Johnson."

"That doesn't mean it isn't murder, ma'am."

Sarah was impressed with Lisa's resolve and decided not to push her to go home. She had clearly processed her emotions and was back on track. "OK, you two. Get some uniform to guard the scene and get back to working through those alibis."

As Sarah went to leave, she recoiled as she almost bumped into someone. "What the fuck?"

"Such a pleasant greeting, Miss Braintree, especially for someone that you wrongly arrested. Would have thought an apology should have been the first thing you said to me, along with your two stooges here. Oh, and there's my lovely Jennifer. Hello, sweetheart." He moved a bit closer and saw the body sprawled on the floor. "Oh, she's struck again, has she?"

Sarah placed a firm hand on his shoulder. "Back off, Mr Godley, this is a crime scene and you have no business here. Please leave."

He stepped away from her contact. "Hey, hey, police brutality as well. Gosh, my article in the *Herald* tomorrow is going to be good." He walked away, cackling like a witch.

Sarah looked at Steph. "Get the cordon extended. I don't want him, or any other of those parasites, anywhere near this scene."

She drove back to the station to see DCO Millar, seething at the interaction with Jeff Godley. She knew in her heart that she had jumped too quickly in arresting him, but for Jennifer's sake, she felt she had to do something. She wasn't looking forward to the lies and sensationalist headlines that she was sure Jeff Godley was now cooking up, giving Gerard another reason to have a go at her.

As she neared the station, her heart sank a little bit further as she realised the next job she had to do was notify Mark's next of kin.

# 32

Sarah pulled the team in for a 5.30pm briefing. The mood was solemn.

"I know today has been incredibly hard. Losing one of our own is the worst possible outcome for anyone in the police service. I do want to stress, however, that, at this time, we don't know whether Mark was another victim of our perp. There was no note left at the scene and nothing particularly to suggest it was her. We are investigating whether this was an accidental drug overdose, as an alternative theory to explain what happened. Rest assured, I will leave no stone unturned until we find out what happened to him. At this point, I do not want his details on our incident board. DCO Millar is working with the superintendent in charge of professional standards to investigate this is as a standalone case."

Sarah paused to see if anyone wanted to comment. There was nothing forthcoming.

"We will take updates from each of you shortly, but after that, I have decided to give you all a day off. I know our perp is out there, probably plotting her next move, but if the tragedy of Mark's death has taught me anything, it's that we need to be fresh, physically and mentally, if we are to catch her. After this, I don't want you back in here until 9.30am on Friday morning."

There were a few surprised looks at Sarah's command, but she cracked on.

"Right. Updates, please. DCI Brown?"

"Once we left the crime scene this morning, Lisa and I have been checking the alibis from last night. We have got through about half of them so far and they all check out."

"OK. Jennifer?"

"Likewise, ma'am. The team have processed about half the DNA samples and no matches to our sample. I also have the hair from this morning's scene to process, as well as the other forensic bits I collected."

"Jessica?"

"Cassie and I have been going through the profile in detail. I think we have made some progress."

Sarah looked at Cassandra, *Cassie*, expectantly.

"Well, ma'am, based on further advice from Jessica, we brought down the possible number of suspects from 1,453 single women in the right age range, down to 677. This is based on the assertion that she lives alone. Based on residency records we found that there are around seven hundred or so that seem to live alone. We have reduced this by another twenty-three based on today's work, eliminating those we stopped last night that are clear of our investigation. This leaves us 677 possible suspects."

"That's a good start, DC Kennon, and thank you for helping her, Jessica, but that is still a massive number to process."

"Don't worry, ma'am. Jessica and I still have some parameters we can look at to reduce this down. We can look at personal history, employment records and family records. They should all help us to get the list down. Oh, and if it is all right with you, ma'am, I won't take a day off, having just joined the team. I can quite easily get on with my work without anyone else about."

Sarah smiled, re-assured by the enthusiasm being shown by the new recruit.

"OK, that's enough for now. Please go home and have a rest. I am happy that DC Kennon can continue her work without the rest of us. I'll see you all, refreshed and ready for the next push on Friday morning."

As the team started to make moves to leave, Sarah called Lisa back. They walked into the office.

"Are you OK, DC…" Sarah checked herself, conscious that her commitment to the formality of rank sometimes made her seem overly distant and unapproachable. "… sorry, Lisa?"

"Yes, ma'am. It's been a hard day and thank you for the time off. We all know we can't really afford to take our eye off the ball, but the team appreciate the gesture."

Sarah smiled. "I've been impressed with you, Lisa. You are very quiet and probably let DCI… sorry, Steph, over-exert her rank on you, but I like the way you work. As a result, I have decided to give you a temporary promotion to sergeant within the investigation team. I know it might seem a bit ghoulish so soon after Mark's death, but I need to keep the lines of responsibility clear within the team, and Cassandra can take up the slack at DC level."

"Oh, wow, thank you, ma'am. I won't let you down."

"I'm sure you won't, Lisa. Can I ask you one thing?"

"Sure. Fire away."

"Yesterday when Mark handed round the composites you seemed to flinch, as though you recognised the picture."

Lisa suddenly looked uncomfortable and Sarah wondered whether she had made a mistake in asking the question. A few seconds passed before Lisa seemed to compose herself. "You're right, ma'am. There was something about that picture that made me check myself. I felt like I had seen the image before but couldn't place where."

"Oh, have you managed to recall anything?"

"No, ma'am."

As Sarah watched Lisa's response, she could see her chewing her bottom lip. Nervous, unsettled. "Is there anything else you need to tell me, Lisa?"

Lisa looked at Sarah, liked a rabbit in the headlights, suddenly caught out like a naughty child. She relented under the scrutiny. "It's Mark, ma'am. There is something really strange about this whole case and the way Mark has been investigating it. I have worked with him before and he is… was, a great copper. He would always chase every lead down like a dog with a bone, never resting until he got what he needed, but with this case he seemed… off."

"How do you mean?"

"You must have seen it, ma'am. I mean, we could tell you weren't happy with him. He was sloppy, didn't seem to have any energy or enthusiasm for the case. It was out of character. Also, he didn't like you. Took every opportunity to badmouth you to the team."

Sarah sighed. "You are right, Lisa. I was very unhappy with his work and not surprised by his attitude towards me." There was a brief, uncomfortable pause. "OK, here's what I want you to do. Can you go back over all of Mark's work and see if there is anything that he missed? I particularly want you to focus on the CCTV from the zoo. He seemed vague and dismissive when I probed him for information. Our perp will be on there somewhere, but for some reason he didn't seem to find anything."

Lisa visibly relaxed, seemingly relieved to get it off her chest. "Of course, ma'am. I will get right onto it on Friday."

With that, their meeting ended and Lisa left the incident room. As Sarah mulled over what Lisa had said, she once again found herself staring out of the window, watching the public go about their business, oblivious of the murderer walking amongst them. The dark clouds earlier in the day had dissipated and the early evening sun was beating down once again, raising the temperatures and getting the tourists out and about. Sarah just watched, her mind spinning. When would she strike again... or had Mark been part of her deadly game?

# 33

Lisa sat on the balcony of her third-floor apartment, enjoying the wonderful views across St Aubin's Bay as she necked her third glass of white wine. The rent on the apartment was expensive, taking almost sixty per cent of her income every month, but it was worth it. This was her place of solace, a place to re-charge and de-stress. She loved the sea, and the views of the bay always calmed her. And boy did she need to de-stress today.

Mark's shocking death followed by the heart-to-heart with Sarah had put her in a spin. She was relieved to have opened up about Mark, but his death troubled her. There was nothing that suggested he would kill himself, but there was definitely something going on with him. He was not doing a good job and his obvious dislike for Sarah was unsettling, behaviour that they saw in the perp and that bastard reporter. It was unprofessional. As her mind chased around for an explanation, she thought about the rest of the team. What was it that was making her so unsettled?

As she poured more wine, she knew in her heart that Mark was not the only one that was being odd. Why was Steph being so blasé about everything? Why had she let Jeff Godley rattle her in the interview and why did she give up on questioning him so easily? Like Mark, she seemed to be coasting, treading water, not committed to the cause.

It might have been the wine twitching her conspiracy radar, but she found her mind drifting to the other person in the team that unsettled her. Jessica. What was it about her that intimidated her so much? Was it her uber-confidence, her seemingly unwavering certainty about her profiling work? Lisa envied her. She had always struggled with personal confidence and worried constantly about what people thought of her. She also realised that it was Jessica's face that had stared back at her from the composites they did after the zoo attacks, but her subconscious had dismissed that as ridiculous.

As she tried to relax, the warm sun and the wine started to take effect as her eyes started to droop; the games her mind were playing exhausting her. She wasn't sure how long she had been asleep when she suddenly came to. As she tried to re-focus on the view, her eye was dragged to something that made her bolt out of her seat. She rubbed her eyes, trying to validate what she thought she was looking at. A few seconds later the person she was looking at had gone, disappearing out of view around the corner of the next apartment building.

Lisa sat down. Had she really just seen that? As she moved her arm, she almost sent the wine bottle flying off the side table, catching it just in time before it smashed on the tiled floor of the balcony. The bottle was empty. Her mind started to play games. *You're imagining things, Lisa. You've drunk a whole bottle of wine. It can't have been her. You're drunk and confused.*

Lisa continued to stare at the path where she had seen this person, willing her to come back into view, to help her validate what she had seen. Ten minutes passed and nothing happened.

She stood up to go inside, unsettled by the experience. If she was right, the person she thought she saw had no business being at this end of the island.

\*

Sarah applied her face cream, knowing in her heart that she was fighting a losing battle against the onset of middle age. The dark rings under her eyes were worse than ever, the constant pressure of this case affecting her sleep. She agonised over what to do with the next twenty-four hours. She needed a break, like the rest of the team, but it seemed selfish and irresponsible to even consider this when that woman was still out there, plotting her next move.

Mark's death had been a shock, but she couldn't help feeling a sense of relief at not having to deal with him anymore. Promoting Lisa and getting Cassandra in had been a bright moment in a difficult day, and with Jessica's profiling focusing the investigation, she had a renewed sense of hope. She was sure Lisa would unearth something that Mark had missed and give the investigation some much-needed impetus.

As she tried to keep the positive thoughts going, the devil on her shoulder brought her back to the one thing that might decide exactly how the next day would go. The threats of a story in the *Herald* by Jeff Godley. The world's press had eased their interest in the case, the numbers camped outside the station reducing each day, but she knew they would lap up a local story about police incompetence and do anything to put her back in the spotlight.

She lay down in bed and didn't set her alarm clock. She would let fate decide when she got out of bed.

# 34

Today was the day. The day when she would get her revenge on the man that had caused her so much pain, the man that had turned her into what she had become and the reason for her hatred towards Sarah Braintree.

She needed a good disguise today. This was broad daylight stuff and she needed to interact with the other staff at the care home to get to where she needed to be. In his room, alone and uninterrupted.

She put on her smart business suit, placed the trusty blonde wig on her head and selected a pair of understated glasses which rested on the prosthetic nose she had carefully applied. She was pleased with what she saw in the mirror. She was ready. The Caledonian Care Home was about to get a snap inspection from the Care Quality Commission.

\*

In the end, Sarah's subconscious had woken her at the usual time and she was on her way to the station by 8am. As she neared the building, her heart sank. The throng of reporters had grown again. As she got closer, she couldn't believe her eyes. Jeff Godley was surrounded by the world's press. She hadn't seen the *Herald* but she knew he had made himself today's story. She tried to walk up the path towards the main entrance without being noticed, but as she got to within twenty yards of the door, there was a shout of 'there she is' and the mob turned and descended on her. The cacophony of voices made her wince as accusations and challenges were shouted at her. From the few words she could decipher, as the voices competed for space, it was obvious he had focused on his perception of a wrongful arrest and his personal vendetta against Sarah. She jostled her way past the unruly mob that tried to block her way. She ignored every attempt to engage and finally reached the main door of the station.

As she walked into the main entrance lobby she barked at the receptionist. "Get some uniform out there and put a proper cordon in place. Now!"

Sarah was fuming as she crashed into the press office. Her presence was not unexpected and the comms team maintained an air of calm and authority as their VIP guest arrived unannounced and in a fluster.

The head of PR came straight of her office and handed Sarah the *Herald*, instinctively knowing why she was here. She took a seat at the breakfast bar in their rest area and read the article. She was front-page news.

It was all there. Wrongful arrest, police incompetence, personal attacks on her credibility as chief of police and speculation about the latest murder. Sarah was relieved that the one thing Jeff Godley didn't know was that the victim he had seen laying on the floor, before she manhandled him away from the scene, was Mark. How much worse could this story have been if he had realised that one of her own team was dead?

Thinking of Mark reminded her that the ME was due to do his post-mortem that morning and she was desperate to know whether he would find anything that would explain Mark's death. She also wondered about Jennifer. She had told the team to have a day off, but, like her, she knew some of them would not be able to settle. With the forensics from Mark's crime scene to process, she had a feeling Jennifer would be in. As she thought about her next move, her concentration was broken by the head of PR, who nodded towards the paper.

"A load of nonsense, I'm guessing?"

Sarah looked at her, slightly crestfallen. "Well, Maria, I would like to say yes, but I'm afraid I did make an error of judgement in arresting him before we had a better case against him. The rest of it's just personal attacks on me. Some form of personal vendetta that I'm yet to understand."

"Don't worry, ma'am, we will work this out. I'll start on a press response and get it over to you later this morning."

"Thanks, Maria." As Sarah stood up to leave, her phone beeped. The next predictable thing happened. Gerard wanted to see her immediately. She left from the back entrance of the station to avoid the baying mob and set off for the government buildings in Grouville.

\*

She parked her car a little way down the street from the care home, which was just outside the centre of Grouville. She didn't want any nosey types from the care home being able to link her to a vehicle.

She walked up to the front door, an official-looking leather-bound document folder in her hand, giving the illusion of authority. A middle-aged lady in a care assistant uniform answered the door.

"Can I help you?"

"Yes, my name is Sarah Braintree, from the Care Quality Commission, and I'm here for a snap inspection of your care facility. Please can you get your home manager?"

The assistant barely looked at her fake ID as she scurried off to get the manager, unnerved by this unexpected visitor. A few minutes later, a stern-looking woman, on the wrong side of forty and a poor advert for health and fitness, walked into reception. Her manner was immediately confrontational.

"Can I help you?"

"Yes, as I told your assistant, my name is Sarah Braintree and I'm here from the Care Quality Commission to do a snap inspection."

"Can I ask why?"

"Come now, Mrs...?"

"Wyatt."

"...Mrs Wyatt, you should know that is not how snap inspections work."

The manager sized her up, and she worried she was not buying her story. After a few tense seconds that seemed to last forever, she relented. "OK, let's get this over with. What do you need?"

She relaxed and put on her professional persona. "Great. I want to start by inspecting the common resident areas, followed by the kitchen and laundry. After that, I want to talk to a couple of residents on this list about their care experiences. You will see we have already had authority from their loved ones for them to be involved. I just need you to let them know I will be up to see them in about half an hour."

"No problem. Which residents would you like to speak to from this list?"

She took the list back, the adrenalin flowing through her body threatening to de-rail the calm, professional persona she needed to maintain if this was going to work. She made a point of perusing the list carefully, trying not to let his name distract her. After what she thought was a reasonable amount of time, she announced her decision.

"I'd like to see Ethel McGregor and Michael Brackley."

"OK, I'm not sure you will get much out of Mr Brackley, but their rooms are both on the second floor. I will get one of the care assistants to let them know you are coming."

"That's great, and can I be clear that I do not want any of your staff on the second floor whilst I'm conducting my interviews. I don't want any interference. Is that clear?"

"That's fine. Shall we start down here?"

She followed the home manager into the large living room, occupied by residents in various states of alertness. She made a point of opening up her leather folder and pretended to write notes as she went. Her adrenalin was flowing, the expectation of finally getting to the man that had caused all this pain was threatening to overwhelm her, but she needed to play the game.

The home manager was giving her a running commentary as they walked round and she nodded wisely, asking the occasional inane question to keep up the persona. After inspecting the living areas and laundry, they entered the kitchen. As she walked past one of the counter tops she froze. A large knife had been left on the side. The demons started to rage. *Cut, cut, cut*. She picked up the knife, paralysed by the feelings coursing through her body.

"Are you OK, Miss Braintree?" The home manager had noticed and was staring at her, confused and a little bit suspicious.

Her mind was racing, the demons battling in her head. Eventually, she righted herself, eased her tensed up body and put the knife down. In the calmest, coolest way possible, she turned to the home manager.

"I'm fine. Sorry, I just have a thing about knives. Do you often leave them unattended like this in a room that anyone can come into?"

The home manager's demeanour changed from the suspicious, accusatory vibe she had displayed with her previous question to a defensive, more passive tone. "Oh, god, no. The chefs should know better than that. I will remind them."

She smiled. She had battled through it and was back in control. She decided to ease the tension. "Don't worry, Mrs Wyatt. It's not a major issue, just one to keep an eye on. I'm really impressed with what I have seen so far."

The home manager gave a forced smile and they finished the tour of the downstairs areas without further incident. As they reached the bottom of the staircase the home manager saw one of her care assistants coming down the stairs. "Are they ready for our visitor, Laura?"

"Yes, Mrs Wyatt, all ready."

They walked up to the second floor. Towards the end of the corridor they went to room 29. The home manager opened the door to Mr Brackley's room and encouraged her to enter.

"OK, Mr Brackley, the visitor that Laura mentioned is here. I'll leave you with her."

The door was closed behind her. She waited a few seconds and discreetly locked the door. Across the room the man she had been waiting to exact her revenge on was sitting ten yards away, an oxygen mask over his face, frail and pathetic.

He gestured for her to sit down on the chair next to him, not an ounce of recognition for the woman that was standing in front of him.

# 35

Cassandra was in bright and early. The incident room was empty, everyone else seemingly doing as the boss had said and taking the day off.

She started by looking at the issue of how the perp had obtained the arsenic. A trawl through the dark web soon rendered plenty of dodgy sites that were prepared to sell all sorts of illegal substances. She searched for sites offering advice on how to smuggle these goods into Jersey. After half an hour of delving into the seedy underworld of illegal smuggling, it was clear to Cassandra that there were any number of ways of getting the stuff onto the island. The favoured method seemed to be hiding the illegal substances inside something like a single tube of sun cream, which was part of a multipack order. A cursory glance by a customs officer would find the top two layers of any consignment containing the real product, with the contraband buried in a single tube in the middle of the box. It was basic but effective, as customs had bigger fish to fry.

She knew she could probably do some 'donkey work' by trawling through thousands of import manifests to see if she could find a trail but decided her time was better spent trying to drill down the list of possible suspects based on Jessica's profiling.

She was keeping each snapshot in a separate database; from the 1,500 odd names she had started with to the 677 names that were now staring at her on her laptop screen. Jessica was certain that the perp was an islander and had potentially lived on Jersey all their life. Cassandra looked at residency records and reduced the list significantly. Now they only had 223 names on the list.

They had also discussed what sort of job the perp might have. The basic intel suggested she was a nine-to-fiver as she always seemed to be free in the evenings and weekends. Cassandra applied some basic algorithms, based on job information she could obtain from public records. By removing anyone that was a shift worker, she got the list down to 131.

The final parameter was her family background. Jessica was convinced the perp was an only child, or someone with an unstable family life. The list was down to 106.

*

Lisa sat at one of the outside tables of Bella's coffee shop, which was a short distance from her flat, overlooking the sweeping vista of St Aubin's Bay. She was drinking a strong espresso to try to dull the effects of the mild hangover she had woken up with, while she waited for the bacon sarnie that she knew would rejuvenate her.

As she let the caffeine hit course through her body, she found herself scanning the crowd, watching every person that passed. She couldn't get the image out of her head and was willing the person she thought she saw the previous evening to re-appear, walking along the seafront, validating her paranoia.

Half an hour later, the bacon sarnie a distant memory, nothing had changed. All she saw was stranger after stranger enjoying the nice weather.

She got up and started walking along the promenade, her mind still racing. She listened to the sound of the waves, the screech of the seagulls and the constant murmuring of the public as they went about their business. It always relaxed her. As her head cleared, she muttered to herself. *There's something going on, Lisa, and you need to find out what it is.*

\*

Sarah wasn't sure how long she had been sat in her car outside the government buildings, the never-ending stream of emails on her phone distracting her from getting on with the business of the day. The expected bollocking from Gerard had not happened. In their brief meeting he had been empathetic, asking how her and the team were coping with the shocking death of Mark and dismissing the rantings of Jeff Godley in the *Herald* as 'just tomorrow's chip paper'. He had listened carefully as she outlined the next steps on the investigation and seemed supportive of the independent review of Mark's death.

As she reflected on the interaction with Gerard, she manically scrolled through her emails. Where was the post-mortem report? Was Jennifer in, looking at Mark's forensics, on her 'day off'? Had Cassandra had any breakthroughs? There was nothing.

She looked out the window of her car, cursing herself for sitting here, doing nothing as the perp played her deadly game. She agonised over their lack of traction in the case. Were they ever going to catch a break? When would she strike again? Sarah was about to get the answer.

# 36

She walked towards him, the rage building but she needed to make this last, make him suffer the way he had made her suffer, day after day, night after night.

He took off his mask. "What do you want then, missy? Some inspector, I'm told." His voice was gravelly, whatever illness he had affecting the strength of his voice.

She wanted to rip his face off, plunge the knife that she had been discreetly hiding in her folder into his chest, over and over and over. She calmed herself.

"You don't recognise me, do you?"

He stared at her, no recognition forthcoming. "Should I?"

"I'm Lucy Crohan."

He put his mask back on and took a deep breath of oxygen. After a minute, he took the mask off again. "That doesn't help. I'm no good with names. How am I supposed to know you?"

The blood vessels in her head were pulsing, thirty years of rage coursing through her body. If he was for real, he was delivering the final, gut-wrenching insult. Not even having the common decency to remember who she was and what he had done to her.

"You really are a piece of work. Have you just forgotten what you did to me and all those other children?"

His face changed immediately; the memory jolted. An expression somewhere between curiosity and fear etched on his face. She glared at him, willing him to remember. He said nothing.

The rage was all-consuming. She got right in his face. "You ruined my fucking life, you disgusting excuse for a man."

He put the oxygen mask back on for a few seconds, taking a few deep breaths before speaking. "I don't know what you are talking about. Now get out of my room. You're no inspector."

He put the oxygen mask back on. She was still in his face, the proximity making her stomach heave, but she willed herself on. She grabbed the tube that was feeding the oxygen into the mask, squeezing it to stop the flow. His eyes started to bulge behind the mask as he gasped for breath, the mask misting up with the exertions of trying to get enough air into his lungs.

She revelled in his discomfort but eventually released her grip on the tube. She sneered at him. "Did that hurt, Mr Brackley? Were you feeling helpless, like every one of those poor children that you were supposed to be looking after?"

He went to grab for the emergency call cord that was dangling from the ceiling near his seat, but she leapt up before he could get it, taking the knife out to cut the cord out of reach.

As she held the knife, she almost screamed with the nervous energy that was coursing through her body. She revelled in the fear that was now etched across his face.

"Do you remember me yet... pervert?"

His breathing was becoming more laboured, any attempt at bravado was waning as he looked at the glint of the blade in her hand.

She grabbed the mask and ripped it off his face, every touch, every contact making her want to vomit. She pulled a rag from her pocket and stuffed it in his mouth. His skin started to redden as the lack of oxygen made his major organs go into overdrive.

She willed herself to grab his arm and dragged the knife right along his forearm, blood slowly seeping from the wound. Adrenalin was driving her forward, helping her to fight the demons. She grabbed his other arm and did the same. She watched with joy as the blood trickled down his arm.

She grabbed the rag and took it out of his mouth. He slumped forward as he tried to get air into his body, coughing and spluttering. She laughed. "God, this is fun. Are *you* having fun, Mr Brackley?"

He had no capacity to speak and went to grab the mask.

"Ahaha. No you don't. There's no relief for you, Mr Brackley. I want you to feel even one ounce of the pain that you inflicted on me and all those others. Do you understand that?"

He stared at her, refusing to play her game, fighting to breathe, fighting to stay alive.

She ripped open his shirt, stuffed the rag back in his mouth and scraped the knife several times down his chest, pools of blood appearing with each cut.

She looked up to revel in his fear, but his eyes had

closed. He had passed out. She slapped him. "Wake up, pervert. I'm not ready to let you die yet."

As she went to hit him again, there was a banging on the door. "Mr Brackley, Miss Braintree, is everything all right in there?"

She froze. Whoever was out there was rattling the handle of the door, trying to get in. Someone must have heard her and raised the alarm.

She cursed. She wanted him to die slowly, experience even a fraction of the pain he had caused her, but the game had changed.

She quickly stuffed some smaller pieces of cloth in each nostril and, in a final act of rage and redemption, she plunged the knife into his genitals.

She grabbed the stuff out of her bag and left it by his body. Her latest message for Sarah.

As the banging and rattling of the door became more urgent, she opened the door to the fire escape and quickly descended to the gravel drive below. She walked off the site and found her car.

She got in and let out a loud, guttural scream.

# 37

The home manager grabbed the keys to his room and flew back up the stairs, the care assistant still banging on the door and rattling the handle. She unlocked the door and her knees almost buckled as she surveyed the scene. She pulled the door to, not wanting to look at it a minute longer. "Call the police. *Now!*"

\*

Sarah had just started to drive back to St Helier when the call came in. She had struck again. In broad daylight. A care home in Grouville. She winced at the location. The perp had been so close. Could she have seen her, walking along the road without realising? She texted the team, reneging on her promise of a day off. She put on the blues and twos and sped back to Grouville.

Sarah was the first of the investigation team to arrive, the first responders the only police presence currently on the scene. A uniformed sergeant greeted Sarah and gave her the basics.

As she walked into the reception area, a large middle-aged woman greeted her, looking pale and distraught.

Her voice was cracking but she managed to utter a greeting.

"I'm Mrs Wyatt, the home manager..." She checked herself forcing back the tears. "...it's just so horrible. That woman is pure evil."

Sarah placed her hand on her shoulder, trying to comfort her. "I'm Sarah Braintree, the chief of police."

The home manager looked at her with absolute shock. "What did you say your name was?"

"Sarah Braintree."

"But... but that was the name she gave me. Sarah Braintree."

Sarah couldn't believe what she was hearing. How twisted was this woman getting? Despite the turmoil raging through her brain, she tried to remain professional. "Just part of her evil game, I'm afraid, Mrs Wyatt. This woman seems to have an obsession with me that we are still trying to decipher. How did she get into the care home?"

"She said she was an inspector from the Care Quality Commission, here to do a snap inspection."

"Is that normal?"

"Well, not normal, snap inspections are usually as a result of a direct complaint to the CQC. If they deem the complaint serious enough, they can do a snap inspection without telling us why."

"So her act was plausible to you. Did she look the part?"

"Yes, perfectly well presented. Business suit, ID and an official-looking folder."

"And how was she as she inspected the place?"

"Fine. Normal, I guess… except in the kitchen. She got really weird with a knife that had been left out. She picked it up and seemed to tense up for a minute. I asked if she was alright and she said she didn't like knives."

"Interesting. I assume you could give one of my team a description?"

"Of course."

"Thank you, Mrs Wyatt. Please stay down here with my officers and we'll deal with this. My investigation team are on their way and we will try to get you back to normal as soon as possible. Please keep any residents on that floor in their rooms or move them downstairs. We can't afford any compromise of the crime scene."

The home manager nodded in agreement as Sarah began her descent up the stairs, steeling herself for what she was about to see.

As she reached the landing of the second floor, she saw a uniformed officer standing guard by a door towards the end of the corridor. After a cursory greeting he opened the door and Sarah took in the full horror of the scene.

The victim was sat in a chair, cloth stuffed in his mouth and nostrils, what looked like knife wounds down his arms and torso, and a knife ceremoniously sticking out of his groin area. Sarah was not easily shocked, but the macabre scene made her catch her breath. As she went to close the door, she noticed that there was something on the floor in front of the victim. She didn't want to go into the crime scene until Jennifer turned up with the forensic coveralls, but it looked like a piece of paper with a big question mark on it next to three lollipops.

When the call came in, Lisa had to run back to her flat to get her car. As she drove to Grouville her mind was still racing, trying to explain what she had seen the previous evening. She kept telling herself she was being paranoid, but the more she thought about it, the more she analysed this individual's behaviour, the more she was convinced that something was off.

She was perversely relieved that the perp had struck again, breaking the enforced time off and giving Lisa another chance to watch the member of their investigation team that was causing her to have these mad ideas.

Within twenty minutes, all the investigation team were at the care home. After everyone had taken in the horror of the crime scene, Sarah tasked them out.

"Right, DCI Brown and DC Kennon, can you speak to the home manager and the other staff? Get statements and descriptions of our perp from anyone that saw her. Speak to the residents too, in case they have anything to add. Also, make sure that uniform keep the press and public well away from the home, especially 'you know who'. Jennifer, Jessica, DS Johnson and I will examine the crime scene."

Steph and Cassandra went to find the manager as the others put on their forensic coveralls. Jennifer went in first as the other three stood by the door, not wanting to compromise the scene any more than they needed to.

Sarah spoke first. "Give me your initial view of the scene, Jennifer."

"Well, we will need to get the ME to confirm what killed him, but from an initial view, the cloth in his nostrils and mouth suggests he was asphyxiated. I'm guessing his lung function was not good if he was on oxygen, meaning it would not have taken much to kill him."

"Is there any evidence of strangulation?"

Jennifer lifted his head. "No, the cloth seems to be the only thing that would have caused the asphyxiation."

"What about the wounds?"

Jennifer examined them closely. "Now these are interesting. Whilst I'm sure the act of cutting was extremely painful to our victim, they are quite shallow and would not have killed him. My guess is that the perp saw this as some sort of torture, prolonging the actual moment of death."

Sarah shook her head. "God, this bitch is sick. What about the knife sticking out of his groin?"

Jennifer examined the area. "The knife has gone right through his genitals, but there is limited blood loss in this area."

"What does that mean?"

"Well, it seems possible that she plunged the knife into his groin after he was dead."

Sarah let Jennifer get on with processing the scene and turned her attentions to Jessica. "What do you make of this, Jessica?"

For a moment Jessica didn't speak. "Jessica?"

"Oh, sorry, Sarah, this scene is..." Her words drifted off.

"Are you OK, Jessica? Do you need a minute?"

"No, no, I'm fine, Sarah. It's just, this scene is so different to the other ones you described. This scene is full of rage, seemingly lots of contact with the victim, the rags, the knife. It's inconsistent with the way she killed these other people. They were all hands-off, mostly poisonings. She didn't touch the victims."

"Are you saying this is not our perp?"

"No, I think it's her, but this murder seems more personal. There is a clear escalation here, which is not uncommon in serial killers. We need to find out who this man was. I'm sure he has a personal connection to our perp. The knife wounds, the time she took to kill this man, suggests a type of revenge, payback for something he did to her. Unlike all her other victims, she knew this man."

"OK, Jessica, I will get DCI Brown to look into his background. This is great work."

Jessica gave Sarah a pained smile and carried on. "Another reason I'm sure this is the same perp is that we have her signature back. A note."

"If you can call it that. Why are there no words, goading me, telling me how clever she is? Why just a question mark and three lollipops? It's bizarre. You're the expert on these puzzles, DS Johnson. Do these clues connect to any TV or film?"

"No, ma'am, nothing I can immediately think of. I agree with you, though, the clues are bizarre."

After a few moments, Jessica carried on. "Sarah, I think the lollipops are signifying something about childhood and the knife in the genitals seems to indicate something sexual."

"Sexual!" Everyone turned to look at Lisa, curious about her sudden outburst. She looked a bit embarrassed at first but quickly got her mojo back. "Sorry, but I would have thought the last thing this is alluding to is sexual. To me, this would seem to signify something to do with abuse, perhaps rape. I think she is leaving a clear message that this man did something to her, possibly when she was a child, if the lollipops are another clue."

There was a brief, uncomfortable silence as everyone in the room processed what Lisa had said and, for the first time since she had arrived on the island, considered the implications of someone challenging Jessica's profiling.

Just as the silence threatened to paralyse the room, Jessica let out a little laugh and a broad smile came across her face. "Very good, Lisa. We will make a criminal profiler out of you yet." There was a noticeable easing of tension as Jessica continued. "You are quite right to pick me up on that, Lisa. When I say 'sexual' I mean from this man's perspective. Your assessment is probably right. She is trying to tell us that this man abused or raped her, which of course is about violence and control of the victim, but he would have seen it as satisfying his sexual needs, however abhorrent we might perceive that."

Sarah nodded, seemingly satisfied with Jessica's response. Lisa smiled inwardly. Maybe Jessica's uber-confidence was brushing off on her.

The incident was soon forgotten and Jessica carried on her profiling of the scene.

"I do wonder whether this could be what she was building up to. She talked about several acts. Act one was designed to humiliate and discredit you, Sarah. The victims were just collateral damage in her deadly games. She said act two would give you the why and act three would give you the who. This murder may be her way of telling you what this is all about."

"But, I don't understand. I don't know this man."

"Are you sure? Could you have met him in your childhood?"

"I don't know, Jessica. When you asked me to think about possible reasons for this woman's hatred for me, I spent most of the time looking at my case history. I hadn't found anything from that and hadn't really thought about the other angles you mentioned. The significant moments in my life. My childhood."

"Does this jog any memories?"

Sarah looked at the scene, the note, the lollipops. "No, nothing. I can't think of anything."

# 38

Jeff Godley stood outside the care home with the growing number of press and TV reporters that had made him the morning headlines. He waited with anticipation, hoping to see the crestfallen chief of police. His article had been amazing, everyone lapping up his story of wrongful arrest and Sarah Braintree's utter incompetence. He smiled to himself. *Never let the truth get in the way of a good story.*

The plan was working. Everything she had planned, everything she had prepared for, had gone like clockwork. He texted her.

*Outside the care home. Ready to make more headlines to humiliate our dear friend. Let me know when you are ready for the final act.*

\*

The team gathered in the incident room at St Helier Police Station at 4.30pm, after another challenging day.

Sarah started the briefing. "Firstly, team, let me say how sorry I am that for some of you my promised day off did not work out. I always knew it was a risk. She was never going to slow down. I'm livid that she has once again outfoxed us. We'll take updates and then you can go home. We need to be back on this at full speed tomorrow morning."

The mood in the room seemed quite supportive. Sarah kept checking herself for thinking ill of the dead, but the team seemed so much more motivated without Mark's sulky face and bad attitude bringing the team down.

"Jennifer. Let's start with you."

"Thank you, ma'am. Not much to update from my initial crime scene investigation. We are processing what I collected and seem to have two good fingerprints from the knife. We are seeing if they match the fingerprints from our other crime scenes. Unfortunately, the work has backed up a bit. As well as the new evidence, we are still processing the DNA samples from the evening operation and I'm still waiting for the forensic results from Mark's crime scene."

"What about the ME report on Mark? I still haven't seen it."

"No, it's not come through yet. I can chase it for you."

"Don't worry, Jennifer, you have enough to do. I'll follow that up myself. OK, DCI Brown, can we have your updates?"

"Yes, ma'am. Cassie and I got statements from the home manager, the care assistant that was on shift and a couple of the residents. They described her as being confident and authoritative, very plausible as an inspector. We got a composite done and there are a number of similarities to the other ones we have. She had long blonde hair, but again there was uncertainty as to whether this was a wig or her real hair. She was wearing glasses this time and the shape of her nose seems somewhat different to the other composites. We are wondering whether she is using prosthetics to change her appearance just enough to introduce more uncertainty into our description."

"OK, I guess all we can draw from that is to confirm that this is our perp. DC Kennon. Did you make any progress this morning before this all kicked off?"

"Yes, ma'am. I have found multiple routes on the dark web for obtaining arsenic. It seems the favourite way to get it past customs is to put it in one tube of sun cream, which is part of a larger multipack. Customs just don't seem interested in this type of smuggling. Too small to worry about. I could probably trawl through import manifests to see if I could pick up a trail but that would take some time."

"Doesn't help us that much, I guess. What about the profiling?"

"Having discussed the profiling with Jessica, we applied a number of filters to the woman we had on our initial list. We looked at women that had been on Jersey all their life, those that had a nine-to-five-type job and only children. This knocked out a big proportion of the names and left us with 106 women."

Sarah rubbed her face in frustration. "That's still a large list and is premised on your assumptions being correct, especially as she struck in broad daylight. That doesn't suggest someone with a nine-to-five job, unless she took a day off. Both these lines of enquiry are still leaving us with a massive workload. I'm not sure the perp is going to give us the time to do the leg work. What do you think, Jessica?"

"I'm supportive of the work that Cassie has done. I'm confident in my profiling and the parameters that Cassie has applied to the list. It's just unfortunate that this has left us with over one hundred people to investigate."

"So, what's your advice?"

"My suggestion is that we focus on the latest victim. As I said at the scene, this murder was definitely personal. The other victims were collateral damage, designed to help her play her deadly games with you, Sarah. But, this one is telling us something. She said her second act would tell us the why. I think this is it. She wants us to find out who this man is and how he connects to this case and possibly how he connects to you, Sarah. If we find that out, I'm sure we can apply further filters to our list."

As ever Sarah was uncomfortable that Jessica had put the focus back on her, probing her background, putting her life in the spotlight. Apart from her parents, she never let anyone get close to her, and she found the scrutiny intrusive and unsettling. As she tried to brush it off, she noticed Lisa was itching to say something.

"Do you have an update, DS Johnson?"

"Yes, ma'am, I didn't want to butt into Jessica's flow, but I have got the basics on this man."

Everyone turned to Lisa. She stopped for a moment, realising how much more confident she was feeling within the team. She wasn't sure what it was. The temporary promotion, the realisation that the chief had great faith in her or just the need for her to step up and make her presence felt.

"His name is Michael Brackley, aged seventy-eight. He has been in the care home for the last three years and has severe pulmonary issues, which is why he used oxygen. He was never married and has no children. His sister is his next of kin. The home manager said she thought he ran children's homes on the island before he retired."

There was silence. Everyone was expecting Sarah to respond, but she sat in her chair, staring out of the window, seemingly lost in her thoughts. Lisa looked at the others; several shrugged their shoulders, not knowing what to do.

Lisa broke the silence. "Ma'am. Are you OK?"

Sarah snapped out of her daydream. "Oh, yes, fine, DS Johnson. Children's homes, you say?"

"Yes, ma'am. Has that triggered something for you?"

"Yes, it might have done."

# 39

Lisa sat with Cassie on the outside tables of the Shoreline Bar, cracking through another bottle of wine. Cassie had a small flat just up the road from Lisa's and they had agreed to meet for a drink, trying to forget the stresses of the day.

Lisa hadn't worked with Cassie before. Despite her growing paranoia she felt she could trust her and she needed to offload.

"Cassie, what do you think of the team?"

"Dunno. OK, I guess. Anyone in particular?"

"What do you think of Steph and Jessica?"

"Steph seems like your typical DCI, a bit up herself, a bit closed off. She doesn't seem very friendly or particularly dynamic for such a high-profile case."

"Yeh, I've worked with Steph before and I must admit she doesn't seem to be her usual self on this case. The other times I've worked for her she has been really positive, really driven. It's odd. What about Jessica?"

"Now, there's a piece of work. I don't think I've ever met anyone so confident in their abilities. When we were discussing her profiling, she didn't seem at all interested in my opinions. She just kept telling me to stick to the profile, not to deviate from the path she had set. It was very strange. In the end, I just did what she told me."

"I agree. I know I need to be a bit more confident myself, but her manner is just... intimidating."

They both took another slug of their wine and topped up their glasses.

Lisa broke the silence. "There's something else."

"What?"

"I'm sure I saw Jessica last night, walking around here."

"Why would that be odd? Jersey's not that big. It's perfectly possible for her to be around this area."

"I dunno. She said she is staying in a B&B in Journeaux Street, in St Helier. Why would she be up this end of the island at that time of night?"

"Come on, Lisa, St Helier's not that far away. Maybe she's a walker. Maybe she was having some evening exercise, going to a bar, meeting someone for a steamy liaison."

Lisa smiled. "Oh, god, you're probably right, Cassie. There's just something about her that unsettles me. I think I'm seeing ghosts all over the place at the moment."

Cassie picked up her phone. "OK, paranoia girl, let's prove what a twat you're being. Journeaux Street, you say?"

"Yes."

Cassie tapped away at her phone. "There are two B&Bs on that street." Lisa put her hand to her mouth to stifle a laugh as Cassie dialled the number of the first one. The phone was answered quite quickly. "Oh hi, could I speak to Jessica Fletcher, please...? Oh, you don't have anyone staying by that name. Sorry, I must have the wrong information."

Cassie raised her eyebrows and dialled the second one. The phone rang and rang. Cassie was just about to hang up when a voice came on the line. "Sunny View B&B, how can I help?"

"Oh, hi, can I speak to Jessica Fletcher, please?"

"Erm… I don't think Miss Fletcher is in at the moment. I've not seen her much today. Can I leave a message?"

"No, no, that's fine."

Cassie disconnected the call. "See. Stop being paranoid. She's perfectly kosher."

Lisa grimaced and took another swig of wine. Her mind still racing. *Catch them in a lie.* Cassie had just proved Jessica was telling the truth about where she was staying. Hadn't she?

\*

She paced around her flat. She had done it, killed the man that had ruined her life, but still she felt unfulfilled. She wanted to make him suffer for longer, but someone had ratted on her. One of the old fuckers in an adjacent room must have heard what she was doing and raised the alarm, cutting short her pleasure, her redemption. It didn't help that the bastard had passed out. Even in his final moments he was small and pathetic.

She took off her T-shirt, quickly followed by her bra, and went to the mirror, knife in hand. She started to drag the knife down her chest, following the line of the ribcage, mimicking the cuts she had made on him. She

194

gritted her teeth as the pain coursed through her body. She did a second one. She revelled in the relief it gave her. She opened her eyes, watching the light trickle of blood that had formed at each cut. She smiled. She hadn't passed out. She was strong. She was invincible.

*

It was nearly 9pm as Sarah sat in her garden, drinking a large glass of wine. The weather was holding, the temperature still in the high teens, as the mid-summer light began to fade from the clear Jersey sky.

Sarah's head was throbbing, the alcohol not doing its job of dulling the pain. In a few short weeks she had gone from being completely in control, the poster girl of Jersey life, into a chaotic wreck. Chasing lost causes and looking more and more like the incompetent police chief that Jeff Godley had so enjoyed painting her as in the papers.

The day had been as traumatic as many of the others, but something had changed. The dynamic had shifted. Jessica was right. On this day, the perp had made it more personal. She had killed this man to tell Sarah *why* she was doing this, *why* she hated her so much. *Michael Brackley.*

Sarah didn't remember much about her early childhood. Her adopted parents had told her about her background a few times, when she was old enough to understand. She knew her real parents were a couple of misguided teenagers that fooled around and got pregnant, giving her up as soon as she was born. She was moved from foster family to foster family, until her last set of foster parents got ill and she was put into the Gorey Home for Children. *Michael Brackley.* She played the name over and over in her head.

She was six years old when she was placed in the children's home but only stayed there for three weeks. She had been on the adoption list for many years when fate intervened. Her lovely, beautiful parents had come to the home to meet all the children that were there, and she was thrilled when they picked her. Her memory was patchy, but she was sure the man in charge of the home was called Michael. *Could it be the same man?*

# 40

The next morning, Sarah locked herself away in her office. The team had plenty to do and she wasn't ready for more uncomfortable scrutiny of her private life. She needed some time and space to process what was spinning through her head. The only person she wanted to talk to was Cassie. This latest development had changed the focus and Sarah needed Cassie to dig into this man's life. By mid-morning, Steph had gone to work through the alibis from the evening operation and get the care home statements in order, Lisa was ensconced in the CCTV suite reviewing Mark's work, and Jennifer was in her labs working through the backlog of forensic evidence. Only Cassie and Jessica remained in the incident room. She called Cassie in.

"Thank you for the work you did on the arsenic and the profiling. I didn't mean to sound negative when we had the briefing last night, but both lines of enquiry seem very labour-intensive. Now, I don't doubt your abilities to churn through the work, DC Kennon, but I would like to change focus."

"OK, ma'am, not a problem."

"Can you delve into the latest victim's background?

Find everything you can about him and see if he has a record. If he did run children's homes, we need to find the records of all the girls that stayed in them while he was in charge. I want you to cross-reference any names you find from the children's homes with our original list of women. I'm not doubting the profiling work you did with Jessica, but this has given us a new focus and I don't want to miss anything."

"That's great, ma'am, I'll get straight onto it."

"One more thing. You will probably find my name on that list. I was effectively an orphan until I was six, when I was adopted. I was mainly placed with foster families up until then, but for the last three weeks before my adoption I stayed in a children's home. I have a feeling it was one of the homes he ran."

"Oh, OK."

"Yes, you have probably sussed out that I'm not comfortable having my private life front and central in this case, so please apply some discretion."

"Of course, ma'am." Cassie began to walk out.

Sarah called her back. "Can you go and do this work somewhere other than the incident room? I would rather Jessica was not aware that we have changed focus."

Cassie gave her a conspiratorial smile, walked into the incident room, picked up her laptop and left. Sarah walked out of her office to re-fill her coffee cup from the ever-industrious filtered coffee pot, containing the fuel that was keeping the team going. Jessica didn't look up, consumed in her analysis of the last crime scene. Sarah went back into her office, sipping at the steaming hot coffee as she watched Jessica. She was doing it again.

Sarah had noticed that Jessica kept scratching herself. It had normally been along her arms but today she was scratching her chest and belly. *Weird.*

*

Jeff Godley stood outside St Helier Police Station with the posse of TV and newspaper reporters, the numbers seeming to ebb and flow on a daily basis depending on whether the *Jersey Serial Killer*, as some were now calling her, had struck again.

Since the latest articles, he had become a bit of a local celebrity, his fellow reporters pumping him for information every time they saw him. He wasn't a small fish any longer. He was *the man*, a key cog in this drama, and he loved it.

He missed Jennifer, but she had served her purpose. He had the inside line on everything that was going on, and Jennifer had been a convenient diversion, making the stupid bitch and her incompetent team think she was the only source of his information. He knew he had to be careful not to report something that wasn't in the public domain. One slip and he would be exposed. He was chomping at the bit, waiting for the next revelation that would send Sarah into a spin. The truth about what happened to Mark Adams.

*

Lisa sat in the CCTV suite slowly going through the CCTV from the zoo. The chief had been sure that Mark's work had been shoddy, and for some reason she was convinced he had missed something.

She was finding it hard to concentrate, her eyes drooping from too much alcohol and too little sleep the night before. She tried to remain focused on the soundless imagery as scores of people drifted through the entrance turnstiles. She had seen the chief early in the footage, perplexed as to why Mark had made such an issue of her being there.

As she began to lose the will to live, she suddenly spotted something. She wasn't sure whether she had dropped off as she watched the footage, creating the sense of the images jumping forward. She rewound it a few minutes. People were still streaming through the turnstiles at a steady space and then… there it was. The footage had glitched. The images weren't smooth. People that were at the turnstiles were suddenly gone; the chain of events interrupted. She called the CCTV technician over.

"Brian, can you watch this section of CCTV? There something wrong with it."

They both watched it several times, slowing it down and running it in real time. After the fourth run-through, Brian grimaced. "What you have here, Lisa, is a CCTV recording that has been tampered with. Someone has deleted footage and spliced it back together."

\*

It was just after lunch and Sarah remained in her office, becoming more and more agitated. She had chased the ME off and on all morning about the post-mortems for Mark and Michael Brackley, but nothing had happened.

She needed something to take her mind off the constant nagging about the latest victim. Was he the man that had ran the home she was in? Was this what the perp was trying to tell her? And what on earth was the significance of the lollipops?

As she considered going for a walk, she realised Jessica was stood in the doorway. "Are you OK, Sarah?"

"Oh, yeah, just can't get my head straight about this latest victim. I think he may have some connection to me, but it's all really fuzzy. I don't know what the perp is trying to tell me."

Jessica gave a sympathetic smile. "Just give yourself some time. If this is about your childhood, it may take some time for your memories to recover what you need to remember."

Sarah gave her a pained smile. "Anyhow, enough about me. What are you doing?"

"Well, erm, I have been going over the crime scene again, but that's not what I need to talk to you about."

"Oh, what's up?"

"I have just had a call with my boss from the mainland. They want me back. Some big case is kicking off and he said they could do with me on it."

"But... we haven't finished here. What if she strikes again? I need your input."

"I know, Sarah, I did explain all this, but he seemed quite insistent."

"No, this is unacceptable, I'll give him a ring."

"No, no, please don't, I can handle him. I asked for a few days more, as I have a feeling our perp is getting close to her threatened finale. I'll do my best to hold him off."

Sarah stared at Jessica, trying to judge the situation. "OK, please try to hold him off for as long as possible. I can't afford to lose you n—"

The sound that stopped Sarah in mid-sentence was Jennifer crashing through the door of the incident room and bursting straight into the office. Jennifer tried to regain her breath, having run from her lab. "Ma'am, I'm sorry to burst in like this, but something critical has turned up. The hair we found at Mark's scene is a DNA match with the sample we picked up at the second crime scene."

# 41

Lisa walked back into the incident room, hoping to see the chief alone to discuss the implications of what she had found. The CCTV tech had more or less confirmed that there was only one possible explanation as to who had edited the footage, based on the timestamp of the autosave feature which automatically recorded any changes. It had to be Mark.

Lisa's head was spinning. Why had Mark tampered with evidence? She knew there was only one logical explanation, but she didn't want to consider it. She had to speak to the chief.

As she walked into the main office, she cursed as the chief was in her office with Jessica and Jennifer. The chief had her head in her hands. Something was wrong. She stood for a minute, not knowing what to do, unsure whether her presence would be welcome. A few seconds later, the chief looked up and saw her hovering around, gesturing for her to come in.

Lisa entered. "Is everything alright, ma'am?"

"No, DS Johnson, it's not. Jennifer has just confirmed that the hair we found at Mark's crime scene is an exact DNA match for a sample we found at the second crime scene."

Lisa put her hand to her mouth. "Oh my god. I knew it."

Sarah looked at Lisa quizzically. "What do you mean?"

"I knew he didn't commit suicide or have an accidental overdose. I told you the morning we found him. He wasn't like that. He had been really unsteady on his feet at the end of the shift, like he was drugged or something. It seemed to me that the only thing he would have been capable of when he got home was going straight to sleep. Our perp must have followed him home and murdered him."

Sarah didn't say anything. She looked out of the window at another beautiful Jersey day, trying to process what Lisa had said. Eventually she spoke. "Jessica, what do you make of this?"

"Well, whilst I have no doubt that this makes sense forensically, it makes absolutely no sense from a profiling perspective. If she did kill Mark, why didn't she announce it, celebrate it, like all the others? She is playing a game with you, Sarah, and would not have missed the opportunity to revel in another kill. The lack of any sort of note is perplexing and completely out of character."

Lisa responded first. "Could she have been interrupted? Maybe she had to leave before she could place the note, because someone disturbed her?"

Jessica frowned. "I guess it's possible, but I would still have expected something from her, boasting about her achievements. If she was disturbed, I would have still expected her to communicate with Sarah in some way."

Sarah shook her head. "This is horrendous. We have to now assume that Mark was killed by our perp, based on the forensics. I will speak to the DSUP in professional standards to get Mark's case transferred to our investigation. Please can someone write this up on the board? I also need to brief DCI Brown. Where is she?"

"She's down in the main CID room, working with some uniforms on those alibis," Lisa said. "I can get her for you."

"OK, DS Johnson, that would be great. Jennifer, can you chase the ME again about Mark's post-mortem? This has suddenly become high on our priority list. Jessica, can you review Mark's crime scene again, to see if there is anything we have missed from your perspective?"

They all nodded and started to disperse. Lisa made to leave but stopped. Sarah let the others leave before she spoke. "Is there something else, DS Johnson?"

"Yes, ma'am, it's the reason I came back in to see you. I have been going through the CCTV from the zoo this morning and have pretty solid evidence that Mark tampered with it. There is a glitch on the footage at around 10.30am. The recording jumps forward. The technician looked at it several times and confirmed that someone has deleted part of the recording and spliced it back together. The software automatically recorded the change. It was the time that Mark was reviewing the footage."

Sarah nodded her head, Lisa's words confirming some deep-seated suspicion that Sarah had held in the back of her mind about Mark. She had never liked him. He was unprofessional, his attitude stank and his investigation work was shoddy. Now she knew why. He was working against her, trying to make her fail. But why? She knew there was only one explanation.

As all these thoughts rushed through her mind, Lisa broke her concentration, echoing her suspicions. "Ma'am. Do you think Mark was working with the perp? Do you think the footage he deleted showed her arriving at the zoo and he agreed to delete it for her?"

Sarah picked at a stray piece of cotton on her skirt, her head exploding with the implications of these recent revelations.

"I can't believe we are even entertaining this possibility, DS Johnson, but yes, I think we have to assume his intentions were not good."

"My god, how more fucked up can this get?"

"The problem we have, DS Johnson, is we don't have the answer to the sixty-four-million-dollar question. If Mark was working with the perp, why did she kill him?"

# 42

Sarah gathered the team together for an evening briefing, the events of the day disturbing and overwhelming. Jennifer had finally obtained the medical examiner's report and it added more intrigue to Mark's case. Sarah had to deal with the 'elephant in the room' and started the briefing with an update on Mark's murder.

"OK, I know I have spoken to most of you about Mark's death, but I need to update you further now that Jennifer has obtain the ME's report. There is no doubt that the amount of heroin in his system was the cause of his death. However, the ME has identified the presence of Rohypnol in his blood, although he is unclear as to how this got into his system. You will know that DS Johnson stated that Mark was unsteady on his feet at the end of his shift, and we are sure these were the early signs of the drug taking effect. The ME has no doubt that by the time Mark got back to his flat, he would not have been in a fit state to inject the heroin. This evidence, together with the forensics, confirms Mark as another victim of our perp. We are assuming that the lack of a note is just her way of trying to throw us off the scent."

Sarah paused to let the news settle into the team, a variety of solemn expressions staring back at her.

Steph broke the silence. "What does this mean from a profiling perspective, Jessica? You suggested we should focus on the last victim, that it would give us the *why*, but how does Mark's murder fit into this?"

Jessica leant forward, taking a moment to consider the question. "From a profiling perspective, Mark's death makes no sense. She didn't leave a note and, if the ME's advice is right, she must have touched him to administer the heroin overdose. Both these things go completely against the profile."

Jennifer interjected. "I understand that, Jessica, but the forensics are unequivocal. The hair we found at Mark's crime scene is an exact DNA match for the sample we collected at the second crime scene."

There was general murmuring amongst the team. Sarah cut across it. "Look, I have made the decision that Mark's murder is the work of our perp, and regardless of the profiling anomalies, we need to investigate it as one of two murders in her so-called second act. I can only assume that she is trying to deliberately mislead us about the connections."

Sarah scanned the room. Her little speech seemed to have calmed the room, but she knew she couldn't wait any longer. She had to tell them the full story. She looked at Lisa, who gave her an encouraging nod, sensing the turmoil the chief was experiencing.

"Team, there is something else I need to tell you about Mark. Whilst his death was an absolute tragedy, I'm afraid I have been given evidence that suggests Mark may have been working with the perp…"

The faces now staring back at her were the predictable range of shock and disbelief.

"…it seems certain that Mark tampered with the CCTV we obtained from the zoo. There is a short period of footage that has been deleted, and the timestamp of this change was recorded at the time that Mark was reviewing it."

There was a sudden flash of rage from Steph. "That's nonsense. I've worked with Mark for years. He would never do a thing like that. You've got it wrong. There must be another explanation."

Sarah stiffened but held a calm, authoritative tone. "I'm sorry, DCI Brown. There is no doubt in my mind."

Steph's face was crimson. "You never liked him. You're just trying to fit him up."

Everyone stopped, no one wanting to breathe. The vacuum was pierced by Sarah, her face contorted with anger. "How dare you speak to me like that, DCI Brown. Do I really need to remind you that we follow the evidence in situations like this? And in this case the evidence has Mark bang to rights. Now, I suggest you all fuck off home, before I completely lose it."

Sarah stormed out of the main room, into her office, slamming the door and kicking the contents of her bin across the office. She stood, staring out of the window, eyes fixed at the view of the sea, trying to calm the rage that had been building in her day by day.

\*

Back in the incident room, everyone looked at each other, not knowing what to do. Steph made the first move, picking up her bag and leaving without further comment, her face telling everyone what they needed to know. Jessica and Jennifer closely followed.

Lisa looked at Cassie. "What the fuck!"

"I know. I didn't see that coming."

"You see what I mean, Cassie. Steph is acting weird. There's something up, and if Mark was working with the perp, I have no fucking idea who we can trust anymore."

"I dunno, Lisa, the chief seems like a hard person to get on with. Maybe it's just a personality clash or something?"

"I don't believe that, Cassie. Something is really wrong here."

As they both got lost in their thoughts, Sarah's door suddenly opened. She seemed surprised to see them there, her expression a mix of stress and embarrassment. "What are you two still doing here? I thought I told you all to go home."

Lisa tried to lighten the mood. "Actually, ma'am, I think you told us all to fuck off, but…"

Cassie's face was a picture. She couldn't believe what had come out of Lisa's mouth. There was an excruciating few seconds as the world seemed to stop, waiting for the explosion. It didn't come. Instead the silence was broken by a rising, booming laugh from Sarah.

Lisa looked across at Cassie and puffed out her cheeks. She had read it right.

Sarah filled her coffee cup and sat down. "What would I do without you, DS J… sorry, Lisa? You seem to have an amazing knack of 'getting me'. This whole situation is leading me to a nervous breakdown. Not only is this bitch killing at will but now one of my own officers seems to be in on it and my DCI seems to think emotions trump actual evidence."

"I know, ma'am, this case is getting everyone stressed. We are just not catching a break. I know it's a cliché, but she always seems to be one step ahead of us."

As they all tried to relax their minds, Sarah looked at Cassie. "I'm sorry your first few days in the team have been so volatile, but as you can see this case is making emotions run high."

"It's fine, ma'am, better than sitting at my desk all day trying to track down the digital evidence for the money laundering case."

"Yes, I must get an update from DCO Millar about that. We must be about to crack that case. Would be nice for something to go right under my leadership at the moment."

Lisa and Cassie smiled at the chief, trying to be supportive as the world crumbled around her. Cassie tried to keep up a positive vibe. "Ma'am, I have that information you were looking for about Michael Brackley."

Sarah twitched out of whatever daydream had temporarily invaded her focus on the real world. "Oh, shit, yeah. In all the drama, I forgot about that. I probably should have got you to brief everyone in the team but maybe right now a bit of discretion might be the right call. Tell me what you have."

"The home manager was right. Michael Brackley ran children's homes pretty much all his working life from 1975 until he retired in 2004. He was never married or had kids of his own and retired to a cottage on the north coast before he was forced into care in 2016. His only relative seems to be his sister, Jane, who lives in France. I have started compiling the list of children that he cared for, but it will take a bit of time as not all the records are digitised. That said, I hope to have it done by the end of tomorrow."

"So, it is highly likely that he ran the children's home that I was in?"

"Yes, ma'am, it seems so."

"This must be a significant clue. Jessica was right. The perp is trying to tell me something about this man and my connection to him."

"Yes, ma'am, there is something else, and it's very odd. He has a police record, but access to the information is restricted. It says his record is 'red filed'. I have never seen that before. What does it mean?"

Sarah and Lisa looked at each other, simultaneously coming to the same conclusion.

Sarah spoke. "That is quite concerning. If someone's record is red filed, it means they have committed, or have at least been investigated for, the most serious crimes. I'm afraid his involvement with children might suggest some form of child abuse allegations."

"How do we get at that information?"

"Therein lies the problem. The red files are not digitised. They are kept on paper and stored in a secure vault on Guernsey. As chief, I can obviously authorise extraction of the physical file, but it may take a day or two to get to us."

Sarah stood up, the tension in her body clear for all to see. "DS Johnson. Can you do the relevant paperwork to get that file over here as soon as possible? This might just be the break we have been hoping for."

# 43

She opened her bedroom window, listening to the sounds of the island: the sea lapping against the beach, the screech of the seagulls, the low murmur of people and vehicles going about their business. Normally these sounds, these images, would have triggered her. The demons would win and she would cut herself, to ease the pain. But, today had been a good day. She was ready for the final part of act two. To give Sarah the final clue that should absolutely tell her *why* she was doing all this. One more murder followed by one final act of absolute retribution that would complete her game of deadly connections and nail Sarah once and for all.

She picked up the bottle of whisky. A present for her final victim. Her neighbour, Mr Crossley, one of the few people she had in her life. She called him 'Pops', a vain attempt to make her feel 'normal', like she actually had a family, had a grandfather who would love her unconditionally. A fantasy that was never far away from her thoughts, every day for almost thirty years.

It was a shame he had to die. He had become a friend, as much as she able to rationalise the concept of a friend. She had first met him at the main door to the complex as he struggled with his shopping. She helped him into his flat and he had offered her tea and biscuits as a thank-you – an act of normality and kindness that she found hard to understand. Over the following weeks, she found herself drawn to him. He welcomed her company and they chatted about everything and nothing in particular. She lied most of the time, creating the fantasy of the life she hoped she would have had. He didn't seem to mind.

As the weeks and months went on, she realised he was the final piece in her masterplan. He was her ticket off the island, once Sarah's life had been well and truly despatched to the scrapheap. Through their regular chats, his love of the sea became evident. Most importantly, he had a boat. A beautiful cruiser that would take her to France, away from all this, helping her disappear.

He also started giving her money. One week it was a tenner, then twenty, forty, fifty pounds. He did not believe in banks. The money came from tins stashed around the flat. He never attempted to hide the stash from her. Maybe in some way, it was him telling her it was alright for her to know where his money was. He had no family. He would want her to have it… wouldn't he? She couldn't compute how much was there, but she knew it would be enough to get her away and rebuild her life.

She put on her push-up bra and low scalloped top, which gave her great cleavage. Pops was never subtle about it, always revelling in her overt sexiness and checking out every curve. She often wondered whether his shrivelled pecker ever got hard at the sight of her heaving breasts. She shook at the thought. *Disgusting men.*

She left her flat and went down to the ground floor,

knocking on his door. A few seconds later, the sounds of chains being moved and locks being turned preceded the door opening.

As he pulled the door open, his face lit up, first staring at her breasts and then her face. "Lucy, my dear. How lovely to see you. Come in. Come in."

"I have a bottle of whisky, Pops. Thought you might want a quick one on this lovely evening."

"Of course, my dear. Get the glasses from the kitchen and pour us both one."

It didn't take long. The arsenic took effect quickly, his face contorting with pain as the poison took his body. She watched with a hint of something. Was it regret? She didn't feel things like normal people, but something about this was churning her up inside. She realised a tear had escaped from her eye. She shook her head and brushed it away. Pops was great. He was going to die soon anyway. He would have wanted to help.

She sprang into action. She found the keys to the boat. She started piling through the flat, opening tin after tin, thousands of pounds piling up in front of her.

She went back into the living room where Pops was slumped in his chair. She left the note on his body and turned to leave. She stopped and looked back. "I'm sorry, Pops."

# 44

It was 7am as Lisa stood on her balcony, eating her toast and enjoying the warm breeze. Why was it always the case that the best weather came when you didn't have time to enjoy it, working your arse off through the heat and humidity of a lovely summer? Half a day off in two weeks was beginning to take its toll, and Lisa needed a pick-me-up. She walked back inside and started to make herself a second coffee. As she idly went about the task, it suddenly hit her. *The coffee.*

She paced around the room as the kettle bubbled to its boiling point. She started to speak out loud, to no one in particular, hoping that saying the words might rationalise the absolute fucked up thoughts that had now entered her head.

"The coffee. The chief said the ME wasn't sure how the Rohypnol got in Mark's system, but we had a coffee at the end of the shift."

The kettle clicked off. She poured the steaming water into her cup. She sipped at the burning liquid.

Could she be right? Someone could easily have slipped the Rohypnol in the coffee. It couldn't have been the chief or DCO Millar, which left only one other person that was there that night. The person who handed round the coffees. *Jessica*.

*

Sarah sat at her breakfast bar, contemplating the previous day's events. She knew she had been unprofessional, blowing up like that at Steph, but this case was taking her places mentally that she had never been before. Chaotic and out of control. Maybe she had made a mistake in taking personal command. Everyone knew she had broken all the command protocols in the book, but when you are the big boss, no one dare tell you otherwise, and, in the end, she was sure she had made the right decision. The perp had made this personal, had vindicated her decision. She knew she was a difficult person to get on with, her stellar career accelerated because she never let anyone get close. As a senior officer, and more importantly as a woman in this profession, she had to rule with an iron fist, take no shit and get the job done. There was no time to worry about people's feelings. They were police officers, for god's sake. Resilience came with the job.

After a few moments she made a decision. She texted Steph. *DCI Brown. I want you to take a few days off. I can see you have been affected by Mark's death and the allegations of corruption against him. Sort your head out and I will see you in a couple of days.*

*

Steph lay in bed, wide awake but with no motivation to get up. Her phone beeped. She picked it up and opened the text message. It was from the chief.

"Fucking bitch," she muttered to herself. "Yeah, I'll see you in a couple of days."

\*

She walked out of her flat down to one of the few public telephone boxes still available on the island. Mobile phones had become such a fundamental part of everyday life, but there were still times when the anonymity of a public phone was necessary, and today was one of those days.

She did feel a bit of remorse that Pops had sat there all night, dead and decaying, but she had to wait to call it in. She had to be away and out of her flat before the police arrived. She couldn't risk some over eager copper doing door-to-door enquiries in the complex and exposing her. She would go to her back-up location and wait. She called the emergency line, giving a false name and address, putting on her concerned neighbourly voice… *old man in flat 1… not seen him for days… worried about him… blah, blah, blah.*

She set off for St Helier and waited for the glorious ending to act two.

# 45

Sarah, Lisa, Cassie, Jessica and Jennifer all arrived at Flat 1 of the St Aubin's Bay Plaza, a small complex of flats with lovely sea views, set back a short way from the main coastal road. The first responders had ultimately kicked the door in when they could not get a response from the owner, a Mr Crossley, quickly calling it in as soon as they witnessed the grisly scene. The officers had secured the scene with tape and waited for the detective team to arrive. They had quickly concluded that the *Jersey Serial Killer* had struck again.

As the group stood outside the flat, looking in at the scene, Jessica posed the question that everyone was scared to ask. "Where's Steph, Sarah?"

Sarah looked at the group, her face serious and unflinching. "I've given her a couple of days off. Mark's death hit her harder than she cared to admit. She needs some time. She'll be back in a couple of days."

There were a few furtive looks between the team, no one really sure if Sarah was telling them the truth. The moment of uncertainty was quickly forgotten as she tasked them out.

"Jennifer, can you go in and start processing the scene? Jessica and DS Johnson can join me inside the tape.

It looks like we have another note and we need to profile this quickly. DC Kennon, can you manage the cordon, please, and get the uniform to do door-to-door enquiries in the complex?"

Everyone did as they were told, wary of the chief's mood. She had been the first of the team to arrive and was clearly agitated when the rest of the team piled into the small foyer one by one. The closeness was uncomfortable; the chief not speaking, just waiting and stewing. Jessica had broken the tension asking about Steph, but they were glad to get out of the claustrophobic space.

Jennifer went under the tape and started examining the crime scene. Sarah, Jessica and Lisa did the all too familiar routine of putting on their forensic coveralls and stood at the extremities of the main scene.

Sarah spoke, irritated and impatient. "Give me your initial assessment, Jennifer."

Jennifer gently moved the victim's head to examine his face. "I think it's pretty obvious that this is another arsenic poisoning, as he has the same physical characteristics as our other arsenic victims. Looks like it was administered in this whisky glass."

"What about the time of death?"

Jennifer did a rudimentary examination. "It's a guess at the moment, but based on lividity, I reckon this was done sometime last night. I reckon he has been here at least twelve hours." Jennifer could sense Sarah's impatience. She picked up the note with tweezers and bagged it. "I'm guessing you'll want to read this?"

Sarah stepped forward and grabbed the evidence bag, not looking forward to reading the latest goading. As she stepped back away from the main crime scene, she held the note in front of her. Lisa and Jessica leant forward to read it. She twitched at their closeness. She would rather have read it on her own, but she knew they had to move quickly if they were ever going to catch this *bitch*.

*Hello, Sarah, long time no speak.*

*Are you enjoying act two of our game of deadly connections?*

*This one's been a blast. Have you worked it out yet? It's been a bit more cryptic this time. I wanted to see if you had any gumption, any problem-solving skills, instead of relying on your team of so-called detectives.*

*You see, I promised to reveal the why, and the clues are all there… if you are only clever enough or humble enough to work them out.*

*But, I'm guessing you are still floundering around, too arrogant to see what is right in front of you, so here is my final clue.*

*The answer is as easy as A, B, C, and if that doesn't help you work it out, ask a Belgian, but not a Frenchmen.*

*I'll see you soon for act three. The final act, where I reveal myself and finally destroy your life.*

There was silence as all three read it over and over.

Sarah broke the weird reverence that seemed to hang over the situation. "What do you make of this, Jessica?"

"Well, putting aside the riddle, which I have no idea about at the moment, we seem to be back to her signature

221

move. The arrogance, the confidence, the need to play games with you, Sarah, is all there. It's interesting she still hasn't admitted to Mark's murder. I think her reference to this being more cryptic is her way of challenging you to make the connection, which we have done, of course. I think the biggest concern is that she is escalating quickly. This murder is very soon after the victim in the care home and her reference to act three shows an impatience to get this game finished. You need to be careful, Sarah. She could be plotting this so-called final act as we speak."

Sarah took the words in with limited emotions, trying to hide the inner turmoil that was coursing through her body. She did what she always did in these situations: kept asking questions. "Come on, DS Johnson, you're the riddles expert. What does this mean?"

Lisa shook her head. "Err, I don't know, ma'am. There's something… but I just can't get it at the moment. Can I take this away and have a think? I need some head space."

"Of course, but work that brain, DS Johnson. If Jessica's right, we don't have much time."

*

Lisa took the bagged note out into the small garden that surrounded the complex, sitting on a bench that was dedicated to '*my loving wife Mavis, who loved to sit in the garden and look out to sea*'. Lisa sat down, a headache rapidly forming as the stress consumed her.

*If Jessica's right… if Jessica's right…* the words were haunting her. She had to get out of there. Just being in the same room as Jessica made her want to vomit. She was involved in this somehow, just like Mark, and she had the front to act as though she was the chief's right-hand woman, her every word like some religious gospel. She stared at the view, the note lying on her lap. She rubbed her chin. "Come on, Mavis," she muttered to herself, "give me some inspiration. Tell me what to do."

Lisa wasn't sure how long she had been sat there, staring out to sea, when she realised someone was walking towards her.

"Hey, Lisa, what you doing?"

Lisa looked round, relieved it wasn't anyone else in the team. "Oh, hi, Cassie. I'm… god, I don't know what I'm doing. This whole situation is so fucked up."

"Why? What's happened now?"

"It's Jessica, Cassie. She's not who she says she is. She's involved in this somehow, just like Mark was. I don't trust her."

"Come on, Lisa, don't start all your conspiracy nonsense again. Don't forget, we checked her out and she was kosher."

"No, Cassie, all we did is confirm she was living where she said she was. I found something… well, thought of something that puts her in the frame."

"Though of something?"

"Yes, about Mark's murder. The ME said he wasn't sure how the Rohypnol got in his body, but just before the shift ended the chief, the deputy and Jessica brought us coffees. I'm sure someone put it in Mark's coffee because not long after he drank it, he started being unsteady on his feet. Now, it can't be the chief or the deputy, so it has to be Jessica."

"But you don't have any evidence to back that up?"

Lisa looked at Cassie, a mix of rage and resignation competing for space in her mind. "She's involved, Cassie, and we need to find out why."

After a few moments of uncomfortable silence, Lisa fixed her gaze back on Cassie. "Have you finished those lists from the children's homes yet? The perp is going to be on that list. I'm sure of it. I don't know what this murder is about yet, but that second victim is the key. There will be a connection to the chief somehow."

Given Lisa's rising mania, Cassie thought it wise to share. "You might be right, Lisa. The chief told me in confidence that she was in a children's home before she was adopted. She's asked me to find people on the list from the children's homes that fit the profile."

"Have you found anyone?"

"No, I've only just started working through the lists. It was supposed to be my priority today before this all kicked off."

"You need to get out of here, Cassie, and get that work done. It's vital we find this woman and work out how Jessica fits into all this."

"I can't, the chief's got me managing the cordon and the uniforms doing the door-to-doors."

"Don't worry about that. I'll take that on. Get back to your computer and find what we need."

Cassie smirked as she moved away. "OK, scary boss lady."

Lisa watched as Cassie walked down to the seafront, her mind still spinning. She hoped to god that she could trust her.

She stood up. She needed to make sure that all was in order with the cordon and check in with the uniforms taking statements. Thankfully, Jennifer, Sarah and Jessica were still processing the crime scene and had not noticed her extended absence.

She chatted to the various officers that were assisting. The cordon was holding, at the end of the long path leading up to the complex, the press numbers growing by the minute. Reports from the officers that had gone door-to-door had been unhelpful. People had either not seen or heard anything, or were not at home.

As Lisa contemplated what to do next, she realised she was still carrying the note around. She read it again. Slowly, the cogs began to whirl. She put her hand to her mouth.

"Shit. I've worked it out!"

# 46

Jennifer moved away from the main crime scene, as she gave the chief the nod to get the coroner's team to move the body. She moved into the kitchen, treading carefully and scanning the scene, looking for anything out of place. Two things caught her attention.

"Ma'am, can you come into the kitchen?"

Sarah walked towards the kitchen, making sure she followed the route that Jennifer had taken to minimise forensic compromise. Jessica followed.

"What is it, Jennifer?"

"Two things, ma'am. There is a glass here, the same style as the one the victim was drinking out of. It looks like the inside has been swilled out with water, but the outside hasn't been cleaned. I think I can see quite a pronounced fingerprint on it. This might mean that someone was drinking with him. Someone who he was comfortable letting into his flat and sharing a whisky with."

Jennifer bagged the glass as Sarah's mind began to race, and she blurted out what was on her mind. "Why does the perp keeps leaving forensic clues like this? She doesn't seem the sort to make mistakes. I think I'm right in saying, aren't I, Jennifer, that we have two DNA samples and at least three sets of fingerprints?"

"Yes, ma'am, that's right, but unfortunately no hits from police records or any of the women we stopped and searched on the evening operation."

Sarah looked at Jessica. "What do you make of this?"

"It fits the profile in the sense that she is clearly full of bravado, confident in the game she is playing. I have to conclude that she is deliberately leaving these clues, almost like she wants to be caught. I must admit, I have been considering a theory that she wants you to find out who she is so that her so-called final act is some sort of face-to-face confrontation. As I said earlier, she is escalating quickly. You need to be on your guard, Sarah."

Sarah slowly nodded her head, acknowledging Jessica's words but unfazed by the threats. There was something strangely compelling about the prospect of meeting this woman. She shook herself back to the present.

"You said there was two things, Jennifer?"

"Yes, ma'am, look at all these empty tins. Biscuit tins, tea caddies, sweet tins, all scattered around."

"What of them?"

"Well, what do older people sometimes keep in tins?"

"Money."

"Exactly. I think the perp knew this man and knew where he stashed all his money. I think she has cleaned him out."

"She hasn't done that anywhere else. How odd."

"Yes, ma'am, it is odd, but I think both these clues tell me that our victim knew his killer."

227

*

Lisa peered into the flat of the victim. Jennifer, Jessica and the chief were in the kitchen, deep in conversation about what they had found. She waited for a pause in the conversation. "Ma'am, could I speak to you, please?"

Sarah looked round. "Of course, DS Johnson." She looked back to Jennifer. "Let me know if you get anything else."

Sarah began to walk out of the kitchen, closely followed by Jessica.

Lisa flinched. She didn't want Jessica involved in the conversation. As Sarah approached the door, Lisa took a gamble. "Err, ma'am. Could I speak to you alone?"

Lisa tried to avoid Jessica's gaze, but as she glimpsed up, she saw something different in her eyes. A piercing look, unapproving... no longer the bright and breezy uber-confident woman that she had worked alongside for the past few weeks. The look was darker... evil.

Lisa looked back at the chief, willing her to comply. "Oh, yeh, I guess so, DS Johnson. Jessica, can you finish off here with Jennifer and update me on any developments?"

Jessica turned around, keeping her gaze fixed on Lisa, an unnerving smile on her face as she walked away.

Lisa was spooked, but she walked out into the garden, back to Mavis's seat, confident that she was far enough away from the flat to be out of earshot.

As they sat down, the chief eyed her quizzically. "What's up, DS Johnson? Why didn't you want Jessica here?"

Lisa was silent for a bit, not knowing how to articulate her mad thoughts. The chief seemed so invested in Jessica. She wasn't sure how her accusations would be taken.

"DS Johnson?"

"Ma'am, I'm sorry, but I don't trust her. I don't know whether it's a reaction to finding out that Mark was crooked, but I'm seeing ghosts round every corner. I don't know whether we can trust anyone in the team and Jessica in particular unnerves me. She's just too perfect. She seems to have such absolute confidence in everything she says and does. That's not normal."

Sarah nodded, a sympathetic expression on her face. "She is very good at her job and you could learn a thing or two from her about self-confidence."

Lisa grimaced. This was exactly what she feared. The chief was going to defend her. "I dunno, there's just something off about her."

The chief smiled. "What does DC Kennon think of your suspicions?"

Lisa was taken aback. How did the chief know she had been using Cassie as her sounding board? "Oh, err, to be honest, she thinks I'm being paranoid."

The chief nodded, the non-verbal's telling Lisa that she needed to move on. After a tense few seconds, the chief spoke again. "Was that it, DS Johnson?"

"No, no, ma'am. Sorry. Forget I said anything. I wanted to speak to you about the note. I think I worked it out."

"Oh, wow. Spill."

"It's another TV connection. She says '*ask a Belgian, but not a Frenchman*'. She's referring to Hercule Poirot, the

Agatha Christie detective. It was a common thing across all her novels that Poirot was mistaken for a Frenchman and regularly corrected people to state he was Belgian. There was a TV series that covered all the Poirot stories. It would seem to fit our perp's obsession with using film and TV references in her riddles."

"OK, I don't watch much TV, and I don't read Agatha Christie, so I'll bow to your greater knowledge."

Lisa smiled. "The other part of the clue – '...*it's as easy as A, B, C...*' – refers to one of the Poirot mysteries, *The ABC Murders*. The thrust of that story was that the killer was murdering people in alphabetical order. The first victim had a surname beginning with A, the second with B and so on. Our last three murders are exactly the same. Adams, Brackley and Crossley. A, B, C."

Sarah was taken aback. "Oh my god. You're right. What does this mean?"

"Think about it. She said act two would be about giving you the *why*. In the Poirot story, the other murders are ultimately distractions to hide the real intentions of the murderer. Poirot eventually works out that it was the second murder, the B murder, that was the real motivation. This fits with our theories. Our second murder was Michael Brackley, the one Jessica said was more personal. The perp is confirming that the murder of Michael Brackley is the *why*."

# 47

The rest of the day had been full of industry. Jennifer and Jessica had spent most of the day processing the crime scene. They had found more empty tins in the other rooms of Mr Crossley's flat but no further significant forensic evidence. Lisa and Cassie had gone back to the incident room, working the evidence, focusing on completing the lists from the children's homes and checking them against the profile.

Sarah agreed to let everyone concentrate on their tasks ready for a briefing in the morning. She sat at home, eating a microwaved lasagne that she was sure shouldn't have been that chewy, but ate it all the same, grateful for the brain fuel.

As she washed it down with a glass of wine, her mind wandered back to the chat with Lisa in the garden. Why was she so sure that Jessica was corrupt? She had been highly recommended by the chief of the Major Crime Agency on the mainland for her profiling skills and Sarah couldn't fault the quality of her work.

Sarah mindlessly strummed her fingers on the kitchen table. Since Lisa had been promoted to temporary sergeant, she had blossomed, no longer the meek little rabbit scared to talk and constantly bowed by Steph's presence. Sarah was becoming increasingly reliant on Lisa's level head and dogged determination in steering the investigation. Could she really ignore her concerns?

She re-filled her wine glass. As she took a big slug of the wine, she agonised over what to do. Mark's betrayal had shaken everyone, and perhaps Lisa was right to start throwing suspicion around the team. Steph in particular had always been a worry for Sarah. Her performance on this case was patchy at best, not as bad as Mark, but not befitting of someone at the DCI rank. On the other hand, Jennifer had been consistently good at what she was doing, especially considering the trauma she experienced with the scumbag Jeff Godley. Cassie also seemed to be a young, vibrant and skilled copper.

Sarah rubbed her face in frustration. What on earth should she do with all this? Her team was small enough as it was without it splintering into factions. She poured the last bit of wine out of the bottle and stared out of the kitchen window, searching for inspiration.

A few minutes later her phone rang. She picked it up to look at the caller ID. It was Jessica.

\*

Lisa sat on her own at one of the outside tables at the Jolly Roger pub, a short walk along the seafront from her flat. A pleasant breeze was coming off the sea but, as she nursed a gin and tonic, her mind was full of noise, competing for space in her muddled brain.

She tried to focus on the positives. Cassie had made

good progress and they should have a list of names from the children's homes in the morning. Based on the latest riddle, Lisa was now certain that they had to find a woman who was somehow connected to Michael Brackley and the chief. She knew that if Cassie found the chief's name on the list, it would help focus the investigation considerably. The lollipops were a crude clue, but it supported the idea that whatever had triggered the perp to start this deadly game had happened in their childhood.

The connections seemed more and more tangible, but what concerned Lisa was the red file on Michael Brackley. It was due to arrive the next afternoon and Lisa had a horrible feeling she knew what it was going to say. If she was right, it might go a long way to explaining this horrific situation.

As her mind wandered to the other murders in this so-called game of A, B, C, her gut tightened as she thought about Mark. If he was working with the perp, why had she killed him? Had Mark stepped over a line? He surely hadn't been killed just because his surname began with A, a convenient fit for her sick game. There was no doubt she was unstable and Lisa couldn't work out why Mark would get himself involved in such a horrendous situation. He was a police officer, for god's sake. He had vowed to serve and protect, not endorse senseless killing after senseless killing. That brain worm kept festering. Lisa hoped it would resolve itself, and soon.

She took another swig of her G&T, trying to ignore the nagging thoughts that had hardly been off her mind for the past few days. *Jessica*. The chief had dismissed her fears, which had come as no surprise to Lisa, and even Cassie thought she was paranoid. But, the more she thought about it, the more she was convinced that Jessica was up to no good. They knew nothing about her. She had been foisted on them in the panic to make some progress in the case and everyone just accepted her. No questions asked. Lisa knew she couldn't let it lie.

As she tried to relax, her attention was suddenly drawn to a figure standing across the street, about fifty metres further up the promenade. A slim woman with long blonde hair and dark glasses seemed to be staring at her. Lisa sat up, straining to see more. The woman didn't move. Lisa stood up. The more she looked at this woman, the more she realised she looked exactly like one of the many descriptions they had of the perp. She stared at her for a few moments. The woman didn't move.

A minute passed, nobody moving. She continued to stare. Lisa made a decision. She started to walk towards her, ever the copper. Go towards the danger. As she navigated out of the pub seating area, the woman turned and started walking in the opposite direction. Lisa picked up the pace, closing the distance with every step. The woman continued to walk along the promenade, crossing the road towards the more built-up area as Lisa tried to close the gap further.

Lisa began to run. "Hey, you, stop. I want to talk to you." There was no response. Lisa was about thirty metres away, the woman still walking in the opposite direction. As she closed the gap further, the woman suddenly took a right turn, between a pub and some houses. Lisa got to the turn; the woman was up ahead. Lisa shouted again. No response. The alleyway began to curve round to the left and Lisa temporarily lost sight of her. She quickened her pace. As she navigated the curve of the path, she cursed as she neared the end of the alleyway. It opened up into a heavily built-up area, with paths going off in several directions and no sign of the woman.

Lisa stood, scanning the different paths, hoping for a flash of blonde hair that would alert her to the direction the woman had taken. She scanned and scanned, but nothing changed. She had lost her.

It was getting dark and Lisa took one last look around before giving up for the evening. She walked back up the alley and onto the main promenade, turning for home. As she fixed the image of the woman in her mind, she wondered whether she had been completely irrational. Was the woman really staring at her? Was it a coincidence that she turned to walk away as soon as Lisa walked towards her? Lisa screamed in frustration, garnering a few strange looks from passers-by.

She reached the turn off from the promenade that would take her to the complex where her flat was. As she walked up the dimly lit path, she heard a noise. A crack of a twig, or something like it. An animal? A person? She stopped and looked around, the fading light and lack of streetlights not helping. Nothing happened, nothing moved, no further sounds.

Lisa shook her head. *Stop seeing ghosts round every corner*, she muttered to herself. She turned to walk towards the entrance to the flat complex.

Within a second her world went black.

*

"Miss Johnson, Miss Johnson, can you hear me? Can you open your eyes?"

Lisa's eyes fluttered open. There was a kind, friendly face staring down at her. It was a doctor.

Lisa tried to sit up. "What happened? Where am I?"

The doctor started shining a light in her eyes. "You're in A&E. It seems you were assaulted outside your flat. One of your neighbours found you and called an ambulance."

It all came flooding back. The woman staring, Lisa chasing, losing her in the housing estate, the funny noise outside her flat and then... blackness.

As she tried to re-orientate herself a familiar voice came from behind the doctor. "So, what have you been up to, DS Johnson? I thought work had finished for the day?"

Lisa looked around the doctor, who was still fussing about, checking Lisa's vital signs. It was the chief.

Lisa was suddenly manic. "It was the perp, ma'am. I was drinking in a pub just near my flat and this woman was staring at me from across the road. She was slim and had long blonde hair, just like the witness descriptions we had. As I walked towards her, she turned and... well, walked in the other direction. I chased after her but lost her. About ten minutes later someone bashed me over the head by my flat and—"

"Whoa, whoa, Lisa, slow down. You have a nasty bang on the head and we need to make sure you are OK. There's plenty of time for you to tell me what happened tonight."

"There's not time, ma'am. I didn't see her face, but as I got closer to her, the body shape... well, it confirmed what I have been saying. It wasn't just our perp. It was Jessica!"

The chief smiled at her, a smile that Lisa could see was laced with pity. A smile that told Lisa the chief was still not with her on this. Lisa was just about to protest when the chief floored her.

"You need to stop this thing about Jessica. I checked the time of your assault based on the ambulance response logs and I'm sorry to tell you that at the time you think Jessica was running away from you and bashing you on the head, she was on the phone to me."

# 48

The next morning Sarah sat in her office, her head thumping like a raccoon in a trash can, brought on by too little sleep and the never-ending stress. Her phone rang. The caller ID told her that the stress was not going to get any better any time soon.

"Morning, Gerard, what I can do for you?"

"Solve this fucking case, Sarah. The committee gave me a roasting this morning. The dead bodies keep stacking up and you seem to be floundering around grabbing at thin air. They want some results, Sarah, or... well, I think it's obvious what will have to happen."

Sarah went to respond, to try to defend herself, but before she could muster any sort of defence, Gerard had hung up. She couldn't believe it. Was that it? Was she now just a punching bag for his bad moods, not even given the chance to update him on the progress she was making?

She screamed in frustration; her coffee cup was launched at the wall. The cup shattered into several pieces. Another metaphor.

"Ma'am, are you OK?"

Sarah looked up, her gaze quickly moving between the

shattered cup and Cassie's concerned face. "God, yeah, sorry, DC Kennon. Bad phone call."

"I'm sure you're allowed the odd smashed cup, ma'am, considering the stress you are under."

Sarah smiled. So many people seemed to hate her, but Cassie and Lisa were different. They seemed to understand her. They were in tune with the stresses and the strains that she was under.

"Thank you, Cassie. What have you got for me?"

"I went in to see Lisa this morning. She seems really chirpy and wants to get back to work."

"Hmm, she needs to rest. She had a nasty bash on the head last night. Is she still going on about Jessica?"

Cassie looked shocked. "Oh, you know about that?"

"Yes, she has been bending my ear about it for a couple of days, but she needs to stop. Just because Mark was corrupt, it doesn't mean everyone should be under suspicion."

"I know, ma'am. She was manic about it the other night, saying she had seen Jessica wandering around near her flat, when she is supposed to be staying in St Helier. I did tell her that it was perfectly possible for Jessica to be having a drink or something at that end of the island, but she didn't seem convinced. In the end, I rang up the B&B where Jessica is staying to prove she wasn't lying about that."

"That's interesting. She was convinced the woman she spotted last night was Jessica and assumed she must be the person that bashed her over the head. But, I checked the timings. When Lisa was chasing this woman and getting bashed on the head, Jessica was on the phone to me."

Cassie raised her eyebrows, not wanting to doubt her friend but confused by Lisa's absolute certainty with this issue. She looked back into the main room. "Actually, ma'am, where is Jessica and where are the rest of the team?"

"Oh, Jessica texted me to say she wasn't feeling well. She was going back to bed to try to sleep it off. She said she might be in later. Steph is still off until tomorrow and I told Jennifer to concentrate on getting the forensic work done."

Cassie smiled, trying to disguise the churning deep inside her gut. She didn't know what to believe. Lisa was as straight as they came and there was no doubt Jessica was a piece of work, but did that make her a criminal? There was something about Jessica's absence that unnerved her. What if Lisa was right? Was Jessica plotting her next move?

Cassie must have looked like she was daydreaming because the chief bolted her out of her daze.

"Is that it, DC Kennon? Do you have that information I need?"

"Oh, shit, sorry, ma'am. Almost. Lisa and I did most of the work yesterday. I just need about an hour to finish it off and I will come in and go through it."

"Am I on that list?"

"You are, ma'am."

*

Jeff Godley walked into the hospital with the confidence of someone that should be there. He had received a text from her last night updating him on her little game of

240

'copper bashing'. The adrenalin was pumping. To get a picture of one of Sarah's team in hospital would increase his kudos. He could see the headlines now... *Police chief can't even protect her own team*... dominating the front page and ingratiating him further with his growing band of international press buddies.

He walked up to the floor that Lisa's ward was on, diverting into the storeroom. He found what he was looking for. A spare set of scrubs. He quickly put them on, grabbed a clipboard, put the fake ID on and walked down the corridor.

He nodded to other members of staff and relatives as he walked, trying to seem like he belonged. No one batted an eyelid. He went into the ward and made a point of walking past Lisa's room, not wanting to seem too obvious. He busied himself at the nurses' station, pretending to consult notes, the busyness of the ward allowing him to blend in. A few minutes passed. He scanned the ward. It was go time. As he reached Lisa's room, he tentatively peered in. She had her eyes closed. Perfect.

He got his phone out and started frantically snapping away. As he took the last one a voice came from behind him. "Can I help you, sir?"

Jeff discreetly slipped the phone in the pocket of the scrubs and turned to face the voice. It was another copper.

"Are you a doctor, sonny?"

"No, sir."

"Well, I'm pretty sure you can't help me then."

The officer looked at him suspiciously. "I'm guarding DS Johnson. She was assaulted last night and we need to make sure that the aggressor doesn't try again."

"Well, sonny, I suggest you do your job better. I just walked in here unchallenged a few minutes ago. Where were you? If I had a weapon, she would be dead by now."

The officer's face dropped; his bravado gone. "Oh, sorry…" he looked at the fake ID, "…doctor, I was just going to the toilet."

Jeff smiled. "Don't worry, son, no harm done." With that he walked off. Mission accomplished.

*

It was late morning and Cassie had finished the work. She walked into the chief's office.

"Ma'am. I'm done."

Sarah looked up. "Great, DC Kennon. I'm on tenterhooks. What have you found?"

Cassie was nervous. She had not expected what she had found. The chief looked at her expectantly.

"I have the full list of girls that were in the homes he ran. Not surprisingly, with almost thirty years to cover, the list runs to nearly nine hundred names. I could have done some profiling on them to reduce the list, but as we suspected, we found your name on the list. I thought it made sense to concentrate on the girls that were in the home at the same time as you."

Sarah was transfixed. "And?"

"Well, ma'am, there were thirteen girls in the home at the same time as you. Apart from you, only six of them really fit the profiling we have been working to."

"OK, are any of the names of particular interest?"

"Yes, ma'am, there is one."

"Who?"

"To be honest, ma'am, I don't know what to make of it. It's Steph… Steph Brown was in the children's home at the same time as you."

# 49

A hush descended over the room. Sarah's face was fixed in shock. "Steph? Are you sure?"

"Yes, ma'am, I've been back over the records. It's definitely her."

Sarah turned her seat to stare out of the window, the view of the sea often a foil for her deepest thoughts. Cassie didn't speak, letting the chief take it all in.

She turned back to Cassie. "What does this mean? Are we really saying that these riddles are telling us that she is the murderer? That just doesn't make any sense."

"Actually, ma'am, I did some checking. If you think about when the murders were committed, the team were generally not on shift. The first murder was on a Saturday afternoon. I checked and Steph was not working. Murders two and three were in the evening. I understand that you had all gone home for the evening on those respective days. The zoo murders were based on contaminated water bottles being left around the zoo. That could have been set up in the morning before the team were together, as I understand your op started around noon. The witness statements on that day talk about seeing this woman, but they seem patchy and unreliable. We also have to consider that due to Mark's apparent involvement, she may have been working with other people. Then we look at our ABC murders. Mark was murdered straight after your shift ended. Steph could easily have followed him home and killed him. Lisa told me you had coffee at the end of the shift. Any one of you could have put the drugs in his coffee to set it up. The murder of our key victim, Michael Brackley, was committed on the day you told the rest of the team to take a day off and she is conveniently off again when Mr Crossley was murdered."

Sarah was mesmerised by what Cassie was saying. Her head felt like the volcano had finally erupted in her brain. She shook her head, over and over. "This can't be right, DC Kennon. Why would she do this? She is a police officer, not a serial killer. And what has this got to do with me? I don't remember Steph being in there; in fact, I don't really remember any of the kids that were in there. I was there for such a short time. I'm even struggling to remember that Michael Brackley was the man running it. It's all so dark and confusing."

Cassie didn't try to justify her pitch. She had learnt to let the chief process news like this.

A few minutes passed; Sarah's concentration fixed on the sea view once again. Suddenly, she sat up from her slouched position, like a meerkat sensing danger. "My god. The forensics. It can't be Steph, otherwise we would have got a forensics hit. Standard procedure is to screen all officers at the crime scene to eliminate any evidence anomalies."

Cassie grimaced, trying not to seem too patronising to the chief. "By that logic, ma'am, it would also rule out Lisa's mad ideas about Jessica, but..."

"What?"

"Well, I have a theory about this issue too. Although you are technically the SIO, Steph has been undertaking many of the tasks that you should have been doing, including having full access to the DNA and fingerprints databases."

"What are you saying? You think she has tampered with her record?"

"Yes, ma'am. I think we need to consider it as a possibility."

Sarah stood up. "Come on, DC... err, Cassie, we need another coffee."

They both went back into the main room, filling up their coffee cups from the rapidly reducing pot that had been on the brew all morning.

They stood in silence, both stymied by the incredible revelations. Cassie could sense the chief was still struggling with the notion that Steph was the murderer.

"Where's the rest of the list, Cassie?"

Cassie was taken aback by the continuing use of her first name by the chief. Was this some attempt to seem more human, show some humility?

"It's here, ma'am." Cassie chose to stick to the formality of rank.

Sarah looked at the list.

*Sarah Joseph (now Braintree)*
*Jane Beddows*
*Steph Brown*
*Maggie Granderier*
*Lily Badley*

Sarah shook her head. "I don't remember any of these names. Is it possible that it's someone else on this list?"

Cassie was trying really hard not to seem disrespectful to the chief's apparent unwillingness to believe that Steph was the murderer. She went for a conciliatory tone. "Before Lisa was incapacitated, we had planned today to look in depth at any list of suspects we produced. I can get on with that work as a priority because, at the end of the day, we don't actually have any hard evidence to support my suspicions about Steph."

Sarah looked at Cassie, her face relaxing, like the words she was hearing had somehow comforted her, giving her an 'out' from having to consider that one of her officers had been killing all these people right under her nose. "Yes, please do that, DC Kennon. I have a lot to think about." The formality was back.

*

Lisa sat in her hospital bed, frustrated and jumpy. The doctor came in and looked at her chart.

"Doctor, I need to get out of here. I can't afford to sit her doing nothing. There is a serial killer on the loose and we need to nab her."

The doctor didn't look up, his eyes fixed on the notes he was reading. "Miss Johnson, I can't in all honesty discharge you yet. You are showing signs of concussion. You are not medically fit to be chasing serial killers.

Now, please rest and I will review your progress again later."

Lisa punched the bed in frustration. She texted Cassie. *Come in and see me. I'm going stir crazy. Bring your laptop. We need to keep going. If these bastard doctors won't let me out, I'll work from my sick bed.*

Cassie replied almost instantly. *Can't just now. We have a list of six girls that were in the home at the same time as the chief. I'm doing a deep-dive into their lives. Will come and see you as soon as I can. There is a doozy in here. You'll never guess who is on the list. Steph Brown!*

Lisa read the text and almost dropped the phone. Steph was in the home at the same time as the chief. They surely weren't considering that she was behind this?

Lisa read it over and over. She put her head back on the pillow and closed her eyes. Had she been looking in the wrong direction? Was Jessica for real? Had her worries about Steph's attitude been because she was their perp? *Mind-blowing.*

# 50

Jeff Godley finished off the 'copy', attached the pictures from the hospital and sent the story to his editor. On any other day this would be front-page news for the *Jersey Herald*, but, if everything went as she planned this evening, there would be another story that would blow it out of the water.

He rubbed his hands with glee. *Showtime!*

*

It was late afternoon and Cassie was getting close to finishing the 'deep-dive' she had done on the other five girls that were in the children's home at the same time as the chief and Steph.

Nothing tangible had emerged until she got to the last name on the list. Lucy Crohan. Her registered address was in the same block of flats as the third victim. She started frantically reading through the statements that the uniforms had taken from the door-to-door enquiries, both on the day of his murder and from some follow-up they had done that morning.

The first batch of statements, from the day of the

murder, gave her nothing, other than a note to say that the person in flat 12 was not at home when they called. She checked the update from the morning's work. Again, she wasn't at home when they called. *Interesting*, she thought to herself. *A coincidence or someone not wanting to talk to the police?*

She started to read through the detail of what the officers had gleaned from the neighbours that were in. On the penultimate one, she found something interesting, something that made Lucy Crohan a credible suspect. One of her neighbours had said she was a good friend to Mr Crossley, spending lots of time with him.

She leapt from her seat and walked into the chief's office. Sarah was reading a file, head in hands, not noticing Cassie's presence in the doorway. Cassie cleared her throat.

Sarah looked up. "Oh, DC Kennon, what can I do for you?"

"Are you OK, ma'am?"

"Yes… well, no, actually. This is the red file on Michael Brackley. It's not good reading."

Cassie sat down in the chair opposite Sarah. "What does it say?"

Sarah's eyes seem glazed, like she was holding back tears. Cassie worried that she was crossing a line. She was just about to try and divert the focus of the conversation somewhere else when Sarah spoke.

"He's a child abuser, DC Kennon, or at least he was investigated for accusations of child abuse. It seems despite some quite compelling evidence his case was never pursued. The case seemed to rely on the corroboration of statements from several children, but the investigation team felt their statements were too unreliable and inconsistent to bring a case against him. This is why the case was red filed."

"When did this happen?"

"That's the thing. The period of time these accusations were made straddles the period I was in the home, and more alarmingly the access log for this file shows that Steph retrieved it from the archives about two years ago when she was on the cold case review."

"Eh, how could she have done that? I thought she had to get authorisation to see these files?"

"She did. I granted it. It was one of many requests that I approved at the time. We had about fifty historical cases under the scope of that review. There was no reason at the time for me to think it odd."

"Is Steph mentioned in the case notes?"

"Actually, not that I can see, although most of the names have been redacted, so I can't be sure. The only name that remains on the case file is the girl who made the initial accusations. Lucy Crohan."

"What!" Cassie leapt out of her chair and thrust the statement at Sarah. "Look at this. Lucy Crohan lives in the same flat complex as our third victim and this statement from one of the neighbours says she spent loads of time with Mr Crossley. Surely both these things make her a credible suspect?"

Sarah read the statement a few times. "My god, DC Kennon, this might be a breakthrough. I could never believe that Steph could be our perp. It goes against everything she stands for as a police officer. I can see that some of the evidence might fit a theory that Steph is our perp, but this must surely change our focus. I want you to do a full profile on this woman for tomorrow's briefing and put out an intel report to all officers on duty that she is a person of interest. Do we have a recent photo of her?"

"No, ma'am, but I will see what I can find."

Cassie sensed that she was being dismissed, but she was disturbed by Sarah's sudden certainty that Steph was no longer a suspect. She decided to risk saying something.

"Err, ma'am, what about Steph accessing the red file? Don't you think that is a bit odd?"

Sarah made a dismissive gesture with her hand. "Oh, I think now we have a credible suspect we can put that down to a coincidence. She was perfectly entitled to request that file as she was a DI in the cold case team at the time. She may not have even been involved in the investigation as a child. I'm sure it's all a big coincidence."

It was now clear it was time for Cassie to leave the room. As she got back to her desk, she had three more texts from Lisa. She was going stir-crazy and was badgering Cassie to come in and see her. She packed up her laptop and decided to go to the hospital straight away.

As she began to leave, she popped her head round the door of Sarah's office. "Ma'am. I'm going to see Lisa and then I will work up that profile later."

Sarah smiled, seemingly OK with their last conversation. "That's good, DC Kennon, give her my best. I'm going to follow your lead and take this file home for a better read. I think this needs the calming power of a glass of red wine."

*

Lisa felt like a caged animal. The nurses and doctors kept fussing around. She knew she should be grateful for their fantastic care and attention, but all she wanted to do was get out of the stiff hospital bed. The perp was nearing the end of her deadly game and Lisa could not sit around doing nothing.

Cassie's text had floored her. Steph in the home at the same time as the chief. She just couldn't see how she could be the perp. They had worked so closely together on the case in the early stages and Lisa hadn't seen anything to be suspicious about. But, as the possibilities raged through her mind, she thought about the profiling. Jessica had said the perp was a textbook sociopath, someone that could blend into normal life without anyone noticing. The problem was, the more Lisa thought about the profiling, the more she felt it was describing Jessica and not Steph.

*Jessica, Steph, Jessica, Steph* – the names kept cycling through her mind. As she tried to clear her mind, she texted Cassie again. She needed her here.

As she waited and waited, she had a sudden epiphany. A way to prove whether Jessica was who she said she was. She frantically searched the internet and found what she was looking for. The number of the Major Crime Agency. She dialled the main number. A friendly voice answered within seconds.

"Oh, hi. Could you put me through to Jessica Fletcher, please?"

There was a brief pause and then, "Yes, please hold the line."

The ring of the connected call was pounding in Lisa's head. Her heart was racing, her hands sweaty. She almost jumped out of the hospital bed as the call was answered. A male voice.

"Hello, can I speak to Jessica Fletcher, please?"

"Oh, yeah, who's calling, please?"

The *oh yeah* floored her. An *oh yeah* that meant the real Jessica was there, in the office, in London. She couldn't speak.

"Hello, are you still there?"

"Oh, sorry, yes. My name is DS Lisa Johnson from Jersey Police."

"OK, hold on." Lisa heard him shout across the room. "Jess, phone for you."

A few agonising seconds passed as Lisa waited. Eventually there was a, "Hi, Jess speaking."

Lisa could hardly speak, but she forced her way through the nausea that was rising from her stomach. "Umm, hi, I'm not sure how to say this, but I'm DS Lisa Johnson from Jersey Police and I was wondering whether you... well, erm... whether you were aware of the multiple murder case we currently have running?"

"Oh yeah, how is that going? I was all set to come over to help you on that one."

"Oh, what happened? Why didn't you come over?"

"The day before I was all set to get on the plane, I had a call to say my services weren't needed any more."

Lisa thought her heart was going to leap out of her chest. "Do you remember who called you?"

"Umm, yeah, I think it was a DCI. Steph someone. Why?"

"Oh my god, Jessica. I think you have just given me the biggest break in this case so far. Someone has been

254

impersonating you. They stopped you coming over so they could take your place. I can't believe it."

"Oh, shit. Glad I could help and let me know if there is anything I can do."

Lisa hung up. She sat in her bed, motionless, staring at the phone like it was some magical being.

As she tried to process what she had just been told, Cassie walked in. "What is it, Lisa? You look like you've seen a ghost."

Lisa put both her hands on her head. "My god, Cassie. Jessica is an impostor. I have just spoken to the real Jessica Fletcher, and worse than that, Steph is involved as well."

# 51

It was just after 5pm as Sarah drove through the iron gates into the family estate and parked up outside the lodge. The red file sat on the passenger seat, goading her, the contents taking her back to a time she had forgotten but was now becoming integral to solving this case.

She walked up to her front door. As she went to put the key in the lock, the door gave. She pushed at it tentatively. "Hello? Mum, Dad, are you in there?"

There was no answer. She stepped quietly into the hall, listening for any sound, anything that would tell her what was going on. Jessica's words were running through her head. *Be careful, Sarah.*

As she passed the entrance to her kitchen, there was a sudden movement from the doorway. She felt a sharp scratch on her neck and within seconds collapsed on the floor.

Sarah wasn't sure how long she'd been out, but as her eyes began to flutter, consciousness returning, she realised to her horror that she was bound to one of her living-room chairs, hands and feet tied up.

She tried to focus, her head fuzzy and her limbs heavy. Her survival instinct kicked in and she forced her eyes fully open, struggling against the restraints. She frantically looked around, trying to find the danger, trying to find who had drugged and tied her up. There was no one there, but as her gaze moved to the other chair, which was now placed a few yards away, opposite where she had been tied up, she saw it. A note.

*Hello, Sarah,*
*Welcome to act three. The final act. The grand finale. A one-night-only event.*
*IT'S MURDER ON THE ORIENT EXPRESS.*

\*

Words were spilling out of Lisa's mouth at a rate that Cassie couldn't keep up with. "Whoa, whoa, Lisa, calm down. You're babbling."

Lisa looked at Cassie, like she wanted to strangle her for stopping her flow. "We need to phone the chief, Cassie. Jessica is a fraud and Steph is helping her. My god, they have been killing all these people right under our noses. I can't believe it."

Lisa was losing it, the weight of what she had just discovered overwhelming her. Cassie tried to calm her down. "OK, OK, hold a sec. I'll phone the chief."

Lisa looked at Cassie, manic eyes staring, willing her on. The call connected and the chief's phone started to ring. After thirty seconds there was no answer. Voicemail. Cassie left a message.

"Shit, shit, Cassie, ring DCO Millar and Jennifer. Someone must be around."

The same thing happened. Two voicemails. Two messages.

"We have to get out of here, Cassie, something bad is happening. I can feel it."

"No, Lisa, the doctor says you have a concussion. Let's get our ducks in a row and as soon as one of them calls we can tell them what we have found out."

Tears were appearing in Lisa's eyes. She shook them away. "Look, Cassie, the real Jessica Fletcher told me that she was all set to come over to help us and then the day before she was due to fly, Steph called her to say she wasn't needed."

"This fits with what I've found today, Lisa. When I found out that Steph was in the home at the same time as the chief, I put a theory forward to her as to how Steph could be our perp. Steph was off shift at the time of every murder, and despite no forensic match she had access to the DNA and fingerprint database. She could have tampered with her record or the evidence that Jennifer has been reviewing. Also, she could easily have spiked Mark's coffee at the end of your shift and followed him home."

"But that theory fits with fake Jessica as well. She wasn't even in the team for the first three but was with us on the night of Mark's murder. If she is working with Steph, the same theory could apply to her DNA and fingerprint record."

"I know, and we think we found out who Jessica really is. There was another girl in the home at the same time as the chief, called Lucy Crohan. She now lives in the same flat complex as the last victim and neighbours said she was really pally with him. If you think about that crime scene, it fits that he knew his attacker."

"My god, Cassie, this is so fucked up. Did you suss out why she is targeting the chief?"

"Not really. It's something to do with their time in that children's home. We got the red file and it seems this Lucy person accused Michael Brackley of child abuse, but it was never brought to court."

"OK, that might explain why she sought revenge on him, but why on earth is she targeting the chief? What can she possibly have to do with that type of allegation?"

"I don't know, Lisa, but it sounds like we are about to find out."

"You're right, Cassie, we don't have a minute to lose. We need to get out of h—"

Lisa didn't finish the sentence. All the machines she was hooked up to started to beep, her eyes drooped and she slumped back on the bed.

# 52

*Murder on the Orient Express.* Sarah stared at the note. She actually remembered watching that film, on one of the rare occasions she actually got time to watch TV. It had Albert Finney in it and they were on a train. *The Orient Express. Of course.* The realisation hit her. He was playing Poirot. Lisa said the last riddle was about Poirot. It confirmed the murder of Michael Brackley as the *why* that the perp seemed so desperate for Sarah to understand. As she sat there, bound and helpless, the information that they had discovered began to process in her mind. The perp had said act three would tell her the *who*. The film must be a clue. She racked her brain, trying to remember the plot. Suddenly, it came to her. Poirot discovered that everyone on the train was involved in the murder. She mulled it over. Jessica, Steph, Mark. Was that what she trying to tell her? That all the team were involved. What about Lisa, Cassie and Jennifer? Surely not. As the possibilities played through her mind, there was sudden movement from the hallway. Part of the answer was now standing in front of her.

Sarah glared at the group. "My god, so Lisa was right. You are a fraud, Jessica, or whatever your real fucking name is, and you, Steph. How could you? Betraying the badge, betraying your profession. You are the worse type of scum. And, why am I not surprised to see you, Mr Godley?"

*Jessica* walked towards her, an amused expression on her face. She stared Sarah down, ramping up the tension. She slapped her hard across the face.

Sarah rode the blow and faced forward, her eyes fixed on *Jessica's*, defiant. "Physical contact. I thought your profile said you didn't like touching people, you fucking freak."

*Jessica* pulled out a knife and held it close to Sarah's face. "Oh, Sarah, what a smart mouth you have. I will get over my contact issues, just for you."

Sarah fixed her gaze on the knife. "What's your plan? If you are going to kill me, then get on with it."

"Ooh, no, no, no, Sarah. We have only just begun. We are not going to make it easy for you. We have a whole evening of entertainment for you to enjoy."

Sarah wrestled against her constraints.

"You see, Sarah, this is my Poirot moment. The moment when I get to speak, to take centre stage and explain how this all went down. To show you my superior intellect. And you played your part so well. Floundering around, not understanding my riddles, letting me kill, again and again."

"I didn't need to work them out. Lisa solved your silly riddles."

"Ah yes, little old Lisa. She was a fly in my ointment. Steph enjoyed bashing her over the head last night as I was on the phone to you. Nice touch, that. Don't you think?"

Sarah glared at Steph and shook her head. "You bitch."

"Now, now. Back to me. You see the last clue was supposed to tell you the *who*, but I'm guessing it passed you by?"

Sarah smiled. "Unlucky bitch. I worked that one out. You're trying to tell me that everyone is involved in this little game of yours, but, of course, that's not true. Lisa and Cassie are loyal to me, even if that idiot Mark wasn't, and I'm guessing Mr Godley here was supposed to be turning Jennifer, but that didn't work out too well, did it?"

*Jessica* had an amused expression on her face. "Well, well. Give yourself a pat on the back. You worked one out. Maybe if you had been that clever from the start, I wouldn't have had to kill all those people."

"OK, I'll indulge you. Why did you kill Mark, if he was part of your merry band?"

"Mark became a liability. His incompetence was beginning to be a problem. I mean, even you began to notice what an absolute dickhead he was. He had to be dealt with, and of course his surname was a happy coincidence for my game of A, B, C."

Sarah shook her head. "You're a fucking lunatic."

*Jessica* struck her again. "Now, now, Sarah. Enough with the name-calling. We have a long way to go and it's going to get really tiring if I have to keep slapping you."

The sudden switch of mood, the sudden flash of anger, told Sarah this was a volatile situation. *Jessica* started to pace round the room. Steph and Jeff watched on, steady and unflinching. Eventually she stopped pacing and once again fixed her gaze on Sarah.

"I have explained the *who*, Sarah. Now let's turn to the *why*."

"I don't think we have finished the who. You haven't told me your real name."

There was a sudden burst of movement. *Jessica* leapt at Sarah, the knife hovering close to her face, her hand shaking with rage. "*How can you say you don't know who I am?*"

Sarah tried to pull her face away from the blade that was glinting in the light streaming in through the window. "You're Lucy."

The mention of her name stopped her. Her face, that was just seconds ago contorted with rage, relaxed and her expression changed to one of curiosity. She tapped the knife against her hand, staring at Sarah, trying to read her. Sarah subconsciously looked to her right, where the red file was now lying.

Lucy spotted the furtive look. She picked up the file and read the first page. The anger was back. "You bitch. You don't know who I am? Do you? I'm just a name in a file to you. My god. You need to die."

"No, Lucy, she needs to know what she has done." Lucy started to pace the room, trying to reconcile what Steph was saying to her. All the while she was pressing the knife into her palm. As she neared Sarah on one of her small laps of the living room, she stopped in front of her, the knife pressing hard against her palm. "This is what you did to me, Sarah. I cut myself to ease the pain. Look!" She pulled her sleeves up, revealing wound marks all along her arm.

Sarah knew she was in trouble but banked on the fact

263

that Lucy needed to complete her 'performance'. She had to keep her talking.

"How on earth can I be responsible for you cutting yourself? I haven't done anything to you. If you are trying to tell me something about our time together in the children's home, then I'm sorry. I don't remember you. I don't remember Steph being in there. I don't remember anything about my time in there. To me, you are Jessica Fletcher, the shit-hot criminal profiler who, up to an hour ago, I thought was helping me catch a killer, not suddenly becoming the prime bloody suspect."

The speech was full of passion and bravado, but Lucy just flicked her head back and closed her eyes. Sarah moved her gaze to Steph and Jeff, looking for some explanation, looking for an 'out'. They ignored her pleading eyes.

The tension was palpable. Lucy hadn't moved. Her eyes still closed. Eventually, she started to let out a long breath, like a safety valve going off in her head. She moved her head forward and opened her eyes. The look chilled Sarah to the bone. A look of pure evil.

A few tense seconds passed and then there was the explosion. "*You stole my fucking life, you bitch!*"

Sarah jumped at the suddenness and volume of the outburst but soon composed herself. "What? What on earth are you on about? How did I steal your life?"

Lucy began to pace again, breathing heavily, trying to calm her rage. "OK, Sarah, I can see I'm going to have to walk you through this step by step, but my god, you are not doing yourself any favours here. It will just make your final downfall that bit more satisfying."

Sarah tried to ignore the idle threats. She continued to

fix her gaze at Lucy. She was not going to be intimidated by the woman that had made her life a living hell for the past month. She would a find a way out of this mess.

Lucy tapped the knife against her hand. She turned and smiled at Steph and Jeff. "Come on, guys. Let's all sit down and tell this dumb bitch why we all hate her so much."

They all pulled up a chair and formed a semi-circle in front of Sarah.

Lucy started the latest part of her theatrical performance. "How long were you in the children's home, Sarah?"

"Err, about three weeks."

"Exactly. Three bloody weeks. Do you know how long we had all been in there?"

The sweeping hand movement that suggested Jeff Godley was also in the home surprised Sarah.

Lucy immediately picked up on her confused look. "Oh, I see. You didn't know that Jeff was in there too, and Mark, of course."

Lucy laughed at Sarah's increasingly confused face and shot a look at Steph. "Not much of a detective, is she, Steph?"

Sarah could see Lucy was in her stride, much calmer but revelling in her so-called Poirot moment.

"Yes, that's right, Sarah. All four of us were in there at the same time as you. All four of us affected by your presence."

Sarah was getting impatient at Lucy's sneering and goading. "That's ridiculous. How can me being in the home at the same time as you, have any bearing on your time in there?"

Lucy shook her head, the rage simmering once again. She got up and tapped the knife on her head, over and over. "You're not listening, Sarah. I told you. You stole my life."

"What are you on about? How can I possibly have stolen your life?"

"Three weeks, Sarah. Three weeks. We had all been in that home for several years, being abused by that monster. We were all ahead of you in the pecking order and I was next to go. I had been there the longest of everyone. I should have been top of the list for adoption. When your parents came into the home, that bastard was supposed to promote me as their first choice and, if I wasn't suitable, it should have been Steph or Mark or Jeff. *Not you*. As I said, you stole my life. You stole the life that any one of us deserved in this posh house, on this posh estate and with rich parents that would attend to our every whim."

Sarah was perplexed. "That's insane. How on earth can you hold me responsible for a decision my adopted parents made? I had no control over that. I was six years old, for god's sake. Have you really all festered on this for thirty years?"

"That man broke me, Sarah. The abuse. Night after night. Week in. Week out. It never stopped and the police did nothing. I was just a name in a file. I was in there another four years before I got transferred to an adolescent unit, so yes, I did fester on it. As the years went by, nothing improved for me. Everything that man had done blighted my life: never being able to hold down a job for more than a couple of months, unable to form relationships with anyone. The hours I spent curled up in a chair, not able to function, watching hours and hours of television, trying to distract myself from the memories of what that man did to me. Then, two years ago, I met Steph again. We relived the horror, the bad memories flooding back once more. She told me about Jeff and Mark. How they had been abused too. We all had to deal with the demons that man had given us. Steph and Mark became police officers, determined to put their pain into something productive. To stop other people suffering at the hands of men like Michael Brackley. As for Jeff here, he just became a wild child. A loose cannon. Being a reporter was the perfect foil for him. Writing untruthful shit about people and suspending himself from reality. As Steph and I talked and talked, my plan for revenge on you and that pervert were set in motion. That puke-inducing ceremony, giving you the Freedom of Jersey, was the final straw. It gave us the perfect opportunity to maximise your humiliation so soon after they lauded you as the fucking heroine of Jersey."

Sarah was torn. The stories were tragic, horrible, but for some reason they had all fixated on the moment that she had got in the way of one of them escaping that evil man. She went for contrition. "I'm... I'm sorry. I don't know what you want me to say. I had no control over the decisions that were made and I'm sorry that man did those terrible things to all of you. I just don't understand why you are blaming me."

Lucy shook her head. "Do you know what he said to me one night when he was abusing me? He said he had to let you go because he couldn't bring himself to fuck the ugly ones. You survived because you were an ugly child and we all suffered because we were cute kids. Does *that* give you some idea why we hate you, Sarah?"

Sarah tried to fight back tears. There was no reasoning with this psycho and her merry band of crims. Lucy pushed on. "You didn't get the lollipop reference either, did you? You see, when he wanted to abuse one of us, he got the rest of the kids to sit in the TV room and gave you all lollipops to keep you quiet. I hardly ever got a lollipop, Sarah."

Sarah knew she was losing. They were revelling in the control they had over here. Her mind wandered to Lisa and Cassie. What were they doing? Would they connect the dots and come and save her? She shook the thought away. *Wishful thinking.*

After her latest tirade, Lucy seemed to have burnt herself out, her head bowed looking at the knife, her focus temporarily elsewhere.

Sarah took the opportunity to divert the attention away from Lucy. "Steph. Come on. You are a police officer. You can't possibly condone what she has been doing?"

Steph's face, which had been steadfast and unflinching, suddenly changed to a look of disgust, a loud, mocking laugh quickly following.

"God, you really are a piece of work. You don't even remember what I tried to do. Do you?"

"What? When?"

"With the cold case review."

"What about it?"

Steph bunched her hands up, trying to quell her rage. Lucy re-engaged, shot a look at Steph and smirked. "The Michael Brackley case was in the scope of the cold case review. I got that red file out of storage and spent ages with Mark going over the original shoddy investigation.

We already had a clear and unequivocal statement from Lucy on file, but the failure of the case seemed to revolve around a lack of corroboration. Mark and I agreed to make fresh statements. We got in touch with other children in the home at the time, including Jeff, all of whom had the same story. I passed a revised prosecution file to you through my DCI at the time. It had real merit. We had a chance to nail that bastard, but you dismissed it. My DCI said you hardly spent five minutes looking at it, before you cast us all aside, once again. So, yes, Sarah, we do blame you. We blamed you thirty years ago, we blamed you two years ago when you couldn't be bothered to re-visit our case and we blame you now."

Sarah held her nerve. They clearly thought they were outlining the case for the prosecution in this theatrical nonsense. She tried to maintain some sort of control. "And what about you, Mr Godley? What crimes do you think I have committed against you?"

Jeff kept the arrogant, self-satisfied expression that seemed to be a permanent fixture on his face. "Oh, I think my girls have outlined our case very well. I'm just glad that I can report every bit of your downfall. We're holding tomorrow's front page."

"What's that supposed to mean?"

"You'll see."

Sarah wrestled against her constraints. She wasn't sure what she would do if she got free, but it was something to do, as the three amigos sat staring at her, amused by her plight.

Sarah flinched as Lucy stood up. "Ooh, a bit jumpy there, Sarah. Frightened, are we?"

"I'm not scared of you, you psycho bitch."

Lucy began to tap the knife on Sarah's head again, with the precision of a metronome. "Now, now, Sarah. You have forgotten my excellent profiling work. I told you, I'm not a psychopath. I'm a sociopath."

"What difference does it make? You are a murderer. A piece of scum."

"Dear, oh dear. If I was a psychopath, you would have rumbled me. I told you. My ability to blend in with normal social situations, to be confident, play a role, was why I was able to be standing right next to you for all that time as you floundered around from one crime scene to the next."

"Lisa saw through your charade."

"Not quickly enough, though, eh, Sarah? She didn't stop this happening, and where is she right now? Oh yes, stuck in a hospital bed with a sore head. Not exactly the cavalry, is it?"

As Lucy's sentence trailed off, she glanced at Jeff and Steph. They both stood up. Sarah instinctively pushed back in her chair, the movement amusing Lucy.

"You're very twitchy, Sarah, but don't worry, we're not going to kill you. We have something much more inventive in mind. Come on, team, time for us to leave."

Sarah was blindsided. What were they doing? She had been trying to delay what she thought would be the inevitable moment of death, but they were walking away. As she tried to work out what was going on, there was another sharp scratch on her neck and her world went black.

# 53

Cassie watched on with horror as the doctors and nurses frantically attended to Lisa. They had been working on her for nearly half an hour, but she was still out. Alive but unconscious. Eventually a doctor barked out an order that they needed another MRI scan. As they began to move Lisa's bed out of the ward, Cassie grabbed at one of the doctors. "Is she going to be OK?"

The doctor looked concerned. "I don't know. Let us get on with our job and we will do our best to save your friend."

Cassie stood alone in the room, the large space where the bed had been a chilling reminder of what they were dealing with. She checked her phone. No one had called back.

She knew she had to move, to do something. Lisa was being looked after and there was nothing else she could do for her. Cassie had a choice to make. Did she go and see the chief at her house or go to the station and try to find DCO Millar? She chose the station. It was closer.

\*

DCO Jo Millar got back to his desk after a gruelling ops meeting. They were about to execute the final warrants for the arrests of the key players in the money laundering case and tensions were high. Co-ordination with Interpol, the CIA, MI6 and French Intelligence had made it doubly difficult, but after nearly four hours discussing the final operational plan, they were all ready to go. He had to phone Sarah to let her know.

Sarah's phone rang and rang. Voicemail. *How strange*, he thought to himself, *she hardly ever lets a call go to voicemail*. He left a message, made himself a well-deserved coffee and sat back down at his desk, trying to catch his breath before the op started. As he picked his phone back up, he realised he had a voicemail from DC Kennon. He was just about to ring her back when his PA came in.

"Sir, the front desk has just sent up this envelope for you. A courier delivered it with instructions that it should be delivered to you immediately."

Jo took the envelope, tentatively examining it. The writing was neat and legible. He listened and sniffed the package. As far as he could tell, there were no signs or smells of anything sinister.

He got out his letter opener and sliced the end of the envelope. He pulled out a single piece of paper.

*Dear Mr Millar,*

*You have been looking in the wrong place. Did you ever consider that the murderer you have all been chasing for the last month might be much closer to home?*

*Have you checked the DNA and fingerprints of all the investigation team, against the samples you collected at the crime scenes? You might just be surprised at what you find.*

*A concerned citizen*

Jo read the note several times. What on earth was this suggesting? It was standard protocol to screen all forensic evidence against the officers on scene, to rule out any inadvertent forensic contamination. From what he knew of the forensics on this case, Sarah and the team had not identified any forensic match. He looked at his watch, cursing this interruption to one of the most important evenings of his police career. He had two hours before he needed to be back in the ops room to command the live op. He grabbed the note and set off to see if Jennifer Colney was still working. He was sure she would re-assure him that the note was just fanciful nonsense.

He went down a couple of flights of stairs to the forensics labs. Jennifer was still working. "Jennifer, thank god you're here."

"Evening, sir. Just finishing up here. What can I do for you?"

"Can you look at this?"

Jennifer took the note, read it, flipped it over to see if anything was written on the back and handed it back to Jo.

"What do you think, Jennifer?"

"I dunno, sir. What are they suggesting?"

"They seem to think we have missed something with the screening of the investigation team."

"I don't understand that. It's standard protocol to screen all investigating officers."

"I know, but why are they suggesting we have missed someone? Did you take samples from Jessica, for example?"

"Yeah, Steph did that as soon as she arrived."

"Cassie?"

"Yes, as soon as she joined the team."

"I don't understand. Is this note just a joke then? Is it another part of the silly games the perp is playing with us?"

They both got lost in their thoughts for a moment, before Jennifer's face turned to absolute shock. "My god." Jennifer put her hand to her mouth. "I've just realised, sir. We didn't screen the chief's samples against any of the crime scenes. I mean, I didn't even think about it, we shouldn't need to..." Her sentence drifted off, her brain shutting down the words, as if uttering them would somehow make the incredible implications of what she was saying go away.

Jo looked at her, stony-faced. "You have to run them, Jennifer. We have to know."

Jennifer logged onto her computer. She got the DNA samples up first that they had collected from the second crime scene and from Mark's murder. She scanned them against Sarah's DNA.

At the same time, she loaded the fingerprint samples into the analysis system and ran them against Sarah's fingerprints.

They both watched the two screens that were processing the results, hardly daring to take a breath. Jo broke the tension. "How long will this take?"

Jennifer looked at Jo, concern etched across her face. "Not long."

Five minutes later the DNA screen popped up a message. 'MATCH FOUND'. A few seconds later the fingerprint analysis screen popped up a message. 'MATCH FOUND'.

# 54

Cassie ignored the lift and flew up the stairs, taking two at a time. She got to the outer office of DCO Millar and brushed herself down. She didn't want to burst in like a crazy lady, even if time was of the essence. She knocked on the door and walked in.

"Hi, can I help you?"

"I'm DC Kennon. I need to see DCO Millar urgently."

"Oh, he's not here. He went down to forensics a little while ago."

"Oh, OK." Cassie flew back down the stairs. She reached the frosted glass door that framed the entrance of the department and fobbed in.

She walked through the main lab towards Jennifer's office. As she reached the doorway, she stopped in her tracks. DCO Millar was staring out of the window and Jennifer had her head in her hands, the unmistakable sound of quiet sobbing coming from behind her hands.

They hadn't noticed her presence, and she felt uncomfortable, not knowing whether to leave or stay. She couldn't wait. "Um, I'm sorry to interrupt, sir, but is everything OK?"

Jo turned around and Jennifer looked up. Jo spoke

first. "Err, DC Kennon, I'm afraid we have just discovered something rather devastating with our case and I must admit I don't know what the fuck to do with it."

"What is it?"

"I got this note delivered to me about twenty minutes ago. Jennifer realised that we had not screened the chief's DNA and fingerprints against our crime scene samples."

"And?"

"We got a match, DC Kennon. The chief's DNA and fingerprints match the samples we recovered from the various crime scenes. This would seem to suggest that Chief Braintree has been committing all these murders."

Cassie screwed her face up. "That's insane. It can't be true. It's—"

Jennifer wiped away the tears, interrupting Cassie's flow. "There's no doubt, Cassie. They are an exact match."

"No, no, no! This is a set-up. It's all part of this perp's game. It's the reason I was trying to ring you both. Lisa contacted the Major Crime Agency on the mainland and spoke to the real Jessica Fletcher. Our Jessica is an impostor and is almost certainly the one doing the killings, but worse than that, DCI Brown is helping her."

Jo's face flashed a look of anger that disarmed Cassie. "Do you have any idea what you are saying, DC Kennon? I have known Steph for nearly seven years and she is a model copper."

Cassie steeled herself. She knew that challenging senior officers was a recipe for shortening your career, but she had no choice. Lisa was in the hospital, having god knows what done to her, and if she was right, the chief was in real danger.

"I'm sorry, sir, I don't mean to be disrespectful to Steph, but the real Jessica told Lisa that Steph was the one that phoned her up to say she wasn't needed. She did it to allow this woman to take her place and impersonate her. We also have a pretty good idea who this woman is. We got a list of all the girls that were in the children's home at the same time as the chief. There was a girl called Lucy Crohan on the list who now lives in the same block as the last victim and neighbours said she was good friends with him. Jennifer, you will remember you said you thought he knew his attacker. She has to be our prime suspect, not the chief. Also sir, we discovered that Steph was in the home at the same time as the chief. The answer to this mystery is linked to the chief's time in that children's home. I truly believe that this Lucy person and Steph are holding some sort of grudge against the chief, related to something that happened in that home, which led to this horrendous killing spree. I believe the chief is in real danger. We should go to her house. Now!"

The room was silent. Cassie wasn't sure she had taken a breath, too scared to pause and give either of them a chance to interrupt her. They all stared at each other.

Jo eventually spoke. "How do you explain the forensics, DC Kennon?"

Cassie looked at Jennifer, putting on her most sympathetic face, hoping that what she was about to say would not rile her up as well. "I'm sorry to say, but I think the forensics are completely compromised. Steph had access to the DNA and fingerprint records of the team. I think if we check them, we will find that they have altered their samples to ensure there was no forensic match

278

and somehow changed the chief's samples to match the evidence we collected. They are framing the chief."

Jo shook his head. "What a mess. How on earth did we not spot this earlier, Jennifer? If we had run the evidence against the chief's samples, we would have picked this up much earlier."

"I know, sir, I'm so sorry, but the command protocols on this case are all over the place. The chief shouldn't have appointed herself as SIO. She should have put in place normal command protocols and stayed as Gold command. I didn't even think about screening her against the crime scenes. She's the chief of police, for god's sake."

"You're right, Jennifer, I'm sorry. I'm having a hard time taking this all in."

Cassie stood in the office, all tensed up liked a coiled snake, sympathetic to the self-persecution that was going on but itching to move on. She cleared her throat, trying to drag attention back to what she felt they needed to do. "I'm sorry, sir, but we need to get to the chief. She's at home and I'm sure if we go to see her, we can sort this all out. I'm also concerned for her welfare. I'm convinced the fake Jessica and Steph are going to carry out their threats about their so-called third act."

Jo looked at his watch. "Fucking hell. I need to be back here running the final stage of the money laundering op in just over an hour. If we are going to do this, we need to go now."

Within five minutes they were in Jo's car and heading for Sarah's house.

*

They arrived at the Braintree estate, which was just on the outskirts of Gorey, within ten minutes. They drove into the main gate and turned immediately left, parking up next to the lodge. Sarah's car was there.

They all bundled out and went to the front door of the lodge, the smell of the lavender bushes that framed the entrance overwhelming their senses. Jo went to press the bell but realised the door was slightly ajar. He pushed it, raising his eyebrows at Cassie and Jennifer. "Hello, ma'am, are you there? It's Jo Millar." No response. "I'm coming in."

They walked through the entrance hall, passing the kitchen on the right, emerging into the main living room. As they did, they were greeted with a strange vista.

The chief was slumped on the sofa, an empty wine glass on the floor and three empty wine bottles strewn around the room. Jennifer quickly put her gloves on and felt the chief's neck. "She's alive but she's spark out." Jennifer picked up each of the wine bottles in turn and sniffed them. She looked up at Jo and Cassie, concern etched all over her face. "It's just wine. I can't smell anything sinister. She seems to have drunk herself into an unconscious stupor."

Jo scanned the scene. "What the hell is this? Jennifer, can you call an ambulance? Cassie, can you do a quick search of the house?"

Jo stood in the room watching Jennifer continue with her initial examination of the scene. His brain started taking him places he didn't want to go. *Is this her giving herself up? Has her conscience finally caught up with her or is this all a set-up? Are Steph and this impostor the people I should be looking for?*

He was suddenly snapped out of his daydream by a shout from Cassie. They both ran into what seemed to be Sarah's bedroom. Cassie stood by the dressing table, her mouth open in absolute shock.

Lined up on the dressing table were three wigs – blonde, red and brunette – a prosthetic nose, a bottle of arsenic and a near empty bottle of anti-freeze.

# 55

Lucy, Steph and Jeff sat on Pops' boat, cheering as Lucy popped the cork on the champagne bottle that she had stashed aboard just for this moment.

"The bitch stole our lives and now she is going to pay."

Steph and Jeff cheered at Lucy's pronouncement and clinked glasses.

"Has the story gone to your editor, Jeff?"

"Oh, yes. The banner says 'POLICE CHIEF ARRESTED FOR JERSEY MURDER SPREE'. I added '*World Exclusive*' to the copy, just to get my editor salivating."

"Are you sure he will print it?"

"No question. He may be a dick, but even he won't miss out on a story this big, especially if he can be one step ahead of the world's press."

"What if he tries to verify the story with the police, Steph?"

"If you got this right, Lucy, they should right about now be overwhelmed with the evidence of her guilt that has just fallen in their laps. At worst they will just say *no comment*, which the press always sees as an affirmation that the story has legs."

Lucy smiled and took a long swig of the champagne, draining the contents in seconds. She let out a guttural scream and threw the glass at the wall of the jetty, a satisfying tinkle of smashed glass filling the air. Jeff and Steph laughed and did the same.

Lucy jumped up from her seat. "We have about two hours of light left. I think it's time we got on our way. Oh, by the way, Steph, did you send Lisa our last riddle?"

"Ooh, no, I didn't. Let me do that now."

*

Lisa's head felt like a hundred elephants had trampled on it as she slowly opened her eyes. She was suddenly aware of several faces staring at her.

"Can you hear me, Miss Johnson?"

She couldn't speak, but she nodded her head slowly.

"Good, good. Now you must rest. You are OK, but you passed out probably due to over-exerting yourself. You have a severe concussion, which will only heal if you rest."

She gave a weak smile and a slow nod.

The doctors and nurses did a few checks, and once they were satisfied that Lisa was OK, they left her to rest.

Lisa looked around. The police officer that had been guarding her wasn't outside her room and Cassie seemed to have gone. She turned her head on the pillow towards the bedside unit. Her phone was laid on top of it. She winced as she rolled her body towards the phone, just about able to reach it. She rolled back and unlocked her phone. She had two text messages.

The first one was from Cassie: *Lisa, I hope you are OK. I'm sorry I had to leave, but I had to go and find DCO Millar. Based on what we've found, I'm sure the chief is in real danger. Will call as soon as I can.*

The second one made her gasp. It was from Steph: *It's Murder on the Orient Express.*

Lisa lay there staring at the text. Her head hurt like hell, but her brain was still functioning. She started an internal monologue.

*Poirot. It's another Poirot reference.* Murder on the Orient Express. She racked her brains, trying to recall the story. *They're all involved. Poirot discovers that everyone on the train was involved in the murder. What is she trying to tell me?*

It didn't take Lisa long. *My god, this is Steph's confession. She saying she's involved. Everyone's involved? No. Cassie isn't, I'm not. Jennifer? No… but Jeff Godley, oh my god, he was trying to get her on the team. Jessica, of course, and…*

That brain worm that had been festering in Lisa's head since Mark was killed, suddenly resolved itself. *Of course, Mark was involved as well. We kept looking for females, but I bet Mark and Jeff were in the children's home as well.*

She ignored the thumping pain in her head and phoned Cassie.

\*

Jo, Cassie and Jennifer stood frozen to the spot. The evidence of the chief's guilt was apparently laid out in front of them.

Cassie broke the silence. "No, no, no. This is a set-up. You can't honestly believe the chief did this. Jessica and Steph have been here, planting this evidence."

Jo shook his head. "DC Kennon, I don't know what to make of this. We have a forensic match with the chief's DNA at practically every crime scene and what appears to be all the tools of her trade here in her house. Just because she is the chief of police, it does not put her above suspicion."

Cassie was losing patience. "It's the fake Jessica and Steph that are responsible for this. They have been playing this game from the minute they conspired to kill our first victim. The stupid riddles, the fake profiling, bashing Lisa over the head. How can you ignore all that?"

Jo didn't get an opportunity to answer as Cassie phone rang. "It's Lisa."

As Cassie walked out of the room, she heard Jo say to Jennifer, "Start processing the scene. I can't ignore this just because it's the chief."

Cassie walked back into the living room and pressed the green button on her phone. The chief was still sprawled on the sofa, no nearer to waking up. "My god, Lisa. Are you OK?"

"Yeh, I've just come round. They say I have a severe concussion and need to take it easy, but that ain't fucking happening."

"Shit, Lisa, I'm glad you're awake, but things here have just gotten a lot worse."

"Why?"

"We are at the chief's house. She is passed out on the sofa, three empty wine bottles strewn around her, but that's not the worst thing. We have just been in her bedroom and on her dressing table are three wigs, a prosthetic nose, a bottle of arsenic and a bottle of anti-freeze. DCO Millar also got an anonymous note about the forensics. They realised that Jennifer had not run the chief's samples against the evidence we collected from the crime scenes and they found an exact match to her DNA and fingerprints. It's fucking mental."

There was a brief silence as Lisa took in what Cassie had just said.

"Are you there, Lisa?"

"Oh, yeh, sorry. It all makes sense now."

"What?"

"I've just had a text from Steph with their last riddle. It just says 'It's *Murder on the Orient Express*'. It's tantamount to a confession."

"I don't understand."

"It's another Poirot reference. In the *Murder on the Orient Express* story, Poirot ultimately discovers that everyone on the train is involved in the murder. They're trying to tell us that everyone was involved, but, of course, that's not quite true. We know that the fake Jessica is involved, and Steph, obviously, but they are telling us that Mark and Jeff Godley were also in on it. Jeff was trying to recruit Jennifer, but when she stopped helping him, he got violent and she walked out. We had been looking for females that were in the home at the same time as the chief, but I'm betting that Jeff and Mark were in there too. They said act three would be the *who*, and this is their explanation. We now know that Michael Brackley's murder was the *why*. Something happened when they all were in that home that they seem to blame the chief for. Maybe it is something to do with those abuse allegations, but I still for the life of me can't work out why they would blame the chief for what that man might have done. But, whatever the reason, they are framing the chief for all these murders."

"I know, I know, Lisa. I have been trying to explain this to DCO Millar."

"He can't possibly believe she is guilty?"

"I dunno, Lisa. He seems to be taking this charade seriously. He's got Jennifer processing the scene when he should be putting an alert out to the airport and port authorities to find the fake Jessica and Steph."

"*DC Kennon!*"

Cassie looked around, cringing at the prospect of what DCO Millar might have overheard. She quickly whispered into her phone. "Gotta go, Lisa, I'll call you back in a bit." She turned to look at DCO Millar, embarrassment obvious across her face.

"DC Kennon, I will make some allowances for your insubordination, as I understand how emotive this situation is, but I will not put up with you questioning my judgement. You know as well as anyone that we process the evidence and draw conclusions from what we find. We would be in breach of our legal duty if we did not treat this scene as a potential key part of our investigation. Now, I agree that it is inexplicable that the chief is our perp, but we must not rule it out until we process the evidence. I will issue an all points order via the control room for this Lucy Crohan person and DCI Brown. If we find them, we will question them in the same way we would question any other suspect."

"I'm sorry, sir."

The uncomfortable air was breached by the sound of the ambulance arriving outside.

# 56

It was nearly 8pm as Cassie walked back into the hospital to see Lisa. The chief had been taken to the same hospital and Cassie cringed when she heard DCO Millar give instructions over the phone to the control room to deploy an officer to guard her and make sure she was cuffed to the bed. As the chief was bundled into the ambulance, she was no nearer to waking up. Cassie had been dismissed for the evening by DCO Millar, with a tone that made it clear she was in deep shit.

DCO Millar had been impatient to get back to the operations room to run what should be the final stage in the money laundering investigation. Cassie was annoyed with his attitude but did have a pang of sympathy that the shit had really hit the fan around their case on the very day when the other big case of the year was about to bear fruit.

Cassie walked into Lisa's room. She was sat up, her eyes were dull and her skin was pasty, but she perked up as soon as she saw Cassie.

"What's going on, Cass?"

"Nothing, Lisa. The chief has been brought in here. DCO Millar has given instructions for her to be cuffed and guarded. He's off running the op on the money laundering case and has Jennifer processing the chief's house. He made it clear I was not to do any more on this case. It's fucking ridiculous."

"My god. What an arsehole. I always thought he was alright, but it just shows how out of touch the senior officers are with what really goes on."

"What do we do, Lisa? Are they still around? Do you think they will have left the island?"

Lisa instinctively touched her head.

"Oh, god, Lisa, I shouldn't be here bothering you like this. You need to rest."

"No, no, I'm fine, Cassie. We are the only ones left that can do anything about this."

Cassie was torn, but she knew Lisa was right. "OK, boss lady. You talk and I will do the heavy lifting."

Lisa gave a painful smile. "OK. Firstly, I think they have done what they set out to achieve. Their plan was initially to discredit the chief in their so-called act one. Act two and three were designed to explain to the chief what this was all about, but it also allowed them to frame her for the murders and get her arrested. I'm sure they are using the distraction of the chief's arrest to plot their escape off the island. If DCO Millar has alerted the airport, it's unlikely they will try that route, unless they are using fake IDs. My bet is they have a boat."

"Won't the port authorities stop them?"

"Unlikely. The bulletin the deputy put out would go to the harbourmaster at St Helier. It's obviously the main port on the island and would almost certainly be avoided by our gang of escapees. The problem is there are smaller marinas all over the island. They could be in any one of them and would barely raise an eyebrow."

"Where would they have got a boat from? Steph doesn't have one, does she?"

"Not that I'm aware of, but we don't know about the fake Jessica or Jeff. Can you look up boat owners on Jersey records and see if they have a mooring registered?"

"Err, yeh, I can try." Cassie tapped away. "OK, we have almost fifteen hundred records here. We need to filter this somehow."

"Get rid of any at St Helier and tell me what's left."

"Umm, that leaves the outlying harbours and smaller marinas around the island. Bonne Nuit Bay, Bouley Bay, Gorey, Rozel, St Aubin and St Catherine."

"Bonne Nuit, Bouley and Rozel are on the north coast. Gorey and St Catherine's are east. St Aubin is south. It won't be too far from where they have been if they want to make a quick getaway, which means it must be Gorey or St Catherine's, if we assume they were at the chief's estate near Gorey. Filter by those two."

Lisa was trying to stay calm, but the adrenalin was pumping and the numbers of the machines around her started to rise. She let out a deep breath, trying to relax as Cassie tapped away.

"There's no boat mooring registered to any of our three suspects in those marinas."

"Damn it." One of the monitors started to beep a warning.

Cassie looked up, concerned, but quickly looked back at her screen when something caught her eye. "Hold on. I've found something. Jim Crossley, our third victim, had a boat mooring registered at Gorey."

Lisa ignored the beeping machine. "That's it, Cassie.

If Lucy was friendly with him, you can bet she nicked the keys to his boat along with all his money. You need to go there now and stop them. Phone for back-up from the control room if you need it. *Go on. Go!*"

Cassie grabbed her stuff and left. A doctor came in to see what was happening with the beeping machine. Lisa waved away his enquiries and shut her eyes. She had done all she could. Would it be enough?

*

Cassie jumped in her car and sped her way back to Gorey. She decided to go it alone for now. She was in enough trouble with DCO Millar without getting the duty inspector to deploy scarce resources on a possible wild goose chase.

It took about fifteen minutes for her to get to the small car park, just on the edge of Gorey seafront. The summer light was beginning to fade and Gorey Castle was lit up, a beautiful backdrop to the vibrant marina that was full of an assorted array of pleasure craft. The weather had been nice all day and the temperatures were holding. The place was packed with people milling around the marina and walking out onto the long stone jetty that jutted out to sea.

Cassie started to run towards the marina, her eyes scanning the boats, hoping to catch a glimpse of Lucy, Steph or Jeff. She cursed as the volume of people slowed her progress. She got to the corner of the long jetty and stopped. She scanned and scanned. *Shit, there's too many boats here. I can't see the wood for the trees.*

She started to walk along the jetty, scanning every boat, looking for something that would give her a break. As she got halfway along the jetty, she noticed a small hut set back from the main walkway. It was labelled as the marina office and someone was still in there.

She knocked on the door and walked in. She got her ID badge out. "Oh, hi, I'm DC Kennon from Jersey Police. I'm looking for three suspects in a murder enquiry that we believe are using a boat out of this marina. Have you seen a group of three people, two women, one man, get on a boat and leave in the last hour or so?"

The guy looked at her curiously. He was very much playing up to the cliché of the old sea dog with his captain's hat and long grey beard, which he stroked as he spoke. "Lots of people coming and going this evening, missy…"

His sentence drifted off as he stared out of the window. Cassie looked at him expectantly, but he seemed to be lost in a daydream. She decided to cut her losses and began to leave.

"…but yeah, I think I've seen the people you're talking about. Caused quite a commotion down here. Smashing glasses against the jetty like a bunch of hooligans. I went out there to tell 'em off, but they just swore at me as they left the marina. No bloody respect these days."

"So they're gone?"

"Oh yeah, missy, about an hour ago, and I've not seen them come back."

Cassie thanked the man and sat down on the edge of the jetty, legs dangling over the side. She put her head in her hands and the tears started to flow.

# 57

It was just past 11pm as Jo Millar walked into the hospital to see Sarah. The money laundering operation had been executed successfully and he was relieved that at least one thing had gone well on one of the craziest days of his career. As he approached the ward, he bumped into the doctor. "Is she awake, Doctor?"

"She is beginning to stir but is not fully conscious or cognisant of her surroundings. You need to know that she was given a strong sedative."

He thanked the doctor and walked towards her room. *So, she didn't drink herself into oblivion then*, he thought to himself. He had a brief chat to the officer who was guarding her room and walked in, closing the door behind him.

As he watched her lying there, cuffed to the bed, he knew in his heart that she couldn't be the perp. He picked up the phone and called the duty inspector. "Inspector, has there been any progress on finding Lucy Crohan or Steph Brown?"

"No, sir, it's been on everyone's briefing this evening and local officers have been to their respective residences, but there has been no sign of either of them. Also, no reports from the airport or harbourmaster."

"OK, thanks, but let me know as soon as there are any developments."

Jo grabbed himself a coffee and sat watching Sarah breathing slowly and steadily, oblivious to the shit that was about to hit the fan. His mind wandered back to his last conversation with DC Kennon. He knew he had been harsh on her, but he could not let junior officers undermine his authority, regardless of the circumstances. Jennifer had texted him to say that preliminary forensic results had Sarah's DNA all over the items that were found in his house. The problem was, they didn't know whether the samples they were testing against were actually Sarah's. DC Kennon had been certain that all forensic exhibits were compromised. He needed Sarah to wake up so he could get her consent to take fresh DNA and fingerprint samples.

He stood up and looked out of the window. The streetlights illuminated the harbour as the night owls continued to party in the bars and restaurants. He was torn. Should he be out there, flooding the island with resources trying to find Lucy Crohan and Steph Brown, or was he standing next to the person who had engineered this sick game?

As he got lost in his thoughts, he was brought back to the present by the clanking of the cuffs against the bedframe. "Jo. Jo. What is this?"

Sarah's speech was slurred, but she was awake, her face in total shock as she realised she was restrained. Before Jo could say anything, the doctor came in to examine her. There was an uncomfortable atmosphere as the doctor checked her over, with Sarah staring at Jo accusingly the whole time. Once the doctor had left, Jo pulled up a seat next to her bed.

The few minutes that it had taken for the doctor to check Sarah over had given her time to get her body working, and she was raging. "What the hell is this, Jo? Why the fuck am I cuffed to the bed like a common criminal?"

Jo grimaced. "OK, Sarah, I am going to take the cuffs off, but you need to know that we have a very serious situation here. I should be talking to you under caution, but out of respect for you and your position, I am going to allow us to have an off-the-record chat first."

Sarah's face was screwed up in confusion. "What are you on about, Jo? What on earth do you think I've done?"

"We have evidence to suggest that you were the one that committed the multiple murders that have taken place over the last month."

"*Evidence!* What evidence?"

"Your DNA and fingerprints match the samples that we found at the crime scenes and we found wigs, a prosthetic nose, a bottle of arsenic and a bottle of anti-freeze in your cottage."

"My cottage. What were you doing at my cottage?"

"DC Kennon was concerned for your welfare. She and DS Johnson are convinced that Jessica is a fake and that DCI Brown has been helping her do all the killings. She insisted we checked on you. When we arrived at your cottage the door was open and we found you unconscious on your sofa with three empty wine bottles strewn around the floor. We checked the rest of the cottage and found the items I mentioned in your bedroom. Jennifer has done some preliminary forensic checks and your DNA is all over them."

Sarah looked away from Jo and rubbed her face. Her mind was racing with the implications of what Jo had said. She turned her face back to him, her expression changing from the rage and confusion that had been ever-present in their opening exchanges to one of vulnerability.

"My god, this is what they meant when they talked about their grand finale. I thought they were going to kill me, but after they revelled in telling me how they had done it, they just left. They injected me with something."

"They?"

"Yes, Lisa and Cassie are right. Jessica is a fake. Her real name is Lucy and she was in the children's home at the same time as me. Steph was in on it too. So was Jeff Godley, and they admitted that Mark had been helping them too before they had to get rid of him. The three of them were there when I got home. They drugged me with something and bound me to one of my living-room chairs. When I came round there was another note and a few minutes later they all appeared. They took great pleasure in telling me how they had deceived me, deceived us all."

"OK, but why? Why did they do all this?"

"Oh, god, Jo, it's so ridiculous. We were all in the children's home at the same time. Our second-from-last victim, Michael Brackley, was the person running the home, and it seems as though he was abusing the children in his care. There's a red file which outlines the allegations that Lucy made against him, but it was never brought to trial due to a lack of corroborated evidence. It seems as though Steph, Jeff and Mark were also abused by him, and Steph joined the police to try to bury the demons of what that man had done to her, by dedicating her life to catching criminals. She tried to bring a new prosecution file to me about Michael Brackley under the cold case review, but I apparently rejected it."

"OK, but I still don't understand why they fixated on ruining your life."

"I was only in the home for three weeks. My parents came into the home to select a child for adoption. Lucy had been there the longest, followed by Steph, Jeff and Mark. They felt that any one of them should have been the natural choice as the next child for adoption. For some reason, my parents chose me, and Lucy in particular blamed me for, as she put it, stealing her life and sentencing her and the others to years more of abuse."

Jo shook his head. "So, DC Kennon is right. Their final act is to frame you for the murders and get you put away. The ultimate revenge for your perceived crimes."

"Yes. Can't you see that? Any so-called evidence you have is completely fake. I don't know how they have managed to get my DNA and fingerprints at the crime scenes, but I can assure you, I had nothing to do with this. I'm the chief of police, for fuck's sake."

"I don't know what to do, Sarah. A lot of what you say makes sense. DS Johnson apparently spoke to the real Jessica Fletcher, so we can get a statement from her to cement that part of a case against them. The doctor did say you had been given a strong sedative tonight, which is why you were out for so long, and I can see you have abrasions on your wrists where they tied you up. If you are right, they used this time as a distraction to get away.

I have an alert out at the airport and ports to stop them if they try to leave, but at the moment, no one can find them. If the forensics are compromised, we need you to consent to us taking fresh samples of your DNA and fingerprints to see if they clear you. If they do, our only chance of convicting them is to catch Lucy Crohan and get fresh DNA and fingerprints, as I'm sure they must match all the samples we have."

"Do it, Jo. Get Jennifer over here so she can sort this out straight away. These bastards have played you like a fiddle and are probably off the island by now. We need to clear this shit up and start looking for them. *Now!*"

# 58

The next morning was a flurry of activity. The *Herald* had printed both of Jeff Godley's stories with the chief's arrest dominating the front page and the pictures of Lisa providing some juicy content to spice up the story. Jo Millar had been in conference with Gerard Le Trousain since 7am agreeing an approach for the press, whose numbers had suddenly swelled again as the story broke with what they saw as the shocking conclusion to the Jersey serial killer mystery.

Jo did a press conference at 8.30am giving lots of non-committal soundbites about how the stories had no substance, how they were carrying on with the investigation, how they had some prime suspects but he was not able to say anymore... blah, blah, blah. By 10am Jo was back in the hospital visiting Sarah.

Jennifer arrived to confirm that she had worked through the night to re-test all the evidence against the fresh DNA and fingerprint samples she had taken from Sarah. Her face was initially fixed with a serious, dour expression, but as she looked at Sarah her features relaxed into a pained smile. "It's good news, ma'am. Your new samples do not match. This confirms that Steph must have changed all the records to show Jessica's... sorry, Lucy Crohan's samples as yours. It's why she was so confident about the forensics at each crime scene. She wanted us to find the samples because it was all part of their plan to frame you. It was such a crude plan, but it worked. I am so sorry that I let you down like this."

Sarah let out a breath that was so pronounced it was like someone had let out all the air from a space hopper in one go. She took a minute to collect herself. "Jennifer, you have nothing to apologise about. They fooled us all. They played us for mugs and we fell into every trap they set. I'm the one to blame. This is my command and I need to be held accountable."

Jo and Jennifer didn't respond. There was an uncomfortable air as everyone subconsciously licked their wounds.

Sarah broke the silence. "Jo, has there been any update on finding Lucy or Steph?"

"No, ma'am, ther—"

He didn't finish his sentence, as DC Kennon arrived, pushing Lisa in a wheelchair. They all turned to look at the new arrivals.

Lisa spoke without any prompting. "Cassie has got something important to tell you all."

They all looked at Cassie expectantly.

She focused her words at DCO Millar first. "The chief's not guilty, sir. You must see that. I've—"

Jo held his hand up to interrupt her flow. "It's OK, DC Kennon. We know the chief is innocent. Jennifer took fresh DNA and fingerprints last night and has re-tested the evidence. There is no match. I'm sorry to both you and DS Johnson here. You have been right all along. Jessica is a fake and is almost certainly this Lucy Crohan person. We also know that Steph has been helping them all this time."

Cassie looked at Lisa, a mix of shock and relief over her face. Sarah filled the void. "I'm sorry too, Lisa. I didn't take enough stock in your concerns about Jessica. Maybe if I had, we could have stopped them."

Lisa looked a bit embarrassed. "It's OK, ma'am."

Sarah smiled. "OK, DC Kennon, what is it you need to tell us?"

"Err, well, ma'am, after we left your cottage last night, I came back to the hospital to update Lisa on what had happened. We started to think about how they could get off the island without being detected. We concluded that they must have used a boat from one of the smaller marinas where there is hardly any scrutiny from the ports staff. We found the public records of boat moorings across all the harbours and marinas. We eventually found that our last victim, Mr Crossley, had a boat mooring at Gorey marina. This seemed to fit with what we found out about Lucy's so-called friendship with him. She obviously befriended him so she could nick all his money and use his boat to get off the island. I rushed over to Gorey marina to see if I could apprehend them."

Sarah was manic. "What happened?"

Cassie looked sheepish but ploughed on. "There was one man in the port office. He confirmed that three people fitting the descriptions of Lucy, Steph and Jeff Godley had been on one of the boats, causing trouble, throwing glasses against the jetty."

Sarah shook her head. "The bastards. Celebrating their victory, by the sounds of it. Where were they when you got there?"

"I'm so sorry, ma'am. They've gone. They've left the island."

# 59

## ONE MONTH LATER

Sarah sat on one side of the large oak table that dominated the main chamber of the government buildings in Grouville. Despite the buildings being non-smoking for over twenty years, Sarah sensed she could still smell the unpleasant, lingering odours of tobacco and cigars that seemed to be ingrained in the wood-panelled walls that adorned each side of the large room. A bastion of male dominance that turned her stomach.

Across from her, Gerard Le Trousain was holding court, surrounded by the six other members of the main Jersey cabinet. He had an air of over-importance as he revelled in the company and the occasion. Sarah had never felt that he had her back during the whole time the multiple murder investigation was going on, and the successful conclusion to the money laundering investigation had done little to temper his mood. She knew what was coming.

"Miss Braintree. You will be aware that we have spent some time reviewing the disciplinary case against you related to the tragic circumstances of the multiple murders this island has suffered over the last couple of months, which I need not remind you included a former member of this very committee. Whilst we are satisfied that the evidence which led to your arrest was fabricated as part of the perpetrators' plan, the unwanted press scrutiny and embarrassment this situation brought to the island of Jersey is intolerable. We accept that your ability to bring this horrific situation to a satisfactory conclusion was hampered by so many of the investigation team being part of the vendetta against you, but your inability to spot the criminal intentions of your team were also considered to be a fundamental failure of your role as chief of the police. The lack of progress in solving this case and finding where these criminals have disappeared to does also not help your case. In conclusion, we have no choice but to request your immediate resignation. You will also be stripped of your Freedom of Jersey accolade, as your actions are no longer in keeping with the principles of the award. You of course have the option to appeal this decision, but with the generous severance package and retention of your pension benefits, we feel you would be best advised not to go down that line."

The room fell silent. Sarah was determined not to be bowed by the sycophantic posturing of Gerard and his team. She looked at every one of them in turn without speaking. She played her thoughts out to herself. *Is this it? Twenty years of service, the last three as their chief overseeing the lowest incidences of crime in Jersey's history and they are going to throw me under the bus because of one woman's determination to play out some twisted game of revenge?* She knew their only motivation was to save face and they had her as their patsy. She shook her head but said nothing, staring them all down and raising the tension in the room. Some of the members started to fidget uncomfortably in their chairs as Gerard stared back with a curious, questioning expression.

After a few more uncomfortable minutes, Sarah stood up. "You will have my resignation by the end of the day." With that she walked out, not prepared to give these bastards a second more to laud their politically motivated actions over her.

As she walked down the sweeping staircase into the lobby, she felt like a weight had been lifted from her shoulders and she allowed herself to smile. As she moved towards the revolving doors, she heard someone shout to her. "Ma'am."

She turned to see Lisa and Cassie sat in the visitors' waiting area. She walked over to them. "What are you two doing here?"

Lisa took the lead. "We wanted to give you some moral support, ma'am."

"Well, you can start by stopping calling me ma'am. From now on it's Sarah. I have resigned from my post."

"What! Why?"

"To be honest, Lisa, I wasn't given much choice, but, you know, I'm kinda fine with it. I'm done with all the political posturing from that bunch of idiots. Throughout this whole sorry episode, they only cared about the bad PR this situation was bringing down on the island. It's time for me to move on and do something else with my life."

There were tears in Lisa and Cassie's eyes, but Sarah shocked them by giving them both a hug, an act of care and humility that they had never seen before.

As they milled around, nobody quite sure what to do next, there was a sudden commotion as someone came flying through the revolving doors.

They all turned to see what the noise was. It was Jennifer. She ran towards them, shaking something in her hand. "Sarah. Sarah. I know where they are!"

Sarah tried to calm Jennifer's manic persona. "What are you on about, Jennifer?"

"Look at this." She thrust a photo of a sprawling farmhouse surrounded by outbuildings and countryside, as far as the eyes could see. "I forgot I had this. I found it at the bottom of my handbag. When Jeff and I were first together, he gave me this photo and said we would go and live there when the time was right. I'm sure that's where they are hiding out. There's an address on the back. It's in a remote part of the Dordogne."

Sarah took the photo. After inspecting it for a few moments she looked at Jennifer and then at Lisa and Cassie. "I can't do anything with this now. It's not my concern."

Jennifer looked puzzled. "Why? Surely this is a significant line of enquiry."

"I've been forced to resign, Jennifer. DCO Millar will be acting as chief. It's his problem now."

They all looked stunned, disarmed by Sarah's apparent willingness to just switch off from the case.

Lisa eventually said what everyone was thinking. "You must want to find them, ma'a... sorry, Sarah. Even if you no longer have the ability to arrest them, you must want the opportunity to look them in the eye when we catch them."

They all sat down. Sarah stared off into the distance, Lisa's words racing around her brain. She eventually turned back to Jennifer. "What are you intending to do with this now, Jennifer?"

"I dunno. I was hoping you would do something with it, but I guess I'll have to give it to DCO Millar."

Sarah's face changed to something more conspiratorial. She leant in closer to all three of them. "Lisa's right. I can't let this go. I don't want any of you to break the law, but I need to ask you all a big favour. Are you prepared to give me forty-eight hours before you take this to DCO Millar?"

They all looked at each other, trying to interpret what Sarah was asking.

Lisa responded first. "What are you planning to do?"

"I want to see if they are hiding out in this place and then I want to talk to them."

"What, alone?"

"Yes, Lisa. They got what they wanted. I'm sure they would be interested to know that."

"That's madness, Sarah. They'll kill you the minute they see you, especially if they think you've rumbled their hideout."

"I don't think so. You have to trust me on this one. You three have been so loyal to me. Treat this as your leaving gift. Give me forty-eight hours and then take this to DCO Millar. I'll do what I have to do and then you can send in the cavalry."

"I agree." They all turned to look at Cassie. She smiled. "I agree. I think we owe it to the chief."

Jennifer and Lisa looked at each other and nodded. "OK, Sarah, it's a deal. You have forty-eight hours."

\*

Sarah got on the next available ferry to St Malo, and by late in the evening she had made good progress to her final destination, stopping in a pretty gite in a lovely rural part of central France, which offered a basic bed and breakfast service.

She ate a light breakfast the next morning, her nervous energy curbing her appetite. She packed up quickly, paid her bill and said goodbye to the owner. She got in her rental car and set off for her date with destiny.

As she reached the Dordogne, she switched to navigating by a local map. She wasn't sure there would be any phone signal as she began to climb towards the remote area that was in Jennifer's photo. As she got closer to the area where the farmhouse should be located, the roads started to get narrower and rougher. After ten minutes of driving along the bumpy tracks it opened out to a small, flat area. She parked up, away from the main track, and got out the map. She looked around, trying to get her bearings from the landscape around her. The weather was mercifully calm and visibility was good.

As she orientated the map, her heart gave a little leap as she realised she was about three-quarters of a mile away from where the farmhouse should be. She grabbed the map and the binoculars. This last bit had to be on foot.

She walked onwards. She hadn't seen another person or vehicle for nearly an hour. Something told her that this was where they would be. As she began to descend into a valley, she saw smoke rising into the sky. She ploughed on. As the track turned a corner, she was suddenly afforded a view of a narrow valley. Bang in the middle of it was a large farmhouse, smoke coming from the main chimney.

She knelt down, keen not to be spotted. She got out the binoculars and scanned the area. At first there was no sign of life, but the smoke from the chimney told her someone was home.

As she scanned to one of the outbuildings, she saw movement. She re-focused the binoculars. It was Jeff Godley. She watched him for a minute as he pottered about. *Where are the others?* she thought to herself. She changed focus back to the farmhouse. A few agonising minutes passed as she saw nobody else. She stopped looking through the binoculars and rubbed her eyes, the intensity of her focus giving her a headache. She kept looking down into the valley with the naked eye. Jeff wasn't enough. She needed them all.

It seemed like time had stopped. She sat in her little hiding place, willing something to happen. A second later it did. She heard the cock of a shotgun and a voice she recognised. "And what the fuck are you doing here, Sarah?"

She held her hands up in mock surrender and turned to look at Lucy. "I just want to talk, Lucy. I'm here alone. No one knows I'm here."

Lucy's face was etched with anger. She shoved the shotgun in her side. "Move!"

They trudged down the valley towards the farmhouse, Lucy periodically shoving the shotgun in Sarah's back to remind her she was there and not to try anything stupid. As they neared the farmhouse, Lucy shouted out, "Jeff, Steph. We have a visitor, and you'll never believe who it is."

Sarah stopped, hands behind her head, as Lucy moved to face her. She heard movement from the side of the building. Steph and Jeff emerged, shocked by this uninvited guest.

Lucy looked at the others. Her expression had changed to one of curious amusement. "OK, Sarah, you have thirty seconds to explain why you are here before I blow your fucking head off, and you might want to start with how you found us."

She went to grab the photo from her pocket. Lucy twitched the gun but relaxed as Sarah slowly drew it out. She looked at Jeff Godley. "You told Jennifer, didn't you, Jeff? She found this old photo that you gave her when you were trying to groom her to be part of your gang. It has the address on the back and everything."

Lucy looked stunned and pointed the gun at Jeff. "Oh my god, you fucking idiot. Is she right?"

Jeff held his hands up. "OK, OK, yes. I'm sorry. I forgot she had it."

Lucy moved the gun back between Jeff and Sarah in rapid succession, seemingly torn as to whom to take out first.

Sarah tried to calm the situation.

"Look, Lucy. Nobody else has this information. Jennifer brought it to me and I convinced her to let me come here and deal with it. No police. No drama."

Lucy trained the shotgun on Sarah. "What do you want? You have ten seconds left."

"You got what you wanted. I'm no longer the chief of police. I was disciplined and forced to resign. I have no authority here."

Sarah winced as Lucy grabbed the gun tighter. She waited for the boom, but it never came. Lucy's hands were shaking violently, but she hadn't pulled the trigger.

"She's lying." Lucy turned to Steph. "She's lying, Lucy. I don't trust her. Just kill her. There's plenty of places we can dispose of her body around here."

Lucy looked back at Sarah, trying to read her.

Sarah went for broke, hoping what she was about to say would work. "I'm not lying. I wanted to tell you all that I understand why you did it. When I was chief of police and in the middle of your deadly game, I wanted nothing more than to solve the case and bang you all up in jail, but when I was sacked everything changed for me. I stopped to think, to look at it from your perspective. I can't condone what you did, murdering all those innocent people, but the more I thought about it the more I could see how much trauma that man's actions had caused you throughout your whole lives. I began to understand why you blamed me for blocking your route out from that hellhole, and Steph, I'm sorry I didn't give your cold case review the attention it deserved. The worst thing was, I came to realise that my parents, the lovely people that could so easily have been your parents, showered me with so much love that the memories of my time in the home became nothing to me. The problem was, I suppressed those memories, but your tragic stories festered in my mind and to my horror I realised something. I didn't always get a lollipop."

Lucy's hands were shaking violently, the shotgun waggling around like someone had put an electric charge through her. A tear escaped and she quickly wiped it away. "What are you saying, Sarah? Are you trying to tell us that he abused you as well?"

"Yes."

Steph interrupted. "She's lying, Lucy. Don't believe a word this bitch is saying. She's playing us. She's led the cops here and is playing for time. Shoot her and let's get out of here."

Lucy turned to look at Steph, an uncharacteristic vulnerability creeping into her persona. She changed her focus to Jeff. "What do you think, Jeff?"

"Once a bitch, always a bitch. I agree with Steph. She's playing us. Kill her."

Lucy turned back to Sarah, the gun locked and loaded. "I agree. You're lying. That bastard told me that he couldn't fuck you because you were so ugly."

Sarah went for bravado. "Oh, and he proved to be such a stand-up character. Why would he lie?"

There was a tense stand-off as Lucy stared Sarah down, the shotgun constantly trained on her.

Sarah put on her most convincing, unthreatening expression. "Please, Lucy. You have to believe me. I have come here today, on my own, unarmed, not as a police officer but as someone who is truly sorry for what they have done to you. You've turned me into a normal human being, someone who thinks about other people rather than her career path. This is the first time in my life, I've really understood what it means to care about people."

There was a snort of derision from Steph, but Lucy seemed to be buying it. She put the shotgun down. "OK, Sarah. Let's assume that I'm inclined to believe this epiphany you've had. What do you expect to happen here?"

"Nothing, Lucy. This is the only copy of the photo. Jennifer trusted me to deal with it and hasn't got the details of your location to give to anyone. I'm the only one that knows where you are. Now I know that probably gives you another good reason to kill me, but I'm trying to make this better, make amends for my part in this and I guess plead for clemency, urge you to spare my life."

Lucy looked at Steph and Jeff. They both shook their heads.

Sarah made her final move. "OK, I'm going to walk away now. If you choose to shoot me in the back, then I understand, but while you are deciding whether to do that remember that you got what you wanted. You humiliated me, you got me sacked and they took that stupid Freedom of Jersey accolade from me. You ruined my life and reputation, and I can no longer live on Jersey. I'm on my way to live in Spain."

She turned around and started to walk back up the path to freedom. She didn't dare look back. She had to hope that they had believed everything she had said. She had lied about the abuse but felt it was the only way she could get any empathy from Lucy. She made it twenty metres before she heard movement. She carried on, bracing herself for the impact of the gunshot. There was the sound of a scuffle, interspersed with a "No, Steph!" shout from

Lucy. The gun went off. Sarah stopped. She had not been hit. It seemed as though Lucy had stopped Steph from firing at Sarah and the gunshot had been diverted by Lucy to fire innocently in the air. Sarah walked on. There was still one more round in the chamber. Forty metres. She didn't look round. Voices were raised, the clarity of what they were saying fading with every step. She was now at the top of the hill, the commotion down in the valley was barely audible and no one had shot her.

As she moved over the brow of the hill and out of their sight, she quickened her step. She risked looking around. No one was following her. She was now twenty metres from where she had parked the car.

As she got closer to her car, she heard the sound of multiple police sirens and the re-assuring *thud, thud, thud* of helicopter rotor blades in the distance.

She got in her car, let out a huge breath and drove away.

# ACKNOWLEDGEMENTS

My first acknowledgement must go to my Dad, who sadly passed away in July 2020 after a year long battle with cancer. He was one of the greatest supporters of my writing and I'm sad that he wasn't able to finish reading this book.

Massive thanks to my immediate family for their support and love in an incredibly difficult year. Their encouragement and positive feedback about my writing has helped me to keep focused. Particular thanks go once again to my alpha readers, Jacky Wade, Karen Warner, Hannah Wade and Anthony Cooper who review, uncomplainingly, all my drafts and always steer me to a better final story.

Thank you to my son, Thomas Wade, for his continuing support in keeping my website up to date.

Thank you to Troubador Publishing for their support, through their Book Guild arm, in getting this book published and marketed.

Finally, a massive thank you to my readership. Your continued support and positive feedback about what you are reading, gives me so much pleasure and I hope I can continue to entertain you with this and future books.

# ALSO BY COLIN WADE

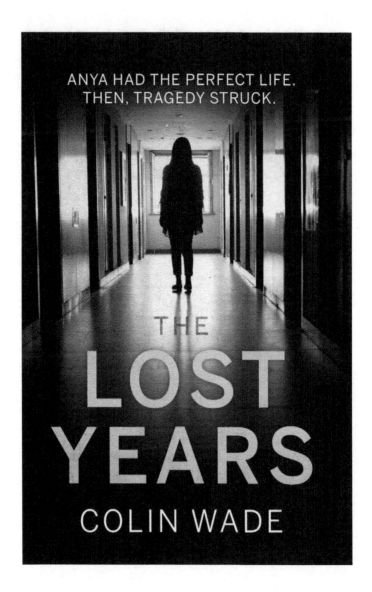

ANYA HAD THE PERFECT LIFE.
THEN, TRAGEDY STRUCK.

THE
LOST
YEARS

COLIN WADE

Anya had a wonderful upbringing. Loving parents, private schooling and a place at Oxford University. The perfect life. Then, tragedy struck. Her parents were killed in a car accident and the grief made her life spiral out of control. She descended into addiction, fuelled by the bad company she was keeping. As she flunked University, she was admitted to a mysterious clinic where two years of her life were lost, apparently being treated for her severe addictions. Her memories of her time in the clinic were limited and she came to refer to this period as her 'lost years'.

A few months after being discharged from the clinic she met Rob. It was love at first sight and she believed she had found her soulmate. They established a new life together, living in the lovely village of Goring in Oxfordshire and running his art gallery. Just as Anya started to feel her life was back on track, horrible nightmares started to invade her sleeping hours. She was getting visions of her time in that clinic and the doctor that had treated her, both things she had always been uneasy about. The nightmares were forcing her back there, goading her into finding out what really happened to her.

As the nightmares continued, her reluctance to share what was happening to her caused a strain in her relationship with Rob but eventually she was forced to confront the horror and they set off on a journey to uncover the truth. As they begin to search for the truth, a nerdy guardian angel with a penchant for hacking comes to their aid, fuelled by his own search for justice. As this unlikely trio dig deeper and deeper they uncover a shocking conspiracy that goes to the very heart of the British establishment and puts all their lives in danger.

# ALSO BY COLIN WADE

FROM THE AUTHOR OF
**THE LOST YEARS**

GREED, BETRAYAL, CONSPIRACY, MURDER.
**CAN SHE SURVIVE?**

# PLUTUS
COLIN WADE

Alice Bidebecker is the best Senior Counter Intelligence Analyst the NSA has ever employed but, after a little under a year in the job, she is feeling underappreciated and disillusioned by the lack of recognition of her work in the male dominated work environment. During a particularly difficult week, she is approached by a strange man in the park during her lunch break. He wants her to work for him, to protect his secrets using her extensive cyber expertise. He claims to be working on a major scientific breakthrough and offers her a new life in Europe and millions of dollars for her services. After agonising over what to do, the toxic work environment, the realisation that she no ties to her US life and a heartfelt note from her now deceased mother convince her to take up the offer and leave the NSA without warning. Her disappearance sparks a major crisis in the US intelligence services, as they desperately try to find her and seek explanations for her apparent betrayal.

As the initial investigations get underway, a link is made to a missing Professor and his assistant from the University of Minnesota, who had been working on some highly sensitive infectious diseases studies. As the full extent of the scientific project is revealed in the ultra-secure European hideaway by a bunch of ruthless business men from the US and UK, Alice begins to realise that not everything is at is seems and her world spirals into crisis. Thrust together with the Professor and his assistant, Alice has to rely on the help of one of the guards, her cyber geek friends in the virtual world and ultimately her old team to tackle the crisis head on.

Greed, betrayal, conspiracy, murder. Can she survive?